The Sweetest Delights in Life

Christine L. Henderson

*"When you find the one you love,
it's one of the sweetest delights in life."*

The Sweetest Delights in Life
Christine L. Henderson
www.christinelhenderson.com

Copyright © 2022 Christine L. Henderson
Revised Second Edition 2024
ISBN 9798849330228

CHAPTER 1
A New Start in Texas

Even before the timer buzzed, Jasmine Cattrell had already begun walking back to the oven. The fragrance of green chilis, garlic, and roasted chicken had reached the perfect level, letting her senses know the savory empanadas were ready. She put on the stained oven mitt, opened the door, and reached into the oven to retrieve the aromatic delights.

The rush of heat assaulted her nose and eyes. When the air cleared and she could gaze at the golden-brown plump empanadas, she broke out in a grin the size of Texas.

After taking a moment to do a happy dance, she held up the tray for one more delightful whiff before her brow furrowed. It had nothing to do with the empanadas but her memory of her now ex-boyfriend, Stefan, who often told her not to waste her time on baking when she could easily order whatever she wanted from a nearby bakery. To him, cooking was like work and if it didn't add a profit to his investment accounts it wasn't necessary.

Yet for Jasmine, it was a creative outlet for her energies when they weren't working on marketing campaigns for their clients. Now it was a holding place until she could resume her previous career again. Ten years ago she landed a job in Los Angeles with one of the top agencies that took her to the other side of the country from Falcon Creek, her small-town Texas home. Now she was back, not so much by choice but by necessity.

However, being home again had its perks, like creating something new for the bakery that was her own creation. Today was the trial run for the savory pastries. Her gut told her they would be a hit. Her mom wasn't so sure. For the last eighteen years since her mom had taken over the bakery, they had only sold sweet treats and cakes.

Her thoughts drifted back to her previous dream job in L.A. with a six-figure income, a boyfriend who lavished her with gifts, and her condo with a fantastic beach view. Who knew it could disappear so quickly. When a major embezzlement of company funds was discovered, the company deflated like a popped balloon. But the final blow was discovering her boyfriend was cheating on her.

As Jasmine reached over to cut into one of empanadas, the bells chimed on the front door announcing a new customer's arrival. She removed the oven mitt, straightened her long white apron, and walked out of the kitchen. As she reached the front display counters, she began her canned response, "Welcome to Sweet Delights - -" but stopped, as she double blinked in surprise.

The person who sauntered into the bakery was a gorgeous guy with the most remarkable deep blue eyes. His broad shoulders were covered by a dark brown leather jacket over a muted plaid shirt. His crisp jeans enhanced his long legs, and his alligator boots finished the picture of a calendar perfect Texas hunk. The only thing missing from the image was the Stetson hat. She immediately dubbed him as Dreamy Eyes.

A group of teenage girls followed behind, whispering and giggling as their eyes stayed transfixed on him as they walked toward the display counters. Though there was probably fifteen years in age between them and Dreamy Eyes, that didn't stop their preening to catch his attention.

Jasmine smiled and pushed away an errant ringlet of hair that had fallen over her eyes. Her eyes darted to her apron and smiled, seeing that it still looked crisp and clean to make a good first impression. Her gaze automatically turned to the left hand of Dreamy Eyes to see if he wore a wedding band, which he didn't. *Now why did I do that? I've no time for dating or even the slightest interest.*

The face of her ex-boyfriend, Stefan, flashed through her mind. He had the same stunning good looks as this stranger. And look where that had gotten her. What she thought they had as a committed relationship, he saw as something more fluid. Discovering his betrayal still caused a knot in her stomach. The last thing she wanted or needed was a new relationship.

No chance of that happening with Dreamy Eyes. He looked more like an out-of-towner than a local. Still, she could appreciate a good-looking male and there was nothing wrong in doing a little flirting if it would improve bakery sales. It wouldn't go any further than that.

Jasmine leaned forward and smiled. "Who can I assist first?"

"It would only be fair to let these young ladies go first," he replied in a velvety voice with a slight Texas drawl that could melt your heart.

His smile had a warmth and sincerity that was disarming. A blush rose on the girls' faces as she felt the heat rise on her own cheeks. *Thank heavens his gaze is on them.* Jasmine fanned her face, then stood by the glass case displaying the cookies and Danish. With a dazzling smile and a sweeping gesture of her arm, which would have made a beauty pageant contestant proud, she asked, "So, ladies, what sweet delights could I interest you in today?"

As she worked on their order, she glanced over at Dreamy Eyes. He probably was one of the many sightseers who filled the shops here on Market Street throughout the year. His gleaming white smile gave him the air of an actor you'd see in a commercial. And those deep blue eyes grabbed your attention and wouldn't let go.

When it was his turn, he leaned his hands on the counter and winked. "Heard you got some of the best pastries in town. What would you suggest?"

With an awkward smile, Jasmine straightened up and dusted off any imaginary crumbs from her apron. Like the teens, she couldn't take her eyes off him, but she had an excuse since he was her customer. His straight black hair was scattered over his forehead as if he'd just finished a game of touch football, minus the sweat.

She cleared her throat and stepped over to the display case nearest to him. "We have locally sourced blueberries this time of year. You might like one of our blueberry and pecan scones. Or perhaps the blueberry cheese Danish may be more to your liking."

"Locally sourced, you say," he said with a twinkle in his eyes. "Did you pick them yourself?"

"No," Jasmine replied, as the heat of a blush rose on her face. *Thank God, he's probably passing through. The last thing I need is to lose my head again over some man. Stefan taught me what a mistake that was.* Rather than face him, she turned her gaze to the trays and focused on their looks. *What is happening? Why am I feeling so awkward?* "There's, um, a local farmer who, um, brings them to us. Which would you like? Or do you want both?"

"What's your favorite?"

Jasmine faced him again, this time with more composure. With a broad smile, she replied, "I'm the baker, so I like them all. My favorite of the day depends on my mood. What kind of mood are you in?"

This time he was the one whose face turned red, like a kid caught by his mom taking a treat from the cookie jar without permission. He cleared his throat and ran a hand across the back of his neck. "I'm in a good mood and interested in trying something new."

Jasmine nodded and tapped a finger to her lips. "Hmmm, then you would want something sweet and flaky that will melt in your mouth like the Blueberry-Cheese Danish. But then again, the scones have a great buttery texture. If you add a dollop of cream and jam, it's as if you've gone to England for High Tea. Both are my own recipes and a favorite with the locals and tourists alike."

He chuckled and threw up his hands in surrender. "Then why chose only one? Let me have both." He placed his hands on the counter, leaned forward, and his gaze followed the lines of the back-display cases. "Do you have fresh coffee as well?"

"Today's brew is a nice Guatemala Antiguan roast. Do you want any cream?"

"No, black is fine for me. It doesn't compete with the pastries this way."

When she handed him the cup, their fingertips touched, and she felt a spark.

He must have felt it, too, because his hand flinched. "That was a bit electrifying. Hope it's got a good caffeine jolt as well." He laughed and then took a sip.

"Do you want your scone warmed?"

He nodded and sat at the closest table while she prepared a scone and Danish for him. She perused the choices in the trays and picked ones that looked especially photographic. Though she pretended her reasons were purely business related, she did want to impress him.

Once again, the door chimed. This time the customer was a middle-aged woman she'd known for years. "Hello, Patricia. What can I do for you today?"

"I'm looking for your mom. I need an assortment of desserts for my Women's Club luncheon."

"She's out getting supplies. Could I help you plan your event?"

Patricia waved her hand. "No need to, Jaz. Your mom has been handling my special orders for years. Just have her call me when she gets back." With a quick wave goodbye, she was out the door.

Jasmine shook her head and gritted her teeth behind a smile. That wasn't the first time she'd received that response. How long would it take the old-time customers to accept her as an adult, capable of running the bakery and handling catering orders rather than the teenage girl who worked there after school? She plated the Danish and hot scone, added containers of cream and jam and brought them to the table where Dreamy Blue Eyes sat. "Here you go. Enjoy."

"Wow, the blueberry aroma sure comes through when you heat it up." He lifted the plate for a closer whiff and closed his eyes for a moment.

As she waited on other customers coming in and out of the shop, she managed occasional sideways glances at his table. He wasn't scarfing the pastries down in haste, as she'd seen most men do. Instead, he used a fork to break apart the scone and then took small nibbles of the pieces. Half-way through the scone, he finally added the cream and jam. Without finishing it, he started on the Danish. *What's with this guy? Doesn't he like my pastries? Or is he taking his time so we can talk some more?*

When the last of the current flow of customers ebbed away, he stood and walked towards her. *Oh no, did he see her watching him?* She lowered her gaze and busied herself with rearranging the display case.

"Excuse me," he said, leaning over the counter. "Can I get a coffee refill? And do you have anything that's not a sweet item?"

"Didn't you like the pastries?" She held her breath and grabbed at her apron in anticipation of his response.

"No. I mean yes. They were fine. I'd like to try something else." He looked at the displays. "Something smells intriguing. Do you have something else in the kitchen that hasn't been brought to the display cases?"

She straightened her shoulders and smiled. "I've made a batch of chicken, cheese and green chili empanadas. Would you like to try one?"

"Yes, does that buzzer mean they're ready?"

His dazzling smile distracted her, and she forgot for a moment that he'd asked a question. "Oh that, no, that was the timer for cookies I've been baking. Let me do a quick reheat of the empanada."

When she opened the oven door, she put on an oven mitt and pulled out the trays and set them aside for the moment. A hint of chocolate drifted upwards from the tray, which she inhaled with satisfaction. Next, she did a quick 10-second reheat in the microwave for the empanada.

Dreamy Eyes rubbed his hands together, and his eyes widened as she placed the heated item before him. "That's looks like something you'd see in a cookbook. Is this a daily option?"

"No, actually this is the first day we're offering it."

"Hmmm. And I get to try the first one." He picked up his plate, turned, and headed to his table.

Jasmine slipped her hands into her pockets so she wouldn't pull her fingers through her hair. She bit her lip and waited. Though she'd made this recipe many times for friends in L.A., she wondered if she'd forgotten some ingredient or put in the wrong seasoning.

She watched as he cut into the pastry and waited a minute to let the steam escape. Then he let his fork sort through the filling in an examination of its contents. He took a bite and nodded in her direction. "Not bad. The chicken is moist and tender. I can taste a mix of mild and spicy chilis, which blends well with the cilantro and coriander."

Jasmine put her hands on her waist. "Wow, I'm impressed that you can taste the different chilis. Are you a chef?"

Dreamy Eyes lowered his gaze and did a slight cough, which was followed by a sip of his coffee. When his gaze returned to her, he shrugged. "Me, a chef. No, but I do enjoy roasting chilis on a grill.

As he nibbled his food, he asked, "How long have you worked here?"

"I started again about a month ago, but I worked here when I was a teenager."

"So, this is your mother's bakery?"

Jasmine tilted her head. She was surprised he had paid attention to the conversations going on around him. His focus was on his phone while he'd been eating earlier. "Yes, I started helping Mom when I was in elementary school. Back then, all I did was sweep up and wipe down tables. As payment, I was given the opportunity to pick out my favorite treat of the day."

"But you didn't stay. What brought you back?"

She hesitated a moment before answering since she didn't want to sound lame and admit she didn't have any other options at the moment. "I needed a change and one of her employees gave her notice. So, the timing seemed right."

"How is it working with your mom?" He put the plate on the table but still held her gaze.

Jasmine chuckled. "It has its trials. You know how it's said two women can't cook in the same kitchen. When you make that a mother and daughter with their own ideas, there can be clashes."

He nodded and sipped his coffee. "I think I understand. When my brother and I get together for barbecues, there's the regular dispute of whether wood, charcoal, pellets, or propane is the best way to cook."

Jasmine smiled as she listened to him talk. He seemed to love cooking as much as she did. When he explained the grilling experiences he had with his brother, she could imagine being there with them. His expressive hand motions and facial reactions showed her the experience and his joy.

Their conversation about food flowed easily, like old friends swapping stories. While they chatted between customers, she'd bring him a new order of a cupcake or pastry and stand by his table as he'd ask about the recipe and nibble a bite or two. He finished none of the items, but Jasmine thought this was his way of prolonging his stay, which had already exceeded an hour's time.

Other tourists came in and she no longer had time to chat with him. As the line at the counter grew longer, she felt relief at seeing her mom enter the shop. Without hesitation, she slipped behind the register to tally up the orders while Jasmine filled them.

After the crowd thinned, Dreamy Eyes returned to the counter once more. This time he asked for a to-go order of her mom's lemon tarts. Jasmine tried not to show her disappointment as she handed him the last order, which her mom then rung up. There was only a quick goodbye as he picked up one of their business cards and waved before she turned to the next customer. With a sigh, she watched him walk out the door and get into the SUV across the street. Definitely a tourist. Locals would drive trucks. Dreamy Eyes had a spotless gun-metal-green Land Rover.

Several minutes passed before the bakery was once again empty of customers. Her mom started scanning the receipts, stopped, held one of them up and stared at it.

"What is it Mom? Is there something wrong with one of the charge slips?"

"No, it's the name on it. Seems familiar."

"One of your regulars?"

"No, it was that good-looking guy who was sitting at the front table when I came in." Her mom stared at the credit card receipt and then threw her hands over her mouth. "Oh, my, do you know who we had in the shop today?"

Jasmine leaned against the counter and crossed her arms over her chest. "Who was it?"

"Trevor Lassitor." Her mom clapped her hands together. "I hope you were nice to him."

Jasmine scratched her head. "What makes him so special?"

Her mother clucked her tongue. "I thought you read the Tasty Bites section of the *San Antonio Times.* He's one of the food critics."

Jasmine slumped into a chair. Wow, did she read him wrong! It wasn't about flirting. Instead, he was pumping her for filler in his review. That's why he kept trying more items.

She ran her hand across the back of her neck and tried to remember some things he'd said. *Did the like what he ate? Or was he pretending? Would he give the bakery a good review? If it's not positive, maybe he could come back for a re-evaluation."*

Only she knew restaurant critics didn't do follow-ups to improve their reviews. But maybe, just maybe the review would be fine. At least, that's what she hoped.

CHAPTER 2
Trevor's Impressions

After Trevor got in his Land Rover, he glanced back at the bakery for one last glimpse at Jaz. At least that's the name he heard regular customers call her. Was the name short for something? Or was it a nickname? He hadn't asked her name since he was there for his job. He needed to remain objective as he was critiquing cooking skills and standards of service for his column. This was only a bakery. Usually, he'd get a few items, maybe eat one as he watched other customers responses, then take the rest in the Rover with him. But it was different with Jaz. He'd spent way too much time with her and found it hard to leave.

Now he was behind in his schedule, and he'd have to play catch up. Good thing his Hill Country feature story included an overnight stay to complete a weekend getaway. The stops he didn't have time to do tonight could be finished tomorrow, which meant he would leave in the afternoon instead of the morning.

Yet her smile and easy banter stayed embedded in his mind. His heart beat a little faster as he recalled the way wisps of her wavy auburn hair kept falling over her sparkling blue eyes. He had wanted to reach over and slip them away. "No, I need to stay professional," he muttered as he slammed the palm of his hand on the steering wheel.

Her shop would be only a paragraph or two out of the entire featured article. Yet, when that first initial spark occurred as their hands touched and their eyes locked, made him wish time would stop. When she described her pastries, he felt a kindred spirit in her desire to create something satisfying instead of only filling. Her enthusiasm was clear in the animation of her voice that rose in delight, her eyes that flashed in excitement, and her long delicate hands that told the story of what she did. The passion she showed tugged at his heart.

Passion for food was the reason he became a food critic and rated restaurants according to his standards. For him, dining out wasn't about keeping up with the latest trends of unusual food pairings but to find culinary experiences that appealed to the palate and sensory perception as well.

Their conversation showed she felt the same way. She wasn't afraid to take chances or create new twists in food and spice pairings. For the most part, the pastries she offered were top notch, with only a couple flaws in preparation. Not even top chefs got new recipes right the first few times. He'd seen that in his restaurant reviews. Creating something unique and delicious took a lot of trial and error to get just the right blend of flavors. Yet, her baking style wasn't the only thing that piqued his interest; it was Jaz herself. He wanted to see her again and not for a food review.

He blew out a heavy breath and started his Rover. *Stay focused and be professional. Can't let my personal interest in Jaz color my thinking. This is business.* Still, her final smile as he left the bakery drifted through his mind and he longed to return to see her again.

His next stop was Frostbites for ice cream. The shop already had five customers ahead of him when he entered. For most people, this would have been an annoyance, but the delay gave him time to mentally work up the layout his story. An ice cream shop visit was a quick in as it should have been for the bakery, except for his meeting with Jaz. He rubbed his face and shook his head; he had to get her out of his memory. Can't mix business with my personal life - at least not until the review was published. He'd complete her review without bias, but her response to what she read could determine if she would want to see him again.

CHAPTER 3
A Chance Meeting

When the bakery closed two hours later, Jasmine still had Trevor on her mind. Though she worked with her mom prepping for the next day, she did it by habit without giving it any real attention. She used the time to recall if she'd said something, anything that could reflect on the business in a negative way. Trevor seemed to like everything, but was that an act to catch her off guard? *Why did I ignore how he only nibbled at his food? I should have tried to draw him out more about what he liked.*

"Are you upset me with me for taking extra time off this afternoon?" Mom huffed after locking the door.

Jasmine cocked her head and frowned. "Why would I be upset with that? You had errands to run and the shop was quiet when you left. I can handle the shop on my own. You returned at the right time when the afternoon rush was at its fullest."

"Well, I should have returned earlier, but my doctor's appointment took longer than expected."

Jasmine's attention riveted on Mom. "You didn't tell me you had a doctor's appointment today?"

"Nothing to worry about, only a standard check-up," She patted Jasmine's cheek. "While I was out and about, I ran into Sara who told me what a great job you were doing in the bakery."

Jasmine threw up her hands in exasperation. "Are you using your friends to spy on me?"

Mom stepped back and shook her head. "What's going on with you? Why are you so touchy? You know I have faith in you. I always have. My friends make me feel even prouder when they say nice things about you."

"Well, not everyone apparently shares your opinion." Jasmine's nostrils flared and she exhaled deeply. "Patricia Vasquez came in today and wants you to do the desserts for the Women's Club luncheon."

"That's great, Jaz."

Jasmine rolled her eyes. "Mom, please, it's Jasmine. Jaz sounds too cutesy and girlish."

"Well, you'll always be my little girl." Mom reached over and gave Jasmine's cheek a pinch.

"Yeah, yeah, I know. But I don't like other people thinking I'm a little girl." In mock drama, she slapped her hands to her cheek and raised her voice to a high childlike pitch.

"I'm just a widdle girl. I don't know what to do."

Mom smirked and shook her head. "It can't really be that bad?"

"But it is. Miz Vasquez made it seem like it was too much for me to handle. She wouldn't even discuss it with me. Only wanted to deal with you."

"Oh, honey, Patricia didn't mean anything by that." She gave Jasmine a hug. "It's her first few months as the Women's Club President. She's afraid of mishandling the event by underestimating. I've done their events so many times. I could do them in my sleep. What she needs is someone who can plan and execute the event and let her take all the credit."

"And you're good with her acting like it was all *her* plan?"

"Of course, I am. As the Bible says, 'Do unto others as you would have them do to you.'"

Jasmine sighed. "That's the Golden Rule."

"Yes, a bit of a paraphrase from the Bible." Mom patted Jasmine's shoulder. "In Titus 2:7, it says that in all things we are to show ourselves to be a pattern of good works That's what I do for Patricia."

"In Luke, it also says a laborer is worthy of his wages." Jasmine put her hands on her hips and furrowed her brows. "You are charging for your services? I know the

Women's Club can certainly afford it and it's not a charity case."

Mom wrapped her arm around Jasmine's waist, and they walked together to the car. "Yes, I do get paid by the Women's Club and by Patricia when she wants to do a little more than their budget will allow. Don't worry about me or the business. God's in control and I do my part. And I'm counting on you to use your marketing skills to bring in more customers and grow the business. Got any fresh ideas to bring in more business without running me into debt?"

While Mom drove home, Jasmine chewed on a fingernail and pondered some suggestions she had for the bakery. Tapping her fingers on the dashboard, she began slowly. "I've got some ideas for promotions that won't cost too much and recommendations to reduce waste through product analysis."

"What's always worked for me is having sweet treats for celebrations and everyday enjoyment. The smell of fresh baked chocolate chip cookies is hard to resist as well as the almond paste flaky croissants. Our regulars love them. That's what's kept them coming back. You don't need to change something that works already."

Jasmine turned toward the window and frowned. *There she goes again, with the "what's always worked for me." There's so much more she could do to raise revenues.*

Nothing has changed since high school. She doesn't want my opinion, only my agreement. Why am I even staying here? I seriously need to find a new job that will challenge me as soon as possible.

"However, I do like the idea of mixing it up a bit with something new. Regulars would have something different to try along with their old-time favorites."

Jasmine's head pivoted and she stared at Mom wide-eyed. "Really? You're willing to try something new."

Mom reached over and patted Jasmine's leg. "Of course, I am. Just don't overwhelm me with a major overhaul of the business. After all, your empanadas were a hit and sold out today. You created a winner. C'mon, hit me with your best marketing idea – remember not too extravagant. Show me what you learned in the big city."

"Well, since you brought it up. Here's a concept I've worked out in my head for a few days to jump-start the business. We'll do a new pastry contest." Jasmine took a deep breath. "We could add three or maybe four new choices to the menu. Maybe a new streusel, cookie or pie"

"Only in small batches at first to test it out."

"Right. We'll do a poster for each one with descriptions of their flavors to entice customers to buy. I can put together some graphics and add photos from my computer, so you won't need to hire a graphics designer. If they try the new items, they get two votes. If they buy anything else, they get one vote. That will let us know more of what we should consider adding."

"It's like a baked goods election," Mom said.

"Right. All votes will include the entrant's name. We'll have a jar for each of new items with the votes going in the jar of their choice. At the end of the month, the pastry that gets the most votes will become a standard on our menu."

"And if the others do well, we'll add them, too."

"Uh-huh. You've got it, Mom. But here's the fun part I hope can create some real buzz. We'll draw a name out of the jar for the most popular pastry as our winner. That person will have naming rights for the new pastry."

"What if someone came up with a really weird name?" Mom asked.

"I've thought about that, too, as it is a possibility. We'll limit the number of letters so it will fit on the menu board and we'll have final approval."

"And then that pastry will become a standard."

"As an award-winner."

Mom squeezed Jasmine's hand and beamed. "I'm so glad you're back in town. God surely knows how to answer prayers."

Jasmine squeezed her hand back. "Yes, today our cup overflowed with business. Hope tomorrow will be the same. Tired me out, but it felt productive."

"All my running around wore me out as well. I'm ready to kick my shoes off and have a simple dinner. Any suggestions?"

Jasmine leaned back into the seat and closed her eyes for a moment. Almost immediately, her eyes flashed open and she hit her hand against her head. "I can't believe that I forgot I planned a girl's night in with Savannah and Lexie."

"When is that supposed to happen?"

"According to the time on my phone, in about 20 minutes. I need to take a shower and clean up. I'll never be ready."

"I'm sure they will understand. Call and tell them you're running late."

They pulled into the garage and Jasmine hopped out of the car as she made her call. "Savannah, it's been a bear of a day. I'm walking in the door now. I'll be there in 35 minutes. What do you want me to bring? ...Dessert, of course... And some of my special sodas, sure... I'll see you soon."

Jasmine headed for her mom's well-stocked, oversized pantry that could feed an impromptu gathering of twenty or more friends at a moment's notice. She'd surely find something there to fit her needs. Rummaging around, she noticed a case of assorted Italian sodas and picked up four of the liter-sized bottles. The sodas were something she'd loved as a teen and her mom always made sure there were enough available for her and her friends. She stashed them into a couple of the nearby cloth shopping bags. Next, she headed to the refrigerator and pulled out two blood oranges, a lime, a nectarine, a small container of fresh strawberries and some fresh herbs as her secret ingredients. She slipped all of these items into another shopping bag. "You don't mind if I take a few things with me, do you?" Jasmine turned expecting to see her mom over by the stove waiting for the kettle to boil, but she wasn't there. "Mom, where are you?"

"In the living room."

Jasmine walked into the room carrying the shopping bags. "What are you doing in here?"

Mom had her eyes closed and was slumped in one of the soft upholstered chairs with her feet on a matching ottoman. "Needed to relax a bit. Guess I did a little too much running around today."

Jasmine sat on the edge of the ottoman and put a hand on her mother's knee. "Do you want me to stay and make you something to eat?"

"Don't worry about me. I'll be okay. Just need a little breather." Mom patted Jasmine's hand. "With those bags in your hands, I can see it's like old times when you'd raid the pantry to have a picnic with friends."

"And if you don't mind, I'm going to raid tomorrow's day-old basket at the bakery. I seem to recall a few items we could use for dessert."

"That's fine. Go ahead. Glad you can jump right back in with friends."

Jasmine smiled and nodded. "You know, I wasn't sure I'd be able to. We all went our separate ways in the last ten years since I moved out. I've kept up with them sporadically through social media. As I got more involved with my new friends in California, keeping in touch the way we used to do fell by the wayside."

Her mom chuckled. "Yes, I remember those long calls when you were a teen."

"Yes. Everything was so dramatic in high school. We had to discuss every little bit of minutia as if our life depended on it. Who has time for that today?"

"Apparently, the younger generation. Your cousins constantly have their fingers on their tech toys doing tweets, texting and who knows what else."

"Well, it's the quickest way to keep in touch. Only tonight, we'll see each other in person as soon as I get ready." Jasmine left the bags by the door, then gently squeezed her mom's shoulder before leaving the living room.

Jasmine rolled her eyes as she walked into her bedroom. It was the same room with pale peach walls and striped curtains from when she was growing up. Her mom didn't change it into a hobby room or workout room like other parents did when their children left home. No, it was held in suspended animation in hopes Jasmine would return and they'd continue to live together as a family until she started one of her own.

When she returned for summer visits in her college years, she ignored the look of her teen years' time-warp room since her stay was temporary. Now that she was living here in a semi-permanent situation, it bugged her. She wasn't some naïve teen anymore and didn't want to feel like one. It was time to bring this room up-to-date. But not tonight. Tomorrow. Or whenever she could find the time.

After a quick shower and change into fresh clothes, Jasmine started to walk out of the room and then turned back. She walked over to the wall by her dresser, pulled down a poster of Britney Spears and tossed it in her trash basket. *That was my past interest and a minor start on a makeover.* With a sense of satisfaction, she left the room.

Her nose followed a comforting scent from the kitchen. Mom was now sitting at the table. "I see you've got the old standby of scrambled eggs and toast for dinner."

"When you're tired and hungry, it really hits the spot. Especially with a hot cup of tea."

"Savannah is having spaghetti and meatballs, another great comfort food. I feel a bit guilty that I didn't make something special at the bakery today."

"Even the baker needs a day off. I'm sure they'll like whatever you can pick up at the bakery. Go have fun."

Jasmine leaned over and kissed her mom's cheek before heading out the door. "See you later. Don't wait up." With a chuckle she added, "Not that I plan to stay out late anyway."

Mom called to her before the door closed. "Yea, yea, sure. I know you girls. You get chatty and lose all sense of time. Enjoy."

CHAPTER 4
Rekindling Friendships

After leaving the driveway, Jasmine turned on an oldies station and started singing along with the words of "Who let the dogs out?" She smiled, recalling the times she sang that song with her friends when they were feeling blue. It was their way of proclaiming the teasing from others didn't matter, they were insignificant, yappy dogs. As class outcasts, they formed an emotional support squad. If it weren't for her two friends, Jasmine didn't know how she would have survived elementary school through high school.

Back then, she was nicknamed the Pillsbury Dough girl, which still made her wince. She'd lost the weight by getting on an exercise regimen and improving on the foods she ate. Gone were the days of sampling everything in the bakery. The only sampling now was a nibble or two.

Since the stores around the bakery had closed for the evening, it was easy to find a parking space. Jasmine stopped in front and headed for the door. Once inside, she turned on the main lights and headed to the counter.

She perused the basket of today's unsold baked goods and picked up an assortment of cookies. That would do for tonight. If Savannah had ice cream, they could make ice cream sandwiches as a special treat. When she opened the door to the car, she saw a dark colored Land Rover pass by. Was it Trevor? No, that was too much of a coincidence. He'd be long gone from Falcon Creek. But his smile was still vivid in her memory,

Savannah lived on the other side of the downtown area. Jasmine drove through the newer commercial area and glanced at the restaurants. She saw the backlit sign for Fresh, the latest trendy restaurant. The side parking lot looked full and she noticed a green Land Rover illuminated by one the lot lights. Trevor was getting out of his car. She caught her breath and bit her lip. Should she pull in and talk to him? What would she say if she stopped? "Why didn't you tell me you were a food critic?" That wouldn't change anything. Instead, she continued her drive to her friend's house and prayed for good words in his review.

A few minutes later, she pulled into Savannah's driveway. Jasmine slowly walked toward the front door taking the time to admire her friend's expertise with landscape design. The front lawn looked like the perfect "how to" example from home and garden magazines. Flowering plants and shrubs in differing heights dotted the lawn to create a flow of color and texture. Greenery continued up the front steps and onto the porch with an assortment of potted plants. Having a green thumb was not one of her talents, but maybe she could learn a few tips from Savannah while she was back in town.

Her two friends must have seen her car lights flash across the driveway as she pulled in. The front door swung open even before she rang the doorbell. She placed the bags with her supplies on the porch as her friends came to greet her. They threw their arms about her in a three-way hug amongst squeals of delight.

"I am so glad you're back in town. It is so much more fun visiting in person than on the phone or social media," Savannah said. "I'm glad I was persistent in getting you to come over.

"I know, but this past month I've been so busy with trying to get into the flow of work at the bakery and getting out resumes that I ran out of time."

"Well, tonight is all about fun. Time to relax. The dynamic girl trio is together again," Lexie added as her face broke into a huge smile.

Once inside, Savannah asked, "How do you like my place? It's not as big and fancy as I used to have with Derek, but it's less work. And when it's only me taking care of it, it's so much easier."

Jasmine let her gaze roam about the living room. The walls were a tawny beige like the colors of the beach and her furniture looked soft and comfy with the azure blue throw pillows and blue and tan print upholstery. The assorted pictures on the walls displayed some of Savannah's favorite places and happy candid shots with her adorable three-year-old daughter. Gone were any pictures of Savannah's ex-husband. Their fairytale marriage of high school sweethearts disappeared because Derek couldn't apparently remember the line in their wedding vows that said forsaking all others. In return, Savannah forsook him since he had no interest in changing.

I like what you've done," Jasmine nodded. "This place says kick off your shoes and be at peace, which is what I'm going to do right now."

Savannah laughed. "It may emote peace now, but when my little peach blossom, Carolinda, is here, there's a constant uproar of giggles, screams of delight, or chants of no, no, no. She's a handful, but I'm thankful to have her in my life."

"Where is she tonight?" Jasmine asked.

With a frown, Savannah replied, "She's with her dad. He gets these occasional bouts of wanting to be a father and show her off."

Lexie started singing, "Who let the dogs out? Woof. Woof. Derek is a dog. Woof. Woof."

"That is sooo funny," Jasmine said. "I heard that song on the way over. I remembered the times we sang it about the jerks we encountered."

"If he's showing her off, it's to impress some new lady he's dating and hoping to make the moves on. Derek certainly fits the bill for being a dog," Lexie replied.

"Hey, he's got his good points, too, even if he was a mistake for a husband," Savannah replied with a playful tap on Lexie's shoulder. "He's never late with child support and helps out with other costs as well."

"Speaking of mistakes, I hope I didn't make one myself today," Jasmine added as she unpacked her grocery bags. She smiled as she glanced at the Henckels knife set in the butcher block. This was a gift she'd sent to Savannah when she moved into this house. Since she was starting over, Jasmine had wanted her to feel good about the new kitchen, and what better way to do that than with a quality knife set that would last longer than most marriages. "Okay, if I make myself at home?" She pointed to the butcher block of knives on the counter,

Savannah waved her hand as she sat by the breakfast bar. "Sure, go ahead, Do your magic."

Jasmine smiled and started chopping the fruit on the bamboo cutting board she found next to the butcher block. "As I was saying, I think I messed up at work today."

"Did you botch a recipe by using salt instead of sugar? My mind tends to drift off when I'm doing a recipe. I forget if I've added two teaspoons or three," Lexie said as she sat on a bar stool next to Savannah.

"I know what you mean, Lexie, I used to forget how much I added sometimes. That's why I always keep the item I'm measuring in my hand until I'm finished with it. I also make sure I drop the ingredients in separate sections so I can actually see what's been added."

"That's a great Idea, Jasmine. I'll have to try that. But it still won't make me an all-around good cook like you," Lexie chuckled.

Jasmine raised an eyebrow. "Well, maybe if you actually spent some time cooking or taking cooking classes instead of having guys wine and dine you like the princess you are, you would be a better cook."

"Wow, point taken. But that is an idea. I could take some classes. That could be another way to meet Mr. Right who can cook." Lexie tapped her finger to her cheek. "But how can I take an advanced class to find him, when I'm just a beginner?"

"That is a dilemma." Savannah said. "Maybe you can start as a novice with a guy and let your love for cooking grow with a love for each other."

"Well aren't you the romantic?" Lexie replied.

"Always. So, what was the mistake you're talking about, Jasmine? Did you hear from Stefan and he's trying to lure you back to L.A.?" Savannah asked.

Lexie threw her arms up as if pushing that idea away and raised her voice. "No, no, no. That hunk in wolf's clothing is not going to whisk our girl away again. I'm just getting used to having our trio together again."

Jasmine raised two fingers in the air. "Scouts honor. I will not let him back in my life again. However, he's trying to be helpful. I've received a couple of texts from him this week. He says he's been putting out feelers for a new job for me. I think that's sweet, but I've learned my lesson with Stefan. Just because he was a great business mentor, didn't make him a perfect boyfriend and potential marriage material. He taught me a lot about business, but I was totally blind to his interest in other women." She scrunched up her nose, put down the knife and placed her hands on the counter. "He was my mistake in L.A. and I've learned my lesson."

"Ooh. I know what you mean. When a guy gets under my skin, it's so easy for me to slip into this fantasy reality of happily ever after and totally ignore what's happening for real," Lexie replied as she snapped her fingers. "That is until I finally wake up to the truth."

Jasmine recalled how life had changed for Lexie. In high school, she wore dorky glasses and had a beanpole figure that none of the boys noticed. After high school, the glasses changed to contacts and her figure finally filled out. After college, she'd married one of the guys from high school who she'd always had a crush on. However, the marriage was short lived. She became a widow at twenty-two when he died from an IED blast during a tour of duty in the Middle East. Since then she'd had numerous boyfriends, but no one came close to her first love.

"Well, I'm done with seeing romance through rose-colored glasses. I'm going to devote my energies to being the best mom for Carolinda and steer away from dating, The next Mr. Right will be Mr. Right Forever and he'll have to find me and prove himself to me." Savannah said as she walked over to the oven to check on the dinner.

Jasmine pointed the tip of the knife in the cutting board. "Making decisions for my life is now number one. It's not getting back with someone like Stefan who doesn't appreciate me." She picked up the knife and continued cutting the fruit. "Savannah, could you get me a large pitcher or punch bowl to mix this all together? And some glasses."

"If today's mistake wasn't about Stefan, what was?" Savannah asked as she pulled the needed items out of one of the cabinets.

Jasmine continued. "I feel a little stupid telling you this, because I should have realized who he was by his actions. But here goes. A food critic came in the bakery today. He was there for over an hour and we talked a lot. I'm not sure if I said some things to him that could make me, or the business look bad."

Lexie leaned forward on the counter and her eyes grew big. "Wow, I've never met a food critic before. They're always so mysterious. You never see their pictures. Was he fat, old and grumpy?"

Jasmine stopped her work as the image of Trevor popped into her mind. She saw his eyes twinkling with mirth as he described a grilling disaster. "No, quite the opposite. He had these gorgeous blue eyes and looked like he stepped off the page of some fashion layout."

"Sounds like he got your attention. Is he still in town?" Lexie asked.

"Yes. I thought he'd leave after he finished at the bakery, but I saw him getting out of his Land Rover at the parking lot of that new restaurant called Fresh."

"Hmmm. A Land Rover. Sounds like the man has money. I like that." Lexie said.

"Or he overspends like he does," Savannah added.

"Yeah, guys can be big spenders until the bills catch up to them." Lexie sighed. "I remember one blind date who had his credit card declined when we were at a restaurant. I was so relieved he had another card that was accepted. I didn't want to get stuck with the bill."

"You don't believe in helping out your date with the dinner check?" Jasmine asked with a smirk on her face. "Or was he a case of, 'Who let the dogs out? Woof. Woof.'"

Lexie laughed. "Oh, he was certainly a woofer. Did nothing but complain about this or that from the time we sat at the table. I couldn't wait to say good night and goodbye. No more blind dates for me."

"Did he tell you he was a food critic?" Savannah placed a pitcher, a long-handled spoon and three glasses next to Jasmine.

"No, he didn't. While I waited on him, he paid cash. Then with his final order he paid by credit card. Mom recognized his name, Trevor Lassitor, as she sorted through the credit card slips."

"I've read his column. He's really interesting. Sounds like he has a passion for food and hates it when restaurants don't have that same zeal. When he sees problems with a restaurant, he doesn't mince words, he lays it on the line." Savannah grimaced. "However, he's not like some TV show cooking judges who are downright mean. I hope he saw your passion and skill."

"How could the man not consider her one of the best in this town?" Lexie waved her hand in the air. "This girl can bake circles around anyone I know. You don't have to worry about a thing."

"From your mouth to God's ear and then whispered into Trevor's." Jasmine high-fived Lexie before returning to mixing all her ingredients and pouring them into glasses. She added some ice cubes from the nearby ice bucket. "Ladies, here's your beverages."

Savannah raised her glass, "To Jasmine, may she get the good review she so richly deserves."

While her friends each sipped their drinks, Jasmine waited for their reactions. She smiled when she saw their heads nod in satisfaction.

"What do you call this," Lexie smiled broadly before taking another sip. "It's fantastic."

"Summer Breeze."

"Ooh that fits." Lexie half-closed her eyes. "I can picture myself lying in a hammock and sipping this on a summer day."

"You should add this to the menu at the bakery." Savannah put down her glass and headed over to the stove to check on the dinner.

Jasmine laughed. "I can't add everything you like on the menu. It's only a bakery and not a restaurant."

Savannah pushed her lip out in a pretend pout. "Why not? You should always use my suggestions."

Jasmine laughed. "When you can find the funds to make it into a restaurant, I will."

"Speaking of restaurants, it's time to eat." Lexie opened the oven door and took a deep whiff of the garlic bread before she slipped the fragrant crustiness into a basket and brought it to the table.

Savannah followed with the steaming bowl of spaghetti glistening with a thick, chunky red sauce with slivers of fresh aromatic basil and topped with savory meatballs, which she placed at the table's center. Jasmine brought in the pitcher with the remaining Summer Breeze concoction. Once their glasses and tossed salad were in place on the table to finish out their meal, they all joined hands and closed their eyes.

Savannah started the prayer. "Heavenly Father, thank you for the gift of friendship and the joy that comes with it. Thank you also for the fellowship we have with you. Bless this food to our bodies and your words to our hearts. Amen."

There was little talk as they passed around the food and filled their plates. Once their taste buds were temporarily sated with the first bites, conversation returned.

"You know I'm always looking for Mr. Right who usually turns out wrong," Lexie said. "Well, I heard this interview on a talk show that said you should write down a list of all the traits you wanted in a mate, like a wish list. Then you're supposed to do another list of what makes you a great choice."

"An honest list about yourself? Most everyone would overrate his or her traits. Now if one of your friends rated you instead, that would be more accurate. Especially if it was one of your good friends." Savannah said as she held up her fork between bites.

"Of course, I wouldn't need to have anyone else rate me. It's hard to find any character defects in my personality since I'm nearly an angel." Lexie smiled innocently and fluttered her eyelids.

Both Savannah and Jasmine laughed with Lexie joining in.

"Okay," Lexie said. "I know I'm not a saint. My biggest problem with men is I'm looking for perfection. I want someone to complete me."

"Complete yourself," Jasmine said. "No guy will ever be perfect, even if they seem like it at first." She immediately thought of Trevor. He seemed so sweet and fun at the bakery until she learned he was a food critic. All that sweetness was for notes to complete his newspaper column.

"Let's give it a try." Savannah rolled up some spaghetti with her fork and spoon. "I'll give it a start for an ideal mate. First off, he'd have to be good with kids, and my Carolinda would have to like him. He could even have some kids of his own and would need a sense of humor. When you have kids, you have to be able to laugh."

"Are you looking for a daddy or a man?" Lexie asked. "I want my man to be good with kids, but I want a husband who wakes up in the morning and the first thing he says is 'I love you' and mean it. I could handle a whole bunch of kids, if I knew deep down, he loved me in capital letters."

Jasmine nodded in agreement. "I think similar hobbies or interests are even more important. I don't want a man who can't take his eyes off the TV during football season. I want them on me."

"You want someone who can cook alongside you in the kitchen. Maybe even in the bakery, and then between the two of you there could be a restaurant," Savannah said before putting a forkful of spaghetti in her mouth.

Jasmine shook with laughter. "You really have this thing about me starting a restaurant."

"Why not? You'd be a hit. With someone else cooking with you, the results would be heavenly." Savannah leaned back in her chair and nodded looking for the others to agree.

"Ooh, I know. You could call it Heaven Scents -- for delights beyond this world." Lexie sang the made-up jingle in her best choir voice.

"Do you two know how many hours it takes to run a restaurant?" Jasmine glared. "Mr. Right and I would have no time for a personal life."

"Then make it a breakfast and lunch place only, so you could have the evenings together." Lexie said. "And you could close Sunday and Monday for more free time."

"Ah, but you know the old adage," Jasmine raised her index finger. "Too many cooks spoil the broth. I don't want to clash with my spouse over recipes."

"Then one of you will have to be out front in the restaurant and the other in the kitchen." Savannah said.

"Or you could specialize only in desserts and specialty sodas like the ones you made tonight. He could do the entrée choices."

Jasmine threw up her hands. "I know you think it would be wonderful for me to have a restaurant, but quite honestly, I don't know how long I'll be here. I really do enjoy baking, but I spent ten years building up my name in marketing and I don't want to throw that down the drain."

"But you've really got a gift for baking. You often told us of the fun you had making treats for your friends in L.A." Lexie said.

"And you know your mom loves having you here." Savannah added.

"I don't want to be boxed in right now." Jasmine bowed her head as she felt a knot form in her stomach. Though she loved being with her friends, she missed the excitement of L.A. and the adrenalin rush of landing a new client. The thrill wasn't here in running a small-town bakery. With all the resumes she had sent out, no doubt a good job offer would soon come in. In the meantime, she'd enjoy time with her friends and hone her baking skills.

"Okay, we'll forget about the restaurant for now. But Mr. Right is out there for you." Lexie raised her glass in a salute.

"Speaking of Mr. Right for you. Let's get back to Mr. Food Critic?" Savannah put her elbows on the table and chin in her hands. "You said he was there a really long time. Wouldn't someone reviewing the food, order it quickly and then leave to take notes in private?"

"That sounds reasonable," Lexie added. "How long was he there?"

"Actually, about an hour, maybe more. We kept chatting in between customers."

Savannah nodded. "Well, I don't think he stayed just for the food. I think he was flirting with you."

Jasmine shook her head. "No, it was for more details for his column." Although she was starting to have a flicker of hope that maybe, somehow, he was interested in her and not only the bakery.

"Okay, Jasmine. Here's the big question. Did he ask for your number?" Lexie tapped her fingers on the table waiting for a response.

"No, he didn't ask for my number, but when he took one of our business cards, he acted like he wanted me to see he took it for a reason."

"Let's have another toast," Savannah said as she raised her glass in the air. "May Jasmine be blessed with a great review and a phone call that leads to a fabulous date."

They tapped their glasses together and then took sips. Laughter mixed with serious and light-hearted conversation about men continued to fill the room as they ate. The clink of ice in glasses, the sound of forks on the plates and bowls scraped of the last bits of food were testaments to the taste and comfort of the food. By the time dessert rolled around, the day's stress and concern for the upcoming review had slipped away.

Though Jasmine missed the friends she had in L.A., she'd never had the same camaraderie she felt at this table. These two women really knew her. They understood her fears and anxieties since they'd lived through many of them together. Being with them again fit like a favorite dress. This time she wouldn't take their friendship for granted as she'd done while living in California. She wanted to keep these friends for life. When the time came for her to move on to a new job, she'd make sure to keep the connection with them strong. Laughing with them over their past romantic mistakes helped put her own past issues in perspective and gave her hope to move on – that is in the future once she was settled in a new job. They also lifted her self-confidence with their expectations of how she could expand the bakery into a lunch spot. The idea did intrigue her as it flitted through her brain, but she quickly dismissed it. Mom would never consider expanding the business like that.

When they all said good night and Jasmine drove home, she did so in silence. She didn't need music as a distraction from the hectic traffic in L.A. This was midweek and the traffic was light. The quiet of the night was comforting and gave her time to reflect on her blessings. These included being home again with close friends, having the time to develop her baking skills, and helping her mom grow the bakery business.

The thought of leaving again left her with a twinge of sadness, but she pushed those feelings away. Being a baker was not her life's work. She savored the thrill of working with clients that grew their business with her marketing campaigns. Sure, she had some opportunity to do that with her mom, but she didn't want to expand her business to more locations. That wasn't enough for Jasmine. She wanted to make a name for herself and even have her own company. That meant she'd continue to send out resumes and network with past co-workers, even if that included Stefan. But with Stefan it would strictly be business.

The timing was uncertain on how long it would take for her to land her dream job again. It could be a couple of weeks or several months. In the meantime, she would stay positive and make the most of her time. With that thought, her mind drifted to Trevor. Did he spend all that time in the bakery only to get notes for his review? Or had an interest in her sparked as the touch of their fingers had. "Arrgh, I can't be thinking about him. The only interest I need have with him is his review."

CHAPTER 5
It's Good to be Home

When Jasmine opened the front door a little after ten, and turned on the light, she was surprised to see her mom sleeping in her favorite chair, feet up on an ottoman and a book open on her lap. She tried to be quiet and tiptoed into the room, but she saw her mom's eyes blink open after a few steps. "Sorry, didn't mean to wake you. Unless of course you were waiting up for me. You can now be assured I came in at a reasonable hour."

Mom laughed. "No, Jaz, I mean Jasmine, I wasn't waiting up for you. Actually, I only sat to read for a little bit. Must have been more tired than I thought."

"Are you sure you're okay? You do seem to tire more easily than I recall from previous visits."

"Don't worry about me" Mom waved the idea away. "There's nothing that me and the Lord can't handle. Tell me about tonight."

Jasmine sat on the edge of the ottoman and smiled. "It was just like old times. We laughed and talked about guys."

"I guess some things never change."

"Well, some things can change. They liked the soda creation I made for them and wondered if we might add it to drink choices at the bakery."

"What drink choices? We only have coffee and tea, not exactly a menu. Besides, if we added cold beverages, we'd need to buy a refrigerated case, soda machine and an ice machine. I don't want to go into more debt. We'll have to wait until we save the money needed to buy the stuff."

"Are there money issues I should be concerned about?"

"No, no, there's nothing to worry about in that matter. Whenever possible, I like to pay for new things with cash, so I don't have to pay the high credit card interest. I believe in being fiscally conservative."

"You'd tell me if you had problems, wouldn't you?"

"Yes, I would. Trust me. There are no money issues at the bakery. I still have reserves from your dad's life insurance policy. It's enough for emergencies, but not enough to stop working. Now, let me get up. I prefer to sleep in my own bed rather than this chair."

"Sure, Mom." Jasmine stood and put out her hand to help her mother up from the chair. "Once we get everything prepped for the oven in the morning and handle the pre-work rush, why don't you come back for a rest?"

"I'm not that old to need morning naps, Jasmine."

She wrapped her arm around Mom's shoulder. "Hey, I'm not doing it for you, but for me. This way you'll be able to come back and fill in for me so I can have something healthier than a sugar snack before the afternoon onslaught of sugar-starved people."

Mom laughed as they walked together down the hall. "I know that's all you want me to think it is. However, I come from a long line of worriers, and I know the signs. However, I'll go along with your idea and take a couple hours off in the mid-morning so you can do the same after lunch. Take some time to see how the town has grown since your visit last year."

Jasmine leaned against the doorframe. "Oh, yes, the booming metropolis of Falcon Creek. What are we? A population of 5,001, not counting tourists when they double those numbers?"

"Don't make fun of this town. I love it. Everyone cares about each other. Our business neighbors on Market Street and here on Cherry Wood are our friends. I bet you didn't have the same closeness when you lived in California."

"You're right there. The best we did was a wave or a brief hello as we passed one another in our driveways while coming home or going to work. For the most part, any friends I had were from my job. From time to time, we'd have food delivered if we were working late. Most lunches were brown-bagged unless we were taking a client out for lunch.

"Sounds like you worked way too much. You know the old adage. All work and no play make —"

"me a dull girl. Yes, I know but Stefan and I did have fun together. That is until the company blew up and he got cozy with someone else in the company. It still surprises me that I didn't see what he was up to."

"Oh, Jasmine, I'm so sorry you had to go through that. But I believe God's got someone else out there for you. In due time, you'll find each other."

"Well, I'm not about to rush into something with a new guy. As I told my friends tonight, I'm going to be man-free for a while. After all, you want me to get a marketing plan together for the bakery. That will fill my free hours rather than wasting them with someone who won't work out."

"I definitely appreciate that idea. However, you need to keep your eyes open."

"And what about you, Mom? Are you keeping your eyes open?"

"Me? No, I don't think so. I had many wonderful years with your dad. I can't imagine finding someone who would fit so well with me again."

"Well, Mom. I think you should take your own advice. I'd love to see you with someone who loves and adores you like Dad did."

"That's not on top of my "to do" list to find a husband. I'll leave it up to God. If he wants me to have a new man in my life, he'll have to bring him to me. I can't imagine trying any of those dating sites."

Jasmine sighed. "No, they're not as easy as they make it out to find a match. I tried it for a few times, and it went nowhere."

"Then maybe we'll have to try the old-fashioned way of match-making by arranging meetings and dates with the sons of my friends."

"Mom don't even think about it. I'm not interested in dating. And I want to keep it that way."

"I could put out a few feelers to see who's available."

Jasmine noticed the twinkle in her mom's eyes as she made the statement. 'Yeah, no. Let's work on the bakery for the time being. And that means we'll be getting up early. Time to call it a night."

Her mom hugged her. "Good night, Jasmine. Pleasant dreams."

"You, too." As she turned toward her room, Trevor's face flashed through her mind. *It wouldn't be bad to have a nice dream about him. No, that's not gonna happen. That would lead to daydreams and I don't want any of that now.*

CHAPTER 6
Hard to Forget

After Trevor finished his dinner assignment and report, he went to the nearby fitness club. He stepped on a treadmill and programmed a 60-minute interval plan. As the machine ran its cycle, his thoughts slipped back to meeting Jaz. Maybe he'd call her after the workout. Then he quickly shook his head. Not yet. After the publication of his review, he could call. He gritted his teeth and blew out a deep breath as he continued his workout.

Ninety minutes later and substantially sweaty from the treadmill and free weights, Trevor headed for the shower. As he put his phone in the locker, it buzzed. The caller ID showed it was his brother. "Hi, Ryan. What's going on?"

"It's Grandma Merle. She had an accident today."

"Is she all right? What happened?" Trevor ran his fingers through his hair and frowned.

"No, she's fine. It was a minor fender bender. I was nearby, so I drove right over and helped her with the accident report. She seemed so disoriented. It had me worried."

"Why? Who wouldn't be a bit shaken up after having an accident?"

"You don't understand. It was more than that. She wasn't sure where she was and how to get home."

Trevor closed his eyes and sighed. "Another sign of dementia. That's not good. What do you think we should do?"

"I want to make a doctor's appointment to have her checked out."

Trevor pictured Grandma Merle in his mind's eye. She was the first person who got him interested in cooking. He remembered her saying, "Don't think your wife will do all the cooking. You need to know how to do it yourself." Then she'd add, "Have you found a nice girl yet?" Heaven help the woman he brought to meet her if she didn't know how to cook.

His thoughts returned to his brother's words. "Getting a medical opinion sounds like a good idea instead of guessing. Do you want me to come up to Dallas to be there?"

"Not necessary for now. I'll let you know after the results."

"Okay, keep me updated. I'm in Falcon Creek doing an overnight assignment. Should I give Grandma a call tonight?"

No, she's resting now. Check in tomorrow."

"Will do. And I'll keep her in my prayers tonight as well."

After Trevor ended the call, he thought about Grandma Merle. Both he and his brother tried to spend as much time as they could with her since Grandpa Mike had passed away. He chuckled thinking how they'd always introduce themselves as the m and m's. Retirement was good for them. They took up golf and moved into an active senior's community outside of Dallas and enjoyed many blessed years there. Trevor envied them and wondered if he'd ever find as deep a love as they had.

Trevor put his phone in locker with his other stuff and locked it. While he soaped in the shower, his mind drifted. *What would Grandma Merle think of Jaz? Man, she got under my skin. I can't stop thinking of her.* He thoroughly washed and massaged his scalp as if trying to wipe her away from his thoughts. After changing into fresh clothes, he pulled out his phone to see the menu of the restaurant he would be reviewing. It would be nice to have dinner with someone else, but he didn't know anyone in Falcon Creek – except for Jaz and he couldn't call her.

The GPS directions had him pass by Sweet Delights. Even though the building sign showed "closed" and only had its bare minimum of night-lights on, he slowed down and looked into the windows to see if she might be there. Not seeing her presence, let out a sigh of relief. Had he seen her, he would have been tempted to stop and spend more time with her. Instead, he drove on.

The next morning Trevor rose early to do a final breakfast review before he left. The restaurant was crowded and as he waited for a table, he listened and watched the reactions of the other diners. Seeing what was left on the plates gave him insight into what was and wasn't memorable. When he finally sat down for his meal, his server handled all the details well, but she didn't engage him like Jaz did.

As he left the restaurant, Trevor reviewed a text on his phone. Oblivious to anything around him, he bumped into someone walking down the street. When he looked up and said, "Sorry, forgive my clumsiness," he was pleasantly surprised to see Jaz standing in front of him. "Well, hello again, it's good to see you."

He watched her reaction turn from a smile to a frown and then a glare, which puzzled him. He gave her his best smile. "Remember me; we chatted for a while at the bakery yesterday?"

Jasmine put her hands on her hips and nodded. "Yes, I remember you. You tried a bit of everything yesterday and asked me lots and lots of questions."

Trevor didn't like how this conversation was going. "That's right." With a half-hearted laugh he added, "I'm an inquisitive kind of guy, I guess. Nothing wrong with that is there?"

"No, under ordinary circumstances I guess not. But it wasn't ordinary." Jasmine mimicked quotation marks with her fingers. "You were doing a review for your column, Mr. Food Critic."

He gave her a sheepish look. "Yes, that's right. So, you recognized my name on the charge slip."

"Actually, it wasn't me, it was my mom. I'm somewhat familiar with your column, but she reads it regularly."

That statement caught him by surprise. His shoulders slumped hearing she didn't recognize his name.

"Why couldn't you be honest with me?" Why did you pretend to be so nice?"

The look she gave him made him feel like he'd been gut-punched. "I didn't pretend. I did enjoy talking to you."

"So you could get details for your column." Her nostrils flared. "Now I've got to worry and wonder what you're going to say in your review." She threw up her hands and then pointed one finger at him. "My mother works very hard to make that bakery a success. It means the world to her. You better not do anything to destroy that."

He held his hands palms up in a gesture to stop and looked straight into her eyes with his brow furrowed. "I have never tried to destroy any place of business. I have always done honest evaluations. I don't appreciate your suggestion that I do hatchet jobs in my reviews. I take what I do seriously."

Jasmine covered her mouth with her hands and then released them. "Oh no, now I've made the situation worse. Forgive me. Don't let my outburst negatively influence your review." She hung her head and started walking away.

The look of sadness on her face before she turned away touched Trevor. He stepped forward, reached for her arm, and gently turned her around. "Don't worry about what you just said. I can understand how you want to protect your mom and help her out. I'm the same way."

She looked up at him and gave a hesitant smile. "Like I told you yesterday, I'm passionate about the business. Sometimes I get a little carried away."

Her honesty captured his attention, as did her expressive eyes and alluring smile. The urge to reach out and wrap his arms around her was strong, but he restrained himself. He slipped his hand off her arm slowly and took a single step away. "I see that. You know I still have to do the review as I see it, right?"

"Yes, of course, but - -"

"No buts. Remember it will be an honest review. That means I will be pointing out the good points of the bakery and the bad. Can you handle that?"

"As long as there are more good points than bad," she said as she flicked her eyelashes and wrapped a few strands of hair around her finger.

Trevor couldn't help but smile as he looked at her hopeful gaze. "Yes, I can say that much. There are more good points than bad."

She blew out a deep breath. "Yes, I can handle that."

"I'll call you or drop by after the review is printed at the end of the week to make sure you can." He tilted his head and gave her a big smile.

"I'd like that. Thank you for being so understanding. I've got to get back to the bakery." She hesitated for a moment as if wanting to say something else. Then she walked away but turned back once. "I'll see you later."

He waved back then put his hands in his pockets and whistled as he headed to his next destination.

CHAPTER 7
Another Chance to Meet

Trevor walked into the San Antonio Times building a week later to pick up his latest paycheck and reimbursement of expenses. He was on his way out when his editor saw him down the hall.

"Trevor, could you come to my office for a minute?"

He nodded and headed towards the editor. "What's up, boss?" He slipped into one of the comfortable leather and wood chairs in front of the oversized carved oak desk where his boss sat. Though this office was in a high-rise stone and glass building, the décor was what you'd expect to see in a Texas ranch den. The walls were painted to give the look of leather. A large brown and white cowhide lay on the floor by a side leather couch. One wall displayed an oil painting of a cattle round up and bore the name of a famous Texas artist.

His boss was especially proud of a Remington sculpture he displayed on the bookcase behind him. The only thing missing was a big stone fireplace with a rack of antlers above the mantle to make you think you were at King Ranch. Trevor had once asked why he chose to have his office look more like a home den, and he replied "Since I spend so much time here, I like to have the comforts of home where I can appreciate them.

"Liked your feature for the Hill Country getaway. Curious about one of your reviews there." Nick looked at his computer screen. "Here it is. Sweet Delights. A bit too cutesy a name for me. What caught my eye is that you actually gave it a four-fork rating for ambiance. Why in the world did you give it four-forks? That is so unlike you."

Trevor looked down for a minute and pursed his lips. What warranted the rating had everything to do with Jasmine. After doing a little digging, he discovered that was her real name. Her passion for baking and her creative take on food is what made the difference. That's what made people come back repeatedly. At least that's how he felt.

Only he didn't write that in the column. Instead the review noted the "welcoming atmosphere." Jasmine and her mother, Belinda, only had brief mentions.

He didn't reference the way Jasmine's hair was piled up on her head with an antique-style hair comb that showed her lovely neck. Or the soft ringlets casually slipping loose that gave her face soft illusions like those you'd see in a Monet painting. He pushed her image out of his mind.

"Hey, the look fit with everything a hometown bakery should be. It was bright, cheery, and showed support for the local high school and a sports team with its sponsorships. Why wouldn't I give them a good rating?"

Nick leaned back in his chair. "With that glowing recommendation, next time I'm up that way, I'll have to try it out. Sounds like the only negative was the empanada, which you gave a two-fork rating."

Trevor nodded. He hated to give that rating, but he had no choice. The filling and the pastry shell didn't work. He grimaced recalling how he had praised Jasmine on the empanada. She was so excited about adding it to the menu. He didn't want to spoil her joy in that moment.

Nick laughed. "Good you only have to sample the food and not clean the plate like you've said your granny still requires."

"That's easy to do with the food Grandma Merle makes. She usually makes my favorites when I come to visit, so I can't complain. Just need to keep the portions small so I can try everything she wants me to eat."

"Got another feature for you. There's an artisan chocolate shop in Falcon Creek with a great idea to promote the local food banks."

"Really? How so?"

Nick typed as he spoke. "It's a local fundraiser for area food banks. You know the concept. Buy a specific product and they donate a portion of the sales to a charity. Nick leaned back and pulled a sheet from the printer. "Here's the contact info. See what it's all about. Check if other businesses are involved as well."

A smile spread across Trevor's face. This could give him another opportunity to see Jasmine. "Sure, sounds great. I'll get on it." Trevor turned and walked out. As he entered the lobby, Giselle Upton, the fashion editor, who was deep in conversation on her cell phone was heading toward him.. He tried to give her space and moved to the side. However, she was in some sort of rant on the phone and using her free hand for expressive reactions and still managed to bump into him.

"Sorry," Giselle said in a meaningless way as if she had brushed away a fly. Then she turned and looked back as if it finally dawned on her that she'd run into him. Her expression changed to a big smile. She reached out with her free hand and caught him by the sleeve. "Ben, I'll call you back. Something came up." She ended her call, dropped her phone in her purse, and then slipped her arm into his with a cozy familiarity. "Trevor, where have you been keeping yourself lately? I've missed you."

"It's good to see you, too." Trevor looked at her practiced pout and the way she fluttered her eyelashes. Giselle knew how to choose clothes to accent her curves and draw attention to herself. They casually dated a few times when he needed a dining partner for his incognito reviews, but he could never see a real relationship with her. "Back from a fashion shoot?

Giselle leaned closer and rolled her eyes. "A ghastly shoot. Can't believe how some people think they know about style when they haven't a clue." She raised one hand in the air as if reading a banner. "I see big discounts in the future for those clothes. That's the only way to get them to move-off the racks."

"Ouch. I'd hate to be the designer who reads that review."

"I write it the way I see it, just like you do. And I love the rush I get from the power. The clothes are a nice perk, too."

"What do you mean by perks?"

Giselle squeezed his arm and shook her head. "You can't be serious. How do you think I have such a fabulous wardrobe? Designers send over clothing samples for me to review all the time. Can I help the fact that many of them happen to be in my size?"

He took a step back. "Doesn't that conflict with you doing an honest review?"

"I only give positive reviews to the designers I like and wear." Giselle sighed. "I would never keep anything I thought was below my standards."

"I guess it's safe to say you won't be wearing anything you saw at today's shoot." He raised an eyebrow as he took a longer look at what she was wearing.

"Never." Giselle threw her head back and laughed. She ran a finger through her long honey blond hair and gave him a smile. "Enough about me. When are we going out again?"

"Wow! That was a quick turn. But we don't exactly date." Trevor removed her hand from around his arm

"We could always change that you know." Giselle gave him a wink.

Trevor put his arms across his chest. "No, I make it a policy not to date anyone I work with. You're a dining companion so I can do my reviews. That's all it is."

"Don't act so serious. I'm teasing you. I know there's nothing between us. However, I do enjoy high-end restaurants and no strings attached."

"Sorry, nothing like that is on my radar. I do have a reservation for a new barbecue place on the Riverwalk, but I don't seem to recall you having much of an interest in barbecue."

"Normally, no. But I could do with something a little more down to earth and zesty."

Trevor's jaw dropped. "You? Really?"

"Oh, Trevor, don't look so shocked. I can do the common person kind of thing. I do have blue jeans." Her eyes twinkled. "Designer, of course."

Though she wasn't his type, he still could smile at her audacity. "So, um I guess I'll pick you up at seven tomorrow?"

"Divine." Giselle gave him an airbrush kiss. "Now, I've got to write up my story. Glad I ran into you." She waved goodbye and walked away.

It was still early enough in the day for him to head up to Falcon Creek. He tapped in the number for the chocolate shop on his phone and confirmed a time to meet with the store's owner. His next call was to Jasmine, but it went to voicemail. He left a brief message saying he'd be up in two days. She'd probably have some issues with his review, but he had no doubt they'd work through it. The idea of seeing her again made him begin to whistle as he walked into the parking garage.

He turned on his car's engine, but stayed in place when his phone rang through the car's display monitor and displayed his brother 's name.

"Hope, I'm not calling at a bad time, but I thought you should know. Grandma Merle had another accident."

Trevor caught his breath. "Is she okay?"

"Her hands and face have some scrapes and bruises. They're doing x-rays for her ankle and checking on a possible concussion. But those injuries didn't happen while she was out on the road."

"Huh? Then how did it happen?"

"According to her story, she got distracted on her way out of the driveway. She saw some weeds in her front yard and stopped to pull them out. You know how she loves her yard. When she got back in the car, she put it in drive instead of reverse and ran into the garage door."

"Is that how she got her new injuries?" Trevor said incredulously.

"The car damage probably shook her up. However, the injuries occurred when she tripped and fell on her porch trying to go back inside. She called me to take her to urgent care. I noticed the garage door right away when I pulled into the driveway. She tried to shrug it off as no big thing, but I'm concerned about her. I don't think she should be living alone."

"Isn't that a bit extreme? Grandma Merle probably needs a little assistance now until she recuperates, that's all. People slip off steps all the time."

"Hey, I'm the one she always calls. I can't keep running over there all the time. At the very least, she needs someone looking in on her daily other than me. With two recent accidents, I think it's time she gives up her car keys. We need to do a family intervention. Could you come up? Dad's out of town on business, but Mom will be here."

Trevor ran his hand through his hair. He could hear the concern in his brother's voice.

"I'll rearrange my schedule and drive up as soon as I can. Where should we meet?"

"Grandma's place. She'll be more relaxed there than anywhere else. Mom's in Austin on an appointment but will be here in about three hours. Can you make it then?"

"Sure. I can be in Georgetown by that time." Once the call ended, Trevor notified Nick about taking time off and cancelled his meetings with Giselle and the candy store owner. He called Jasmine again, but only got voice mail and left a message telling her their meeting was on hold. Hopefully, she wasn't using caller ID to screen calls and drop his.

There was no need to go home first. If he were going to spend the night, he could always wear some of Grandpa Mike's clothes. Grandma Merle didn't give them away after he died. She liked to imagine he was only away for a short trip. In addition, she liked seeing the clothes get some use when he or his brother visited since they were all similar in size.

About thirty minutes outside of Georgetown, Trevor called his mom. "Any news on Grandma Merle?"

"Your brother says the x-rays don't show any evidence of a concussion, and the ankle is only sprained. She'll need to stay off her feet for a bit. Can't have her hobbling around, falling, and next time actually breaking something."

"No, we'll probably need to get someone in to help her around the house. What do you think we should do about her driving? She's had two recent accidents. They weren't major, but --

"They were still accidents. I'm concerned about her driving, as is your brother. She's had that car for a long time and it's just not reliable anymore.

"It has that sentimental value to her of being the last car Grandpa bought." Trevor smiled as his mind flashed to memories of how Grandma's eyes would light up hearing the crunch of the tires on the driveway when Grandpa came home after his day at work. She was so happy to have him home with her. Theirs was a long-lasting love filled with joy in being together. That's the type of relationship he hoped he could grow into when he married. "Hope she doesn't throw a fit when we bring up the idea of giving up the keys."

"You know she will, Trevor. We've got to convince her it's in her best interest. You've got a way with words. You'll figure out what to say."

"Great. You want me to look like the bad guy. She's your mom. Aren't you supposed to have the closer relationship?" As soon as the words were out of his mouth, Trevor wished he could pull them back. Where Grandma Merle showed loved and affection for him, she showed distain for his mother. According to

Grandma's endless carping, his mom never did enough for her. "Sorry, Mom, forget what I said. I'll talk to her."

"I hope she'll listen to you."

"I'll do my best."

Trevor parked in front of Grandma Merle's house, just after his mom pulled into the driveway. He picked up his bag from behind his seat, with his computer and other electronic gadgets he always carried and walked up the driveway.

His mom pulled a couple of shopping bags out of her trunk, then gave him a hug as he stood beside her. While they walked to the front porch she said, "Thanks for coming on short notice. Mother will definitely appreciate the extra attention. Let's have a light dinner first and help her to feel at ease. After dessert we can bring up the driving discussion."

The front door swung open before they even had a chance to knock. With a deep breath and a half-hearted smile, Ryan reached out and gave his brother a quick hug. "So glad you're here. She's been extremely fussy."

Ryan turned and gave his mother a kiss and a hug. Taking her bags, he added, "I'm glad you're bringing gifts. Maybe that will put her in a better mood."

Trevor smiled as he walked in the door. Though the house looked like so many of the others in the neighborhood from the outside, it was uniquely Grandma Merle's on the inside. This was her dream house. Grandpa had given her a blank check to decorate it in whatever way she liked. The Saltillo tiles and soft red clay color on the walls gave it a southwest feel. Wrought iron light fixtures with custom finishes of Texas stars added to the decor.

Original paintings on the walls were side-by-side with photos of Grandma Merle and the artist. Texas Living magazine did a special feature on the home as the décor was so unique, which made her especially proud. She'd framed that magazine cover and story for all to see.

"Trevor, is that you?" A strong, no nonsense voice with a slight drawl called from down the hall.

"Yes, Grandma it's me." Trevor quickened his pace and walked toward the sound of her voice.

"I'm in the entertainment room. You come in here right away."

He chuckled at hearing her call it her entertainment room, since most people would call it a living room or family room. However, her term made sense, as that was the room where she always entertained her guests. When he saw her seated on the couch with her leg propped up, Trevor stopped in mid stride. His brother hadn't exaggerated. She looked like she had been the losing end of a bad brawl with a bruised and swollen cheek and scrapes on her hands. He tried to lighten the situation by attempting a joke. "Wow, Grandma, I didn't know you turned into a professional fighter. Hope the other guy looks worse."

Grandma Merle put up her fists in a pretend boxing jab. "You better watch out, or you'll be next."

Trevor leaned down and gave her a gentle hug and kiss on the cheek being careful of her injuries. "I wouldn't stand a chance against you, so I won't even try." He moved aside so his mom could give her a hug as well.

"Hi, Mom," she said. "How are you doing? I've brought you some things to make you feel better and speed up your recovery." She nodded at Ryan to hand over the shopping bags to Grandma Merle and sat on the chair to the right of the couch.

Grandma Merle peeked into the bags right away. "I didn't know tripping and falling were reasons for gifts, but the thought is sweet. Let's see what you brought." She pulled out a pale blue zippered nubby knit jacket and a matching top. "Well, this is nice, but why didn't you bring me some pants as well?"

Trevor turned towards his mother in time to see her friendly smile disappear and be replaced with a pursed lip grin.

"Well, Mom. I didn't know if you needed any pants."

"I didn't *need* a jacket or top either. But I guess it's the thought that counts." Grandma Merle patted the couch beside her. "Trevor, come sit beside me. Did *you* bring me any gifts?"

"No gifts, Grandma, only me." Trevor sat and clasped her hand. "Really, Grandma, how are you doing?"

Grandma Merle waved her other hand dismissively. "I feel better than I look. Don't worry about me. You're probably tired from the drive. Would you like something to drink? There's always sweet tea and soda, but not those fancy Italian sodas you prefer. Or we could start a fresh pot of coffee. What would you like?"

"I could use a soda. How about you, Mom?"

"A sweet tea for me would be nice."

Grandma Merle pointed her finger at Ryan. "You go and fetch those things and get me some sweet tea, too. Go ahead, now. I want to chat with my other favorite grandson for a bit."

Trevor smirked but quickly hid it with his hand. Grandma Merle was in her queen bee mode giving commands to her subjects as she deemed fit. For the most part, the family let her get away with that attitude. Only not today. She'd need to listen to reason. It wouldn't be easy.

Grandma Merle turned her full attention to Trevor. "Tell me, who's your latest lady love? I hope it's not still that Griselda person."

"It's not Griselda, her name is Giselle." Trevor rolled his eyes seeing the way she scrunched up her face in distain saying Giselle's name. "She's not my lady love. We go out but it's only as my plus one partner for restaurant reviews."

"Good, she's not right for you anyway." Grandma Merle nodded and pointed her finger at him. "When are you going to settle down like your brother, Ryan, and raise a family? You can't let your brother get ahead of you with grandbabies."

Trevor shook his head and put up his hands. "I'm not ready to settle down yet. I still need to find the right girl." When he finished those last words, Jasmine's face flashed across his mind and he smiled.

"What was that smile about?" Grandma Merle reached over and pinched his cheek.

"Nothing really." Trevor didn't want to get into a discussion about Jasmine. What would he say? He'd spent a lot more time than usual with her for his newspaper column. They had a lot in common. He'd seen her briefly since the interview. Now he had to cancel their first date before it even happened. Pretty lame on his part. "Actually, I was thinking about a restaurant review and it made me hungry. Could I fix some dinner for us?"

Ryan walked in with a tray filled with iced glasses and handed one to each of the three seated. He put the tray on the coffee table and sipped the soda he brought for himself.

"No, Ryan can do that. I see him all the time. I want to spend time with you." Grandma Merle patted Trevor on his knee.

"I can do what?" Ryan asked.

"Make us something to eat. Maybe some soup or eggs. My jaw still hurts a bit." Grandma Merle rested her hands on her lap. "Now go."

"Okay, let me see what I can rustle up." Ryan stood and headed for the kitchen.

"Let me see how I can help, too." Trevor's mom rose and patted Trevor on the shoulder as she passed by him. She nodded and added in a slight whisper, "No time like the present to talk."

Trevor knew exactly what she meant. This was a good time to ease his grandma into the idea of giving up her car. He silently said a prayer and asked for wisdom to know the right words to say.

CHAPTER 8
The Bakery Review

Jasmine took in a deep breath after the current rush of customers left. The only people remaining were she and Donetta, a new part-time worker, who was in the kitchen cleaning up. The display cases were nearly empty, and she felt especially vindicated when she noticed only four of her chicken, cheese, and chili empanadas remained. Once she refilled the empty trays, she was ready for a break. She dropped into a chair by a table near the counter so she could easily slip behind the register if needed. On the plate before her, she had a warmed empanada.

The recipe was the same she used when Trevor sampled one. She slammed the folded newspaper on the table, which showed his review of the bakery. As she read, she mumbled under her breath, "So Mr. Know-it-All, you think you're an expert on empanadas. Well, I think you are way off base with your review. People like my empanadas." Her index finger punched at the paper. "I'll show you. I'm gonna do my own sample test."

Jasmine pressed her fork into the crust to let out some steam and then used her knife to make a deep cut. *Looks flaky and nicely filled as he said.* She took a bite of the chicken alone and let it settle on her tongue before chewing. *Good texture. Maybe a little too much salt from the stock.* Next, she pressed her fork against the crust to check its crumble, and it responded nicely. She picked up a piece on her fork and did a nibble at the edge of her mouth. *Good taste. What did he mean it didn't go together?* She had another fork full and closed her eyes to savor it.

The second bite hit her like a ton of bricks when she realized he was right. They didn't work together. The filling needed more of a savory crust to enhance its nuanced flavors. The cheese muddled some of the flavors. It was a matter of less is more. Next time, she'd leave the cheese out. Her shoulders slumped and she grimaced realizing this truth about her food. Still the reality was hard to accept. *Well, he didn't have to mention the empanadas. He could have left them out of the review. He did try lots of other stuff.*

The bells chimed over the front door of the bakery. She turned to see her mom enter with a handful of shopping bags. "I didn't expect to see you back so soon."

"I see you're still obsessing about the review," Mom said as she dropped the bags on a chair besides Jasmine. She pointed to the newspaper on the table.

"Not obsessing, just reviewing it." Jasmine said as pushed out her chin.

"And you're eating an empanada that looks like the one he reviewed. But you're not obsessing about it? Looks to me like you dissected it. From your own analysis, did you agree or disagree about the pluses and minuses of his evaluation?"

"Why would you think I'd do something like that? That idea is absurd. I know it's good based on the sales." Jasmine gaze didn't leave her plate as she ran her fork through the filling.

Mom sat beside her and squeezed Jasmine's hand. "Because I know you. You have always been a bit of a perfectionist and get upset when things don't go just so. You won't please everybody. The best thing you can do is try to sell out the pastry or pie by the end of the day. If that doesn't happen, you start fresh with something else the next day. That's how the business works."

Jasmine sighed. "I know it's just that I - -"

"You want everybody to like what you make. You can't. We all have different likes and dislikes. Do the best you can. And remember God's in control and he's got a plan for us."

"You're right," she sighed. "Taking the words from Scarlett O'Hara, 'Tomorrow is another day.'" I'll keep trying to find the right mix of ingredients tomorrow or the next day. Speaking of which, the contest I set up for naming the three new baked goods seems to be working. They've been our best sellers for the last two days. People are really drawn to the idea of creating a new name." As she winced, she added, "Only I'm afraid to look at the entry suggestions."

"Let's be bold and take a look as soon as I put away these supplies." Mom stood and headed for the kitchen.

Just to be stubborn, Jasmine finished the empanada. She picked up the empty plate and utensils and loaded them into the dishwasher in the kitchen.

Donetta was off to the side sweeping up the crumbs from the floor. She stopped for a moment and pushed her hair away from her face. "Looks like we had a good day. I'm amazed at all the people who come in. I never noticed that before I worked here."

"And you're a great help to us," Jasmine's mom replied. "Why don't you wash up and take a break. Get yourself something to drink and a pastry if you like and sit."

Donetta beamed. "Great. I'd like to try the Red Velvet Streusel. It looks yummy." She headed over to the sink, washed and dried her hands, then made a beeline to the display cases.

"See," Jasmine said. She crossed her arms over her chest and raised her chin as she smiled broadly. "She wants to try the new items just like our customers."

Mom patted her on the shoulder. "Yes, dear, that's wonderful. Now let's go through the contest entry jars to see what they'd like to call them."

Jasmine picked up the jar from the counter that read Entry #1 and brought it to a table nearby. This held the entries for their mixed-berry muffin with orange zest and candied ginger. She carefully took the entries from the jar and made sure none fell to the floor. She selected a folded sheet and handed another to her mom. "Okay, let's read them out loud and when we're done, we'll put them all back in the jar."

"I'll go first," Mom said as she sat down next to her. "Berry Bounce Zinger. That's a good one."

"How about Mixed Berry Mash-up?"

"I liked the first one better. This one says Berry, Berry, Berry."

Donetta sat at the adjoining table and raised her hand in the air. "I've got a suggestion."

"Sorry, Donetta. Employees can't enter. Wouldn't want to risk having your name pulled and customers thinking we rigged it." Jasmine smiled. "But let's hear it for fun."

"How about Triple Berry Treat?"

Jasmine's mom applauded. "That's very good, Donetta. Next time we add something new, that's not a contest, we'll include you in on the brainstorming session." She turned back to Jasmine. "This name the pastry contest has really caught on. Our sales for the past week are up ten percent."

"That's great. The teens and moms traffic is up. Hopefully, this increased interest will bring in more birthday and graduation orders." Jasmine said.

"Speaking of special orders, I forgot to tell you we're scheduled to be a vendor at "Taste of South Texas" held at the Henry B. González Convention Center in San Antonio in two weeks."

Jasmine gasped. "What? We have a catering event in less than two weeks and you're just telling me now."

Mom squeezed her shoulder. "Don't worry. It's not like I just remembered the event. I've been working out the budget and list of supplies for a while. I've even lined up extra help."

Donetta waved her hand. "I'm one of the help. I think it sounds like fun."

"It will be fun and a lot of work." Jasmine's mom went to the counter and picked up a pen and notepad. "Now we have to decide what items we want to showcase."

"Mom, we've got to do this right." Jasmine pulled at a strand of her hair as she faced her mom at the counter. She had seen the invitation to be a vendor but thought her mom had tossed it. The booth space was costly. "That's a big leap of faith for you, but it could pay off. We'd certainly get our business in front of a lot of people. The kind of people who have catered events."

"That's why I'm willing to risk the expense. With my years of catering experience, I have an idea of what types of food work and the sample sizes. We'll need a special showpiece. Something to make us stand out above the competition."

Jasmine tapped her fingers on the table. "It should be something that will travel well, since we'll have to make it in advance." She pulled her cell phone from her pocket and scrolled through the photos. "When I was in California, I had a client who was expanding her catering business. Her food and sugar sculptures were phenomenal. I sat in on one of her classes to better understand what she did. That hooked me. I went on to take a series of classes in creative sugar sculptures. I discovered I had a talent for it. I enjoyed seeing the final results and started making them for special events for friends. Here are some examples."

Donetta and Jasmine's mom moved in closer to see the pictures as Jasmine pulled up each one. "Here's a delicate crown I did and here's a Cinderella carriage. Those are beautiful but would be hard to fix if they cracked. What I think will work is this one. It's a bouquet of flowers. We could put it on top of a tiered cake for extra height."

"Jaz honey, these are so lovely. I'm sure your friends felt special having these done for them."

Donetta pointed to the photo. "They're beautiful, Jasmine. It looks like crystal glass flowers."

"Since it's spun sugar, the texture is a bit like glass. We can box and cushion each one separately for safe travel. The cakes can be frosted with simple designs to highlight the sculpture."

"Oh, honey, those flowers are definitely eye-catchers." Mom squeezed Jasmine's shoulder. "I definitely think it will draw attention to our table. Can you add a monitor showing scrolling pictures of your other works? I think that would be really impressive."

Jasmine beamed. "Glad you like them. They're tedious to do, but I love making them. Doing a scrolling presentation is relatively easy to do. It was a big part of my business." *Thank you, God, for the talents you've given me. Forgive me for misjudging my mom as not valuing my input enough. She's been running this bakery much longer than I've been at playing being a baker. Give me an open heart to be more responsive to her.*

"With God's blessings, we'll make a great team at this event. I'll supervise the baking and you can work on the marketing, so people want to do more than try out our samples." Mom walked behind the counter and pulled up an iPad. "Let me look at the tallies for what we've sold in the last several months to find the best sellers. Since we'll need to make a lot of samples, I want to keep it to a total of six for easier prep work of large batches."

With her fork in the air holding a small piece of the Red Velvet Streusel, Donetta said, "I hope you'll include this. It's my favorite."

"That's a good choice," Jasmine said. "We're selling several dozen daily."

"Okay, we'll make that our first choice. How about those pecan swirls?" Mom asked as she looked at the computer.

Donetta nodded her head enthusiastically.

"Okay, that's two. How about the lemon custard tart with the hint of ginger?" Jasmine replied. This was one of her mom's signature pastries and a perennial favorite with her regulars. "And something in a puff pastry, that always impresses people."

"Agreed. We'll need something savory like an appetizer. How about your chicken empanadas?" Mom asked with a twinkle in her eyes.

Jasmine shook her head and raised her hands. "No, I'm reworking that item. Perhaps we could do a spicy chicken kolache instead. That was something I'd make in L.A. for friends. It's a little bit California and Texas. And maybe something like a roasted veggie cheese puff."

"Great. Sounds like we've got a good start." Her mom waved to someone walking by the window and reaching for the door. "We'll talk more about this later. Looks like we've got a customer." She walked behind the counter and put the computer on the shelf under the cash register. "Welcome to Sweet Delights. What sweet treats could I get you today?"

Jasmine returned all the entries to the jar, rose from her chair, and pushed in the others. Their break was over. Two more tourists arrived and then one of their regular customers put in an order for a princess themed cake for her granddaughter's birthday party.

As she waited on the new customers, she wished there was a chance that Trevor would be the next one to walk in. But that wouldn't happen. There were lots of reviews to be done in San Antonio and he only came to the Hill Country on a rare occasion. Still it would be nice to see him again.

CHAPTER 9
Thoughts of Trevor

The next day when Jasmine arrived at the bakery, she noticed the message light flashing on the phone. The voice mail noted two messages. The first message was from Trevor saying he would be up to see her in a couple of days. She smiled and rocked on her feet in a minimalist happy dance so her mom wouldn't notice. Though his review pointed out the problems with her empanada, she'd come to admit the fact it was fair, balanced, and positive overall. However, her joy faded when the second message put a hold on his planned visit. The message was short and only mentioned a family emergency. *Lord, whatever the issue, please fill the family with peace and comfort.*

The door chimes sounded again as a family entered. "Welcome to Sweet Delights," Jasmine said with a smile. She'd call Trevor to see how he was doing during the first break from filling orders.

On most days, she was grateful for a regular stream of customers, but now it seemed more like it was a prison sentence she wanted release from to call Trevor.

Finally, she saw her opportunity. "Mom, I need to run a quick errand." Without waiting for a response, she headed out the door. This was going to be a private call with no one around to ask her questions afterward. She walked towards the small community park in the center of town that had a lovely three-tiered fountain detailed with vibrant Spanish tiles, a bank of colorful flowers, fragrant lavender and rosemary bushes, and a few benches to sit and relax. She chose an empty one near the edge of the park and tapped in Trevor's number.

He picked up on the fourth ring. "Hello."

"Am I catching you at a bad time? She asked as she wrapped her finger around the bottom edge of her shirt.

"No, actually your timing is great. Grandma is taking a nap and she's doing much better than I expected when I left you a message."

"What happened? Your message said there was some sort of a family emergency? Did it have to do with your grandma?"" Jasmine hoped Trevor didn't think she was being nosy. She'd heard the concern in his voice mail message and wanted to offer a listening ear.

"She had an accident and got a bit bruised up, but no broken bones. The big concern is her driving. The family thinks it's time she gave up the car keys."

"And how does she feel about that idea?" She heard a deep sigh on the other end of the line before Trevor responded.

"Not too well. She got a bit huffy about it and that's when she said she needed a nap. I think the nap is her way of shutting us out temporarily."

Jasmine frowned. "Doesn't sound like an easy situation. I can remember as a teen slamming the door to my room and throwing myself on the bed when I thought my mother didn't understand what I was going through.

Trevor chuckled. "She wasn't that dramatic; she simply gave us the very strong impression she wanted to be left alone."

"Oh, no, I didn't mean she was acting like a teenager–

"I know and I didn't take it that way."

Thank God, he didn't think I was comparing his Grandma to a childish teen. Jasmine bit her lip. "What are you going to do?"

"Probably have an additional discussion with my brother and Mom about what to say when she comes out of her room."

"Should I hang up and call you later?"

"No, please don't. I want to talk to you. I have a new feature story to work on with a store in Falcon Creek. I'll be bringing a photographer with me, but I still want to see you. Could we meet for dinner on Thursday?"

"Dinner for the three of us?" Jasmine kept her voice upbeat and tried to hide her disappointment at his suggestion of a friend date.

"No, no. He won't be with us. He'll only be around for the shoot. After I'm finished with the interview, he's heading off to spend time with his friends. We'll be in separate cars. Dinner is just for you and me."

A broad smile spread across her face at the thought of a dinner date, but then her eyes narrowed, and she tilted her head. "Will the dinner be... business for you as a restaurant review?"

"Well, there is another restaurant I need to review, but we don't have to go there. I can take you wherever you want to go."

Jasmine took a few seconds to think over her response. If she made the decision where they went, then the conversation would center on the two of them. What if they ran out of things to discuss? What if she got tongue-tied and said all the wrong things?

If their dinner were part of a review for him, the meal would be business and they could keep the conversation around their dining experience. Conversation around food tastes and cooking would come easy. "Let's go for your review. I'd like to see how you do your assessments when I'm not the subject of them."

"Okay, I'll pick you up at seven and then drive to the restaurant. I'll need your address unless you want me to meet you at the bakery."

"No, I'd prefer the house. The address is 1437 Cherry Wood. Do you need directions?"

"Not necessary. I'll plug the address into the GPS. However, I have to cut our call short. Mom is flagging me over for a meeting. I'll see you Thursday."

"Wait, I have one question. I need to know how to dress. What restaurant are we going to?"

"It's the Old Grist Mill on the river. A number of people have emailed and asked me to review the place. Hope it's as good as the raves."

Jasmine gulped. "Um, yes. I've heard good things about it, so I'll dress up a bit."

"Good. I look forward to seeing you soon."

After she hung up the call, she stared at the phone. She'd chosen the option she hoped would keep it more business-like. Instead, she would be dining at what was considered one of the most elegant and romantic restaurants in the area. Hardly a place to go when she was trying to hold back from falling for him. *God, is this some sort of joke on your part? Are you trying to tell me something?*

CHAPTER 10
First Date Expectations

Thursday at the bakery was busy, but that didn't stop Jasmine from thinking about Trevor. For some reason, she had the jitters like before a high school first date. She was so obsessed thinking about seeing him she had to ask a customer or two to repeat an order because her thoughts were drifting to the upcoming date rather than filling their sweet treat orders.

At five o'clock when they turned over the sign to show closed, Mom put her arm around Jasmine's shoulder. "Bet you're happy the day's over, aren't you? Now you can finally go home and get ready for your date tonight."

Jasmine felt a flush rise up her face, so she pulled aside and started straightening the chairs around the tables without facing her mom. "It's really no big thing. It's more of a business thing. You know, helping him do his review."

"Uh, huh," Mom replied shaking her head. "Nothing but business. I doubt that. You had that faraway look in your eyes several times today and I saw you tapping your fingers on the counter impatiently as if you couldn't wait for everyone to leave."

Jasmine walked behind the display case and began removing trays. "I don't know what you're talking about. I barely thought about him at all today."

"Right. And brisket isn't the favorite barbecue meat in Texas. Honey, it's okay to admit you're nervous about going out. Dating is like chess. You've got to be careful with your first move as it can change the outcome of the relationship for better or worse." Mom waved. "Go home. Take a hot bath. Relax. Call one of your friends and get some advice. I can do the clean-up and prep work for the next day."

"Are you sure?" Jasmine asked as she dug her fingers into her apron.

"Yes, go get ready. Have fun and give me the details later."

"Thanks." Jasmine hugged her mom and kissed her on her cheek. She walked to the door, but turned back, took off her apron and handed it to her mom. "You're the best."

Mom put her hands on her hips. "Have a good time."

As soon as she got in her car, she called Lexie and they arranged to meet in a half-hour, which would give Jasmine time to shower and wash her hair.

At home, while she waited for the water to warm up, her thoughts drifted to Stefan. Though they broke up, he still hadn't dropped out of her life. He'd texted her that morning with a tip about an ad agency opening in Denver. Though the position didn't look like something she'd be interested in, she still appreciated his assistance in helping her find a new job. She stepped into the shower and shook her head. He knew how to be sweet and caring even while he was seeing other women behind her back. *How could she have been so blind?*

What about Trevor? She wondered as she shampooed her hair. The only things she knew about him were his love of cooking and that he worked for the newspaper. Was he dating others? Had he just ended a relationship as she had? She rinsed out her hair and took a deep breath. *Guess I'll learn those answers in a few hours. No sense trying to figure him out now.*

By the time Lexie arrived, Jasmine had already laid out a few clothes options over the back of the couch. "Here are some of my first choices." Jasmine pointed to the couch.

"Oh, Jasmine, I'm so excited for you. Can't believe your first date is at the Old Grist Mill." Lexie said as she gave her a quick hug.

"Remember it's not really a date. I'm helping him with a restaurant review," Jasmine replied as she tugged on a strand of her hair. And you can't tell anyone that's what we're doing tonight. Remember, he still needs to do this incognito."

"Oh, don't worry about me mentioning his work. I'll just brag on you going out with a hottie tonight in a great romantic setting. Even though it's business, we're going to make sure he notices you. Let's see what works best." Lexie picked up the first dress and shook her head. "No, that's too somber, too black. This isn't a funeral."

"Hey, that's a designer dress. I wore it to several parties in L.A."

"This isn't L.A. You need something with a little more color that shows you're fun and have a great sense of style." Lexie pointed to one of the other outfits. "Now I like that one. Could I borrow it some time?"

Jasmine playfully jabbed her friend's arm. "This is about finding me something to wear, not you."

Lexie held another two-piece outfit out in front of her. "Yeah, I know, but you do have great taste in clothes. We are about the same size; except I'd have to adjust the skirt lengths since you have longer legs than me. This pairing looks good. Try them on."

"Why don't you get us some sweet tea from the fridge while I change?" Jasmine took the clothes from Lexie and headed to her room. "I also need suggestions about what to do with my hair."

Jasmine returned to the living room wearing the sea foam green skirt and silk three-quarter sleeve top, which had soft geometric designs in various shades of green outlined in black. She twirled around to get Lexie's opinion.

"Oh, yes. That works. The color brings out the flecks of green in your eyes. Now let's see what we can add for jewelry." Lexie headed towards Jasmine's room.

While they were looking at the jewelry, Jasmine said, "Can't believe how out of touch I feel about dating. Stefan and I were so casual and relaxed about going out. We planned more for our business dinners. We always wanted to make the right impression of looking successful."

"Oh, I know what you mean. When you're seeing someone for a while, you fall into a regular pattern. With a new guy, there is no pattern, so you've got to wing it." Lexie handed Jasmine a pair of drop earrings with a cascade of silver and green disks and a trio of silver bangle bracelets. "That's when I usually buy something new."

"Well, I didn't have time for that." Jasmine smiled when she saw her reflection in the mirror.

"Looks good so far," Lexie said. "Now let's work on your hair." She walked behind Jasmine and pushed her hair off her neck. "You've got the long, thick wavy hair that guys love, and an elegant neck. Both should be highlighted. What if we pull it up on one side and let it hang loose on the other?"

"I like that idea." Jasmine nodded in seeing how Lexie held her hair up. "Let me find some clips or something to hold it in place." She walked into the bathroom and searched through several drawers.

Lexie stood in the hall and leaned against the wall. "I have a second date with Randy this weekend, but we won't be going to anything as fancy as the Old Grist Mill."

Sensing a note of envy from Lexie she said, "Well, at least yours is a real date, not part business like mine."

"Sure, but you still can enjoy the great food and get to know him some more. We're going out for an afternoon movie and then a casual dinner."

Jasmine brought out a tortoise shell curved comb with a clip and handed it to Lexie. "And I'm sure that will be fun as well. So, Randy passed the first date test?"

"Yes, he was sweet, held up his side of the conversation and even opened doors for me," Lexie replied as she continued to work on Jasmine's hair.

"That does sound good. And no problems with him picking up the tab for the date?"

Lexie's eyes got wide. "No problem at all. When I glanced at his credit card, I saw it was a platinum one."

"Just hope it's not maxed out." Jasmine recalled past issues Lexie had with men and their bad credit.

"Lord willing, he's got the income to back it up." She rolled her eyes. "Not that I'm any kind of a gold digger. I just like the occasional little gift every now and then. That's not too much to ask, is it?"

"Not at all. You're a special lady and you deserve special treatment." Jasmine turned her head to get another view of how Lexie fixed her hair. "And you've done of wonderful job of helping me look great for my date." She hugged Lexie. "Thanks."

"Great, now let's go to the kitchen. I haven't eaten yet and since you're not going to invite me on your date, let's see what's in the fridge."

They settled into the chairs around the kitchen table. Jasmine sipped her sweet tea while Lexie nibbled on some leftover sautéed chicken breasts. In between bites, Lexie said, "This is your first date with Trevor. I wonder if he'll pass your test for a second one."

Jasmine put her hand under her chin. "You know, I'm not sure about our dating. I really like talking to him, but I don't even know if I'll be staying around here. My last job was in L.A. Who knows where my next ad agency job will turn up?"

"Well, you don't have another job yet. So, in the meantime, have a little fun." Lexie leaned forward and grinned while she pointed to Jasmine's ring finger. "Who knows? Maybe 'Dreamy Eyes' will end up giving you a great reason to stay here."

Jasmine laughed. "You are a true romantic. Always thinking that the love of your life or mine is the next date."

"What's wrong with that? Mr. Right Forever is out there somewhere. If he does walk by, I don't want to miss him. I know God has someone for me and I'm keeping my eyes open wide. You should, too."

"Okay, I will." Jasmine chuckled. "But I'm not putting my life on hold waiting for him."

The doorbell rang. Lexie tilted her head and grinned. "Maybe you won't have to wait for him at all." She jumped out of her chair and headed for the door.

Jasmine caught up to her and grabbed Lexie by the shoulder. "Hold up. I don't want you peppering him with questions. Go sit on the couch and let me open the door. Then you can say hello and leave."

Lexie gave her a feigned pout. "Just hello? Not fair. But I know you're nervous, so I'll give you space."

CHAPTER 11
Dining Together Incognito

Trevor turned into the restaurant's parking lot and turned off the ignition. "I'm so glad you could come with me tonight." He smiled and reached for her hand. As their fingers touched, once again they felt a zap of static electricity.

"We're full of sparks when we touch, aren't we?" Trevor said.

Jasmine's throat went dry and she couldn't talk. She just stared at him and got lost in his beautiful blue eyes. *Yes, he was truly Mr. Dreamy Eyes.* After several seconds, she blinked and got her voice back. "I, umm, yes, we do. I haven't been here since they've hired the new chef. I'm interested in seeing his take on the classic dishes."

"Wonderful. We'll both get to see it with new eyes," Trevor replied as they continued to hold hands.

"Are there any rules to the way you do these reviews that I need to know?"

"Glad you asked." Trevor nodded. "Here's how I work." He pointed to his jacket breast pocket. "I have a digital recorder here and a microphone at my lapel. When a dish comes the table, I take a few moments to note the time and my initial reactions to the food without any interruption. After that, conversation is open. The recorder will run all evening." He turned and gave her a lopsided smile. "I hope that's okay with you?"

Jasmine sucked in her breath. "Wait a minute. Does that mean you taped our conversation at the bakery?"

"No, I only did text notes there."

"Good, because I'm sure I rambled on and I wouldn't want a recording of that hanging around."

"There's no need to worry about that."

Jasmine raised her eyebrows and considered the idea. The recorder would pick up everything they *both* said. He could listen to it repeatedly. She'd have to think about what she was saying. "Do others hear this?" she asked as her hands gripped her purse.

"No, no not at all. I would never share it with anyone."

"It feels kind of odd that our whole date will be recorded."

Trevor repeatedly shook his head. "No, not now. Only at the restaurant. Then it's turned off once we leave."

A timid smile crept across Jasmine's face. "You're used to having your thoughts taped and I'm not. Would you make me a promise?"

"What kind of promise?"

"Promise you'll make a copy of the conversation and give it to me. If I don't like it after I hear it, I want to know you'll erase your copy."

He gave her a quizzical look. "As long as it's after I've turned in my report."

Jasmine chuckled. "Of course, I meant *after* your report. I don't want to interfere with your work." She batted her eyelashes playfully. I'm not interfering with your work, am I?"

"Not in the least. I think your presence will make it feel less like work. Now let's go eat." Trevor stepped out of the SUV and walked to her door.

Jasmine opened her door and stepped out only to see Trevor abruptly stop as he reached the door.

"Oops," she said. "Sorry, it's been a while since a guy opened doors for me. We opened our own doors not wanting to be considered the weaker sex."

Trevor raised an eyebrow. "Do you think my actions show I consider you as someone who is weak?"

Jasmine's eyes widened. "No, not at all. I like that you want to open doors for me. You're a true southern gentleman. And I mean that in a good way."

"Grandma Merle always taught me to treat my date like a lady, so you can always expect it from me." Trevor held out his hand.

Jasmine put her hand in his and smiled. "I'll do my best not to jump out so quickly next time." The warmth from his hand felt reassuring and their two hands seemed like a natural fit.

As they walked towards the restaurant, Jasmine caught the rich, sweet scent of the nearby magnolia trees in bloom. The gentle splash from the now mostly-for-show waterwheel by the gift shop surrounded by varying sizes of ferns and shrubs helped to give the impression of a secret forest glade. Strands of a mellow saxophone and melodic piano chords drifted through the air as they drew closer to the restaurant's entrance.

Trevor stepped forward and opened the door for Jasmine. Outside there was an aura of serenity and calm, but inside there was a feel of delightful expectation. As the hostess escorted them to their table, Jasmine heard the occasional muted oohs and aahs from diners they passed. The aroma of garlic, chilies, and searing meat hung in the air and tantalized her senses.

Their table had a view of the recently restored grist mill with its quaint rustic appeal. Soft lights highlighted its features. The hostess held the chair for Jasmine and then gave them their menus.

Trevor leaned forward as he held his brown leather menu. Just above a whisper he said, "I usually like to order at least two appetizers to share, a salad and at least two different entrees with no repeats on the side orders. Because, you know –" He waved his open hand and smiled.

Jasmine fully understood that he did this to have a wider selection of food items to review, but she gave him a fluttering eyes naive look to tease him. "No, what do you mean?" She saw him look around awkwardly as if trying to make sure no one could hear his words.

"You know, my work," he whispered.

She chuckled. "Yes, I understand. I was only teasing you. I like the idea of sampling various dishes."

"Great." He let out a sigh of relief and opened the menu. "I've heard good things about the Crab Cakes with Jalapeno Pesto. The Spinach with Roasted Red Pepper and Goat Cheese Quesadilla also sounds interesting."

"Sounds tasty." Jasmine glanced down at the menu. "What about sharing a classic Caesar salad to see how it stacks up to other versions we've each tried?"

"That works for me. For entrees, what would you think of the Smoked Duck with a Port Reduction Sauce and maybe their Prime Rib Eye with a Chimichurri sauce?"

Jasmine shook her head. "How about making one of those options Smoked Salmon with the Orange Ginger Vinaigrette?"

Trevor nodded. "Okay, let's go with the Rib Eye and the Salmon."

Jasmine sipped her water and looked around the room after the waiter took their order. Animated family groups, quiet couples, and those dressed in business attire holding serious discussions filled the restaurant to near capacity, even though it was not a weekend. However, the scene at a table in front of theirs grabbed her attention. A couple sat there holding each other's hands. The man pulled away one of his hands and reached for the inside of his jacket breast pocket. Jasmine caught her breath as she watched him pull out a ring box and flip it open on the table. His action received a joyous "yes" from the woman and shrieks of delight.

The reaction caught Trevor by surprise, since the excitement happened behind him. He turned to see what caused the noise.

"That sound you just heard was the excitement of a marriage proposal," Jasmine said as she wistfully gazed at the joyous couple.

He applauded with others in the room at the happy event. Then he faced Jasmine again. "I've witnessed that scene in so many restaurants; I've lost count of the times."

Jasmine tilted her head. He seemed so dismissive about something so wonderful and romantic. *Did he have something against the idea of marriage?* Her smile thinned to a straight line. She recalled the times she had mentally planned her future with Stefan, which always included marriage. That event was apparently not in Stefan's plan. Marriage also seemed like something Trevor didn't have in his future either. Not that it was anywhere in her plans either. At least not for now. "Well, I think it was romantic. Are you against romance or is it marriage?"

"You think I'm against romance?" Trevor cocked his head and lowered his voice. "I'm not. However, what we just experienced here is something I don't consider romantic."

"What? Proposing in a candlelit restaurant isn't romantic?" Jasmine crossed her arms over her chest and looked down her nose at him.

"No, it isn't." Trevor gazed at his water glass which he swirled in his hand, then raised his gaze directly into Jasmine's eyes. "Asking someone to marry you should be a private experience at a location that's special for the two people. Later on, they can go to a restaurant or have a party to celebrate the proposal."

His answer caught her off guard. "Really? What places would seem romantic to you?"

"Perhaps a picnic by a waterfall. Or a beach at night." Trevor tapped his fingers on the table. "Maybe even sitting together on a couch listening to the couple's favorite music. What would you consider romantic?"

"A couple of minutes ago I would have said what we just saw. Now you've got me reconsidering." Jasmine gazed off to the side lost in thought. "The idea of the proposal being a special moment between the two of them without an audience is very romantic.

With that idea in mind, I would say the proposal should take place perhaps where the couple first met or had their first date." She pointed to the window. "Out by the side of the grist mill, there are benches where you take in the beauty of the grounds. That would make a perfect setting for a proposal."

"Now you're getting the idea." He gave her a quiet applause with his fingers barely touching. Then he leaned forward, and his voice softened. "Food can be romantic, too, as you know from making wedding cakes and special treats for Valentine's Day."

Jasmine had to break off eye contact to catch her breath. She looked down and reached for her glass as her heart beat faster. Dreamy Eyes was making her feel wistful about romance. "Yes," she nodded. "I hope romance never goes out of style. A large percentage of our business includes wedding cakes and other pastries for the big event."

"Do you do any events in San Antonio?"

"Not really. However, Mom booked us as vendors at the *Taste of South Texas,* which we hope will bring in new clients."

Trevor nodded. "That's a great opportunity for making contacts. I've covered the event for the last three years. The paper does a photo story and I supply the text. I'll make sure I look for you there."

Jasmine leaned back in her chair and smirked "I'll make sure you try only pastries that are up to your high standards, so I get a good review."

Trevor wagged a finger in her direction. "You're still upset with me for what I said about your Chicken and Chili Empanada, aren't you?"

"No, I really understand the reason behind it. I just don't want a second negative critique. Only mention something you like." She gave him a pleading look.

Trevor chuckled, "With the many vendors who will be there, only a few will get a blurb. And yours will be one. The feature story is mainly a promotion of the event and the charities it supports."

"Good." She leaned in closer and whispered. "Back to, you know, your work. Is there anything else I should know about our dining experience tonight?"

"Just tell me your honest, initial reactions to the food. Let me know what flavors you taste," Trevor replied.

"Like doing a wine tasting with food – check the bouquet, or in this case aroma, let it sit on my tongue for a moment and then chew to see what flavors come through."

"The way you described the experience makes it sound like you're the food expert." Trevor nodded his head.

Jasmine chuckled. "I'm hardly the expert. However, I am experimenting with different seasonings and extracts at the bakery."

"I'm still learning, too. When I'm cooking, my mind starts thinking about how this herb will complement that spice. When they work together, there's that great aha moment."

"I love that feeling, like I'm one with the food I'm cooking." Jasmine oohed. "Look, here's our appetizers."

The waiter placed the two appetizers in the middle of the table and placed a small plate in front of each of them. "Enjoy." He bowed and walked away.

Jasmine watched Trevor's movements of putting a serving of the quesadilla and crab cake on his plate, and then she did the same on hers. He tasted a sample, and then she did the same. She waited for him to respond, not wanting to break his concentration.

After a few seconds, Trevor took a sip of water, then spoke. "Okay, I've considered my impressions. Let's see how they're different or similar."

Thus began their evening debate of what they liked and didn't like. In their analysis, they recounted other food favorites, which were triggered by their meal. There was never a lack for words except when they had food in their mouth. As their meal progressed, Jasmine caught herself looking at Trevor in a new way. He was easy to be with like an old friend. Conversation came easy and laughter flowed. She could totally be herself with Trevor.

Critiquing this meal wasn't a competition of who could do a better analysis. That would have been the case with Stefan. *Thanks, God, for letting me see that some men are a better fit than Stefan. No, wait, I didn't mean a better fit. I meant better to be with. I'm not looking for a new partner. I'm looking for a new job.*

Jasmine took a long sip of her drink and concentrated on it flowing down her throat to take her thoughts off Trevor. Then she added. "I've enjoyed our meal tonight. It's been fun."

"Yes, I've enjoyed it, too." His hand slipped across the table and he gave hers a gentle squeeze. This time there wasn't a spark of electricity, but there was a warmth that made them both smile.

They lingered after dinner until Jasmine noticed Trevor carefully surveying the room. "Is there something I'm missing?" Her question seemed to catch Trevor off guard.

"What? No, sorry. Just noticing the dining room is slowly starting to empty. Guess we should leave as well." Trevor motioned to the waiter for their check.

Jasmine thought the dining room looked quite full but didn't question his statement. She reasoned he had a long drive home and wanted to put together his notes while they were still fresh in his mind. Hopefully, he hadn't grown tired of spending time with her.

As they walked to his Land Rover, Trevor offered her his jacket since there was a slight chill in the air from an evening breeze. Once they buckled in their seatbelts, he turned to her. "I hope you don't think I cut short our dinner because I don't like being with you. I would have enjoyed sitting at the table much longer, but I didn't want our presence to stand out. My reviews are all about being anonymous. The restaurant is still about fifty percent full so I'm merely one of many diners for the night."

"I understand. You take your job seriously. I loved watching your facial expressions. It was as if you were doing instant computer calculations as you tasted food to come up with a rating."

He nodded. "You don't mind this evening was part business, do you?"

"I enjoyed the whole evening. I really wanted to see how the new chef changed things around. And our conversation gave me new insights into new ways to prepare old favorite dishes."

Trevor put the SUV in reverse. "Fantastic. Next time, let's make it no business at all, only for us."

Jasmine smiled. The idea of a next time made her want to twirl around in delight, but she was in her car seat and merely nodded. Work realities crossed her mind. There'd be little free time in her foreseeable future. There was a huge among of prep work for the fundraiser in San Antonio. That event might be the next time they could meet.

CHAPTER 12
The Taste of South Texas Event

There was a buzz of excitement around the Henry B. González Convention Center floor as vendors brought in their displays and supplies for the *Taste of South Texas*. The band worked on sound checks with the occasional guitar riffs and drum rolls. Banners with the event sponsors were raised all around the room. Continual bursts of camera flashes from display tables ran through the room as vendors posed with their staff to commemorate the event.

When Jasmine surveyed the area, she estimated there were at least seventy-five other vendors ranging from caterers to restaurants competing for new customers along with their bakery. Their booth was midway into the loop and far enough away from the two bands to carry on conversations with prospective clients. They'd invested a lot of money into this event with supplies, free samples of their best treats, and extra staff. She hoped it would pay off in more catering events and special orders.

"Where do you want me to put these storage cases?" Donetta asked.

"About three feet behind the table and to the left so we don't knock them over," Jasmine's mom replied.

Together Jasmine and her mom laid out the tablecloths over the two adjacent front tables and then set up the poles for their business banner. Donetta laid out elegant silver trays with paper lace doilies on the tables. In front of each tray, tented laminated signs displayed the names of each food item. Donetta's cousin, Robbie, set up the extension cords, secured them to the floor, and to the side of the table legs, so there would be no chance of anyone tripping on them and making the night a disaster.

As they worked on distributing the pastries on the trays, Jasmine's mom tapped her on the shoulder and whispered, "Smile nicely, a news crew is coming our way. Probably setting up a story for tonight's show."

Jasmine automatically ran her hands over her pants before working on the displays of the spun sugar flowers. The roses had turned out beautifully from the pale green stems to the deep red rose petals. As she arranged them around the display tables, she heard the click and slight whirling sound of a camera snapping pictures. She turned and smiled.

Two people stood in front of the Sweet Delights display tables. A man with a beard and hair tied in a ponytail was busy taking pictures from assorted angles. The female had her hair pulled up and wore dangling silver earrings that nicely accented her blue-green and silver print short dress. Her neatly manicured hands held a digital recorder, which she clicked on. "Hello, I'm Chelsea from *San Antonio Style magazine*. Do you have a few minutes for some questions?"

"It would be my pleasure, but let's make sure to include my mom as well. We're a team." Jasmine motioned for Mom to come stand beside her.

"As a mother-daughter team do you ever have any disagreements over what pastries are made each day?"

"Do bluebonnets bloom in the spring?" Jasmine's mom replied with a chuckle. "Of course, we do. But we draw straws daily to see who's in charge."

Jasmine nudged her mom and shook her head. "She's kidding, of course; we don't draw straws. What we do is keep tallies of what inventory sells and what doesn't. When we want to bring in something new, we try it in small batches as a test run. Our customers choices mostly determine what will be in our display cases. They're the ones more in charge."

"What pastries have you tried that didn't make it?"

Jasmine immediately thought of Trevor's review of her Chicken and Chili Empanada. After that, she dropped it from the menu temporarily. Once she reworked the recipe, so all the flavors and textures fit, it was brought back. To let the customers know the recipe had changed, they'd given out samples. Now it was on the menu board once a week and was selling well.

"I can answer that one," Mom chimed in. "One time, I was making Valentine cookies and put in cayenne instead of cinnamon. Now I know Texans like their peppers, but this was too much of the spice. Good thing I noticed the smell wasn't right when I took the first tray out of the oven."

"Yes, a little hot pepper can add a nice kick, but only if used sparingly." Jasmine smiled and then caught her breath. She scanned the area again thinking she had seen Trevor, but now she only saw someone wheeling a tall display case in the spot where she thought he had been standing.

Chelsea pointed to the scrolling picture frame of the displays from previous catered events Jasmine had done. "You've got some talent there. Have you ever been on any of the TV competitions like Cupcake Wars?"

The compliment surprised Jasmine. "No, I haven't." She'd seen numerous episodes of the show that gave bakers a set of unique food items they would probably never have pair together; yet now had to use the odd flavor combinations to make something both edible and artistic. She often wondered how she'd perform on the show under pressure.

Chelsea continued with a few follow-up questions about what they were serving tonight and some of their bakery specials before she moved on to another table.

The band started their first set by leading in with beloved classic country instrumentals made famous by singers born in Texas including Willie Nelson, Miranda Lambert, Waylon Jennings, and George Strait to liven up the cavernous room. The conversational buzz grew louder as the paid attendees started trickling into the venue. Jasmine did a quick review of their displays and brochures to make sure everything was in its place.

"Don't worry, honey." Mom patted Jasmine on her shoulder. "We're good to go. It's show time. Hope the crowd is as large as promoted and brings in new clients."

Jasmine smiled, straightened her chef's jacket and brushed away a few loose hairs out of her face. *Okay, God, you're in control. Help this be a good night for us.* As she heard a familiar laugh, she caught her breath. Trevor. He was laughing with a vendor a few displays away from theirs. Her hand started to rise and wave to him, but then dropped like a stone when she saw a female drape her arm around his shoulder.

The woman wore a sleek backless deep purple silk top and a flared black linen skirt. The ensemble looked like something she'd see in a designer boutique. Her hair hung loosely around her shoulders and gave the too perfect impression of merely being brushed out. That special look could only come from a salon visit earlier in the afternoon. No way she'd even come close to looking that good. Jasmine no longer had that kind of expendable income. She dropped her gaze back to the displays in front of her and began rearranging them. All the while, she hoped Trevor would not see her and only move away.

"Hello Jasmine."

Upon hearing her own name, she felt her heart drop down to the floor. She had looked forward to seeing him again, but never counted on him being with a girlfriend. Not that she had any reasons to think he wouldn't be dating someone. After all, they'd only been on one date and it was semi-business. They'd spoken on the phone daily since then but weren't able to work their schedules to fit in a time to see each other. *What a fool I've been.* She took in a deep breath and turned to face him. "Hello, Trevor. Good to see you again." Her smile broadened when she saw he was alone.

Her mom walked over. "Well, if it isn't Mr. Lassitor." She reached out her hand. "We haven't officially met. I'm Belinda Cattrell, Jasmine's mom."

Trevor shook her hand. "Good to see you again."

"That remains to be seen." Belinda tapped her finger to her lips and gave him a steely glare. "What type of write-up are you going to do on our booth?"

"Mother!" Jasmine gasped.

"Oh, Jasmine, I'm only teasing him." Belinda chuckled.

"Good one, Belinda," Trevor laughed. "But don't worry, judging by what I see in your displays you won't have to worry about the review."

"Thanks, you'll have to excuse me. I have other people to assist." Belinda moved over to the other display table.

Jasmine leaned closer to Trevor and whispered, "Did you mean what you said about a new review?"

"Yes, everything looks wonderful here. I know you've brought the best items to display and they look enticing."

"What would you like to try?"

"Pick out something that you think works best."

"Here's one of our new items. It's currently called Red Velvet Streusel, but that may change." Jasmine handed a sample to him. Her fingers clutched at the edge of her chef's jacket and she held her breath, waiting for his response.

Trevor took a bite and smiled. "This is really good. Rich tasting with a wonderful cream cheese drizzle with almonds. And there's something that makes the flavor pop that I can't quite figure out."

Jasmine smiled and crossed her arms over her chest. "Glad you like it. We did a little extra tweaking on it to give it that special taste." Then she leaned forward and whispered, "The recipe is under lock and key. I am not at liberty to divulge the details, especially to you."

Trevor gave her an appraising look. "So you don't trust me and think I'll blab it to our readers."

Jasmine's eyes twinkled. "Maybe you'll need to come back to the bakery and dissect them like you did on your first visit to figure out the contents."

"I look forward to trying more choices at the bakery as long as you're there to discuss them with me. How long have these been on your daily display board menu?"

"They're relatively new and part of a new marketing campaign. We're trying four new pastries for four weeks. Customers vote for which one they like best..." She babbled on about the contest until she had to suck in a new breath and then she felt her face grow flush. "Sorry about that. I got a bit carried away. We've been having fun with the campaign."

"No apology needed. Sounds like a great idea to build sales. And this streusel is one of the four in the contest, right?"

Jasmine nodded.

"Did you bring the other three so I can vote my pick as well?"

"That's the only contest entry we brought with us." Letting her words get ahead of her brain she added, "If you want to sample all four, that's another good reason for you to come back to the bakery and try them out."

She pursed her lips in a straight-line grin. *What is wrong with me? That sounds so middle-grade and semi-desperate. I don't need to keep pushing him to see me again. I can't forget that woman he was with. I'm probably just a passing interest to him.*

"I really would like to try more of your pastries. You're very talented and I promise to only vote and not critique." Trevor held up his hand up with two fingers extended. "Scout's honor."

Jasmine laughed at seeing his innocent look and started to say something but stopped. The woman she'd previously seen with him had sauntered over and now stood next to Trevor. Her shoulders slumped when she looked at this woman, who looked even more stunning close up. They fit well together. She was tall and slim and wore beautiful triple diamond drop earrings Jasmine could probably never afford. Her perfectly manicured, slender hands had an assortment of rings on them, but none on her left ring finger. Jasmine quickly moved her hands behind her back to hide her clean but stubby nails. "Welcome to Sweet Delights. What may I get for you?"

"Ooh sweets, no. I can't stay here."
Giselle shook her head. "Too much
temptation. But I can't resist *one*." She gave
Jasmine a conspiratorial smile. "What do you
suggest?"

Jasmine wanted to say, "Go find another
boyfriend, I'd like a chance with Trevor."
Instead, she bowed her head slightly. "I think
you would appreciate our classic lemon tart
with a hint of ginger. It's great for parties and
special events." She picked up a pair of tongs
and with great precision moved it from the
tray to a napkin without crumbling the crust
even slightly.

Giselle took a quick nibble and
exclaimed, "Oh, my, this is simply fabulous. It
reminds me of the wonderful custard tarts that
they sell in Lisbon at *Pasteis de Nata*." She
reached over and squeezed Trevor's arm. "I
know you'd never gush like that over
something you ate, but I can." Giselle turned
back to Jasmine. "Seriously, these are really
good. You should be selling them to the
trendy hot spots in town. You'd have a loyal
following."

"Thank you, I appreciate the compliment,
but we're only a small shop. The one
commercial vehicle we have is a standard
minivan We're not set-up for a large-scale
operation."

Trevor put his hand on Giselle's shoulder.
"If Giselle says she likes something, that's a

high compliment. She rarely likes anything. You should look into that option."

Jasmine felt a flush rise up her face again as she gazed into his eyes. "Thanks, again. I'll look into it."

"Come on, Trevor we've got to run. The others are waiting." Giselle discarded the empty napkin in the nearby trashcan, then wrapped her arm around his.

Trevor turned back to Jasmine for a moment. "I promise I'll come up and visit the store in a couple of days. You can count on it."

Jasmine raised her hand in a slight wave and sighed. *How foolish to think he'd be interested in me except for my baking. That Giselle woman is so above my league I wouldn't make it to the tryouts.*

More people drifted over to their tables for taste samples. She welcomed the distraction so she wouldn't think of Trevor. With each visitor, she described the pastries on hand and gave flyers that highlighted the bakery and their catering options.

The crowds grew as the night rolled on and the band did a great job of keeping the guests entertained. The atmosphere was friendly and relaxed. About three-quarters of the way into the event, their supplies started to dwindle, as did those of the nearby vendors.

It looked like the number of guests exceeded the numbers projected by the event coordinators. She hoped those numbers would produce an increase in catering sales. Despite standing on the thick rubber pads over the concrete floor, her feet were starting to hurt. Still she put on her best smile whenever someone came by and showed an interest in what they were offering.

When they were down to their last trays of each pastry they brought, a single man dressed in a neatly tailored and expensive-looking black suit with a crisp black shirt stopped by their table. Besides being impeccably dressed and wearing a large diamond stud earring and a Rolex watch, he stood out since he arrived alone and not with a small cluster of friends as most others had done. His appearance and manner gave the impression of someone who would entertain in a lavish fashion on a regular basis.

"Welcome to Sweet Delights," Jasmine said. "What would you like to try?"

The man didn't say anything right away but looked over what was on the table. Finally, he put one arm around his chest, rested his other arm on it, and pointed to the Lemon Tart. "Tell me about that one."

Jasmine moved to the tray to hand him one, but he held up his hand to decline.

"No, for now, just tell me what makes it special."

Jasmine was having trouble reading him. Did he have some sort of food allergy and wanted to make sure there wouldn't be a problem with something he ate? Or was he another food critic? Whatever he was she didn't want to lose a sale or a good review.

With a flourish of her hand, she pointed to the tart. "This is a classic tart, but we've updated it with a fresh twist by adding ginger. We use only fresh Meyer lemons and turbinado sugar. The crusts are made with Greek yogurt instead of the standard shortening which gives it a rich and flaky texture. The taste is like fresh lemonade on a hot day with a cookie on the side. Cool and refreshing. It's one of the favorites at our bakery."

The man nodded as she gave him the details. Then he went on to ask about the other items.

She described each one in the best way possible to entice his interest. Still he did not ask to try a single sample. Was he a competitor?

After she finished her descriptions, he asked, "If I only wanted to try one, which pastry would you suggest?"

She looked at the table of pastries in front of her and then looked at him. "I think the lemon tart would suit you best."

He nodded. "Then let me try one of the tarts."

Jasmine placed the tart in a napkin and graciously handed it to him. "I hope you enjoy it."

"I'm sure I will." He took a slight nibble, closed his eyes for a moment, and then nodded. "Yes, it is quite good." He pointed to the spun sugar flowers. "Beautiful. Did you make those, or did you buy them from a supplier?"

Jasmine straightened her shoulders and stood tall. "No, they are from the bakery. Actually, they're my own creation. You can see samples on the video screen of the types of events we've catered. Are you planning an event where you need a caterer?"

"Not exactly." He reached into his pocket and handed her his card. "I'm Cooper Benedict and this is my company. I'm only here for a couple of days but give me a call next week when I'm back in my office so we can discuss some ideas."

"Thank you, I'll do that."

He raised his fingers up in a slight salute and bowed his head. "Thank you for the tart. It was an excellent choice."

As he left, she looked down at his card and read the name of the company, Benedict Enterprises. An embossed image of an old movie camera split the space between the two words on the glossy card. Very classy. No address. The phone number looked to be one from L.A., but since most businesses kept their phone numbers even if they moved, that didn't necessarily mean his business was based there. What would he want to discuss? Was he a video director who wanted to sell her a video to market the bakery? He'd left no clue other than the card. With a shrug, she slipped the card into her pocket. *Okay, God, that was interesting. I have no idea what it meant, but I'll follow up to see where the contact may lead.*

While talking to Cooper Benedict, the crowds had begun to thin out. As she looked around, Jasmine noticed many of other vendors were packing up or had already left.

Her mom gave her a quick hug. "Looks like it was a good night. Everyone seemed to like our food and I have a list of names and numbers to call tomorrow and later in the week. How about you?"

Jasmine nodded. "Some people filled out interest cards, and the guy who just left gave me his card. Not sure if he wants to use our services or wants us to buy something from his business."

"Give him a call anyway. He may become a customer now or perhaps later, who knows. Do the footwork, and let God handle the results."

"Sure, Mom." Jasmine put her arm around her mom's waist. "Only wish God could handle the results now and help with the packing up."

"Well, you'll have to settle with the four of us for now. Donetta and Robbie have been doing a great job of packing and cleaning up as we went through the night. They're a godsend in that manner."

"Amen to that. Now let's clean up and leave. I'm exhausted." Jasmine cleared off the remaining trays on the table. She briefly scanned the room but didn't see Trevor. She sighed. Did it really matter if he was still around? He had his friends and his girlfriend to amuse him. The only thing they had in common were being foodies. Good she realized that now. Besides, she didn't need any new entanglements, she'd be moving on to a new job soon.

CHAPTER 13
Changing Expectations

Jasmine was so tired from the "Taste of South Texas" the night before that she reached for the snooze button and was about to give herself thirty minutes more. Then she realized in her half-dreamy state she wasn't in California the morning after a big celebration. There was no time to sleep in. Working in a bakery meant early hours to get the baked goods ready for sale when the first customers walked in the door. She threw her feet over of the bed and stood. As she showered, she thought about seeing Trevor with that gorgeous woman last night. *Guess that's God's way of closing a door and reminding me I need to focus on getting my career in order.*

When she headed into the kitchen, the wonderful aroma of fresh brewed coffee filled the air and made her more alert. Mom was definitely a morning person and always ready with something to eat before they headed out for the day.

"Aren't you tired? How do you manage to get up so early?" Jasmine filled a cup with coffee and then sat at the kitchen table with her mom.

"No, I'm definitely tired, but I couldn't sleep. I've only been up for forty-five minutes, which gave me some quiet time for Bible study. Now I'm ready for company. How did you sleep?"

Jasmine thought for a minute and stretched. "Actually, I slept well. Are you worried about the business? Is that why you couldn't sleep?"

Mom headed over to the oven. She pulled out a couple of golden-brown turnovers, slid them on two plates and brought them to the table with a couple of forks. "The business is better than expected and growing. I just had some issues with sleeping because of extra aches and pains from the event last night. Ready for another big day at the bakery?"

Jasmine smiled broadly. "Mom, you made my favorites, your breakfast turnovers. How early did you really get up?"

Mom waved her hand and grinned. "Oh, Jaz, I mean Jasmine, I didn't make these from scratch this morning. I always have a small batch in the freezer. I took a couple out last night and left them in the refrigerator, so they'd be ready today."

"I loved it when you baked these for me as a kid. It made me feel so special." Jasmine cut into the flaky crust with her fork to let the steam escape. She closed her eyes for a moment to breathe in the scent of aromatic sausage and eggs. "They're so much better than any breakfast sandwiches you can get at a fast-food place. Why haven't you made these for the bakery?"

Mom sighed and shook her head. "We already have the breakfast kolaches with ham and cheese. We don't need another breakfast option. Besides this has always been a special family treat."

Jasmine reached over and squeezed her mom's hand. "Well, it's a family treat that should be shared with others. I know it would be a popular choice."

"I'll think about it."

"I've got a better idea. Let's pray about it."

"They both bowed their heads and held their hands together. Belinda started the prayer. "Heavenly Father, thank you for the food set before us and the hands that made it. We are grateful for the wonderful blessings you have bestowed on us. Thank you for the talents you have given us. Show us the way to share them with others to your glory."

"And Lord thank you for an encouraging and helpful daughter who brings new life to me and the business daily. Amen."

Jasmine took a bite of the turnover and rocked her head back and forth in delight. "Mom, this is sooo good. I love how you've crumbled the smoky sausage and added a little thyme and chives to the eggs that still taste fluffy and creamy in the pastry. You've got to do this as a small batch at least for Saturday morning."

"Okay," Mom sighed. "We'll try it once and see how it goes." She took a bite of her turnover. "Now, I've got a question for you. What happened with Trevor last night? What did he have to say after I stepped aside and got busy with others?"

"Not much. I told him about our name the pastry promotion and he thought it was a good idea." Jasmine kept her head down as she talked. She could feel the heat of a blush rise up her face and hoped Mom didn't notice. It wasn't like she had some kind of crush on him. Okay, it was. However, it was only an idiotic daydream on her part. He had someone else and she had her work until a better job came along. Case closed. She looked up and smiled at her mom. "Oh, there was one thing more. His girlfriend --"

"Girlfriend? Are you sure?" Mom dropped her fork on the plate.

"Well, she had her arm draped all over him in a very possessive way." Jasmine nibbled on a piece of the crust but didn't really taste it.

Mom reached over and squeezed Jasmine's hand. "Maybe she was just a friend who was a bit tipsy."

Jasmine smiled wanly. "Well, maybe… Whoever she is, she said she really liked your lemon tart and thought we should be selling it to restaurants in San Antonio."

"Really? I never thought of taking our pastries down to San Antonio. By the time we added transportation costs to supplies and a profit, it would be hard to sell to the restaurant at a price where they could make a profit as well."

Jasmine tapped her fingers on the table. "Unless we were doing it on a large scale with a full truck or a satellite location in the city."

"Whoa, you're making the bakery sound like a mega operation with trucks and a second location." Her mom laughed. "We're just a simple one shop operation. That's keeps me busy enough with the catering on the side."

Jasmine shook her head. She couldn't imagine why her mom didn't want to jump at a new opportunity to grow the business. "Haven't you ever wanted to dream big, Mom?"

"I'm happy where God has planted me. I know you're different. You had a great career going with that ad agency. I'm sorry an embezzlement shut it down. However, the timing of your job loss was a blessing because I needed someone. I love having you here, but I wonder if you'll be happy staying."

Jasmine stared at her plate. She wondered that same question. The bakery gave her a joy and a sense of achievement when she saw customers faces light up in delight as they bit into the pastries. When she worked on an ad campaign and the client approved it, the feeling was more like she scored a touchdown. There was the challenge of making the next score with another campaign and another client. "Mom, I know you want me to stay here. I do like working in the bakery and being here with you, but I worked hard for the last ten years to make a name for myself in my career. I'm not ready to give that up. I told you I had resumes out when I came here. If something good comes up, I'll probably take it."

"Yes, I understand." Her mother let out a deep sigh as her shoulders sagged. "I know you have your own life and plans. I hoped you'd want to stay. Only please give me at least two to three weeks' notice if you plan to leave. Donetta is a good helper but I need more than her part-time assistance to keep the place running."

"Keep your chin up, Mom. I'm not going to jump at the first offer that comes along unless it's offering the challenge and income I want. I'm going to be picky. At this point, you're the only employer who wants me and I like the job."

Well, I hope it stays that way for a while. However, we can't chat here at the kitchen table all morning. We've got breads and pastries to make before our clients start coming in."

"Give me twenty-five minutes to get ready and then we can go."

After the morning rush ebbed and the bakery was empty of customers, Jasmine and her mom sat at one of tables with cups of hot tea and a muffin to share. They both turned to the door when Mike, the delivery man, for the local florist walked in.

"Good morning, ladies. No need to get up. I can't stay and I'm on a diet, so I won't be taking anything to go. Hope, these flowers make your day, Jasmine." He handed over the colorful bouquet of flowers in a maroon bowl.

"I wonder who they're from." Jasmine took the bouquet and reached for the card that was included.

"They're from Trevor," Mike said.

Jasmine's jaw dropped and she glared at him. "I can't believe you're opening and reading the cards."

Mike laughed. "That doesn't interest me in the least. This order was called in, so I wrote and attached the card for the caller. Hope you enjoy them. Gotta run! Other stops are calling me."

Jasmine's mom grinned at her. "So maybe Trevor does have some interest in you after all."

"Don't make too much of the flowers. The card didn't have any mushy sentiment. He just wrote, *Hope the night was successful. Looking forward to seeing you next time I'm up there.* See, nothing much there." Jasmine covered her mouth with her hand so her mother couldn't see the big smile hidden behind it.

Mom shook her head. "No, I think you're wrong there. It's always a big deal when a man sends flowers. He wants to get your attention. And each time you see the flowers, you'll think of him."

Jasmine stood and picked up the flowers from the table. "Well, then I'll just bring them to the office where I won't see them."

"Oh, no, you won't," Mom said as she took the arrangement from Jasmine. She carried the flowers over to a display case and placed them on the top. "There, now everyone can appreciate their beauty when they come into the shop." She crossed her arms and smiled in satisfaction.

"Okay, have it your way," Jasmine raised her hands in surrender. "Since we have a bit of a lull, I'll follow up on the leads we received last night. I'll make the calls from the office in back." She picked up their two mugs and the plate and headed behind the counter.

"You can hide in there for now, but the flowers will still be here when you come back." Mom called after Jasmine in a teasing manner.

Jasmine sat at the desk in the office and pulled out the info cards they'd collected last night. She was ready to make the follow-up calls, but first she wanted to phone Trevor. One thing she neglected to mention about the card was the rest of the note that asked her to call and gave his number. Part of her hoped the call would go to voice mail, so she could quickly thank him and hang up. The other part wanted to talk to him and see if maybe she was wrong about the woman she'd seen with him.

After three rings, Trevor picked up. Jasmine stuttered in surprise. "Um, hi Trevor. Thanks for the lovely flowers."

"Wow that was quick. I called the order in twenty minutes ago. I didn't expect to hear from you so soon."

"Well, um, the florist is only a few stores away. I know, um, you're probably busy, so shouldn't take, um, any more of your time." Jasmine twirled a few strands of her hair in her finger. Why was she so tongue-tied and timid? Maybe she should have sent him a text so she wouldn't sound so insipid.

"No, please don't. I want to talk to you. I'm writing a report on my computer, but it can wait. Unless, of course, you're too busy to talk."

Silence. It was her turn to talk. She spurted out the first thing on her mind. "It sure was busy last night, thanks for stopping by and giving us some encouragement to expand."

"Oh, you mean what Giselle said about supplying desserts to some of the better restaurants in town."

"Yes, Giselle." Jasmine was glad Trevor couldn't read her thoughts or see her pinched lips. At the event and now, she felt like Cinderella before the magical change and viewed Giselle as the fairy tale princess after the enchantment. In an upbeat tone she didn't feel, she added, "I appreciated her suggestion, but a larger delivery van or truck is not in our budget."

"Hope you won't totally dismiss the idea. Giselle works for the paper, too, and has a ton of contacts. Many of them use catering companies for their special functions."

"So you don't just date, you get to see each other at work as well. That must be nice." Jasmine's response was monotone and her shoulders sagged as she stared at the wall.

"Excuse me, did you say date? Giselle and I do not date. She's done a few food review dates with me, but they're not date, dates. It's strictly business."

Jasmine's head popped up. *I was wrong.* "But I thought by the way she draped her arm around you, that you were a couple."

"Not at all. That's just Giselle's way. She likes to give the impression she's all about the one she's with, when all the while she's looking for the next guy who'll knock her socks off."

"Seriously?" A broad grin spread across her face. *Giselle wasn't his girlfriend.*

"Yes, even though she can turn most men's heads when she walks into the room, I'm not interested. However, there is someone I would like to get to know better."

"And who could that be?" *His answer had better be me or I'm totally going to feel stupid for even thinking he's interested.*

A soft chuckle erupted on the other end of the line. "You want to hear it don't you? It's you, of course. Our personalities fit. I'd like to get to know you better outside of work. Do you think that could happen?"

"I hope so. I enjoyed our time together. Any plans to come up to the Hill Country soon?" The doodles on her pad became little hearts and flower stems in bloom.

"I'm working on a few stories over the next couple of days. I'll be up there next Thursday for a follow-up with the candy store promotion. Could we get together then?"

"I'm going to be busy the next few days with catered parties. By Thursday I should be able to take a break and spend some time with you." She sorted through the interest sheets from the event, but her mind was on seeing Trevor again.

"And I'll check with Giselle to see if she can drum up some business for you."

"Thanks, Trevor, we would definitely appreciate those leads. It would be great to have a growing clientele list in San Antonio and Falcon Creek."

"You will. I've no doubt about it. Have to cut this short to get back to work. Glad you liked the flowers. I'll call you back later when I've got more time. We can talk about what you'd like to do on Thursday in more detail."

"I'd like that. Bye." She hung up the phone and gazed at the note wishing he'd been able to deliver the flowers in person. Thursday seemed far away, but the upcoming parties would keep her occupied and make the days fly by faster.

CHAPTER 14
Being a Good Friend

The next day after the morning rush, Jasmine refilled the baked goods trays then headed back to the office with a cup of coffee to make some marketing calls. Before she had a chance to pull up her list of prospects, her phone rang.

"Urgent friend alert and you can't say no."

Jasmine stared at the phone and frowned. "Uh, Lexie. That's an odd way to start a conversation. What's going on?"

"Yeah, sorry. It's just my mind is ahead of my words. I'm calling about our girl, Savannah. She is feeling like she's had the floor kicked out from under her. And we've got to help her?"

Jasmine caught her breath. "Did something happen to Carolinda?"

"That sweet child, no she's fine. But it's what she said to Savannah. This past weekend Carolinda spent some time with her no-good daddy. You know how Derek likes to show her off to his lady dates and how he's a good daddy and all. Well, it seems that Carolinda overheard his latest girlfriend on the phone bragging about getting engaged."

"And this lady was happy about that idea with him?"

"Uh-huh. Carolinda told her mom she was all gushing and stuff and she wanted to know what engaged was. And Savannah had to explain it to her. That couldn't have been easy."

Jasmine ran her fingers through her hair and sighed. "Savannah never mentioned that Derek was in a new relationship. This change must have come as quite a surprise."

"You're telling me. He should have told Savannah in advance so she would have been prepared for responding to Carolinda. Or they could have told her together, which still would be awkward. This all happened this morning as she was taking her to school.

I ran into her at "Brew Me Right" just after that. When she told me, her voice flip-flopped from anger to sadness. You know, even though they're divorced, I think maybe she thought in the back of her mind that he'd change, and they'd work things out for the sake of Carolinda."

Jasmine's thoughts drifted to Stefan. Would she even be willing to give him a second chance? At this point, she couldn't see doing that; but then the hurt and deceit were still fresh in her memory. She did believe in forgiveness and second chances, but Stefan would have to prove to her that he had really changed.

However, that wasn't the case for Savannah. Derek had moved on to someone new. "First loves are hard to get over, even after a divorce. Despite the fact he was the one who trashed the marriage vows, it's hard to let go when you promise forever."

"Well, we've got to give Savannah some moral support. Let her know we're there for her and God's got a better plan for her. Having pizza at Luigi's always made us feel better when we were frustrated or sad in high school. Let's go there tonight."

"Sure. I can do that. What about finding a sitter for Carolinda?"

"Well, since I already discussed this with Savannah, expecting you to come, too, I asked that question. She says her neighbor, Monique, could probably do it as they have a reciprocal arrangement for a couple of hours when needed. Will six work for you?"

"Sure. We close at five. That'll give me enough time to freshen up and change, even if there are latecomers at the bakery. I'll see you then."

"Great! Keep her in your prayers today."

"Definitely." After she disconnected the call, Jasmine said a quick silent prayer for Savannah. Then her mind slipped back to high school days. Savannah and Derek began dating in senior year.

Prior to Savannah becoming his English tutor, they hadn't spoken much, but studying together changed that. They married after their freshman year in college. Attending different schools made them realize they wanted to be together.

Like many newly married people, they thought they had a lifelong commitment and could weather any storms. She took a few night study classes and worked full-time so he could finish college in four years. Immediately after graduation,

Derek got a job with a great commercial development firm. He quickly made his mark, and they were able to buy a big home in hopes of growing a large family. However, somewhere along the way, he decided that family life wasn't enough for him.

That thought brought on an emotional stab through Jasmine's heart. She had also believed the relationship with Stefan would last. Yet he had cheated on her with two women. There could have been more.

The only apology he made was that he was sorry she found out. For him, they were merely a way to let off some steam.

She certainly let off some steam as she had screamed, "How could you?" What made it worse was the collapse of the company where they both worked.

Looking back, Jasmine could now see that losing her job was a good thing because it would have devasted her to continue working side by side with him on ad campaigns.

The job had also made her a workaholic with her life centered around the company and work friends. Her once daily prayer and meditation had become once a week with Sunday morning services.

God had closed the door to her L.A. life but opened another with her return to her hometown. Though she loved the excitement of brainstorming over million-dollar marketing ideas, being at home and using her creative abilities to bake gave her a sense of joy. Now her only work anxiety centered around making sure they had enough sweets to last the day with only a few remaining, rather than the gut-wrenching blow of losing a major account to another firm.

Yes, life was good, and she had all the time she needed to look for another job. Only she couldn't waste too much time and lose her edge. For now, she was happy to do her best to improve sales at the bakery. She would continue to network and seek out new challenges in the marketing industry, but let God control the outcome. And that gave her a sense of peace.

CHAPTER 15
Night Out with the Girls

The bakery continued to be busy until closing that day. With Donetta there to help with the clean-up, Jasmine could leave once the closed sign showed on the door. She pulled off her apron and hung it in the kitchen. "Looks like we had a good day. Business is picking up with our 'name game' competition."

"Yeah, it's fun watching the jars filled with votes." Donetta wiped down the jars to eliminate the smudged fingerprints.

"And those votes are the reason our goodies are disappearing. I'm glad we did this. Thanks for the suggestions, Jasmine," Belinda said.

"So, you do think I'm adding something to the business," Jasmine's eyes twinkled.

Belinda gave a playful pat on Jasmine's arm. "Of course, I do. I love having you here with me again. But don't stay here looking for more compliments. You've got places to go and people to meet. Give my best to Lexie and Savannah and drive safe."

"Yes, Mother." Jasmine hugged her mom, then waved goodbye. "See you, tomorrow, Donetta."

Jasmine always felt she smelled like she'd been dusted with sugar when she left the bakery, so she took a shower, got into some fresh clothes, and spritzed some perfume on before heading to the restaurant. Before she left, she checked her phone for voicemail and text to see if Trevor might have followed up again. There was no reason for him to do that since he would be there tomorrow, but she had to check just the same. Then she shook her head and smiled. *Look at me, I'm acting like a teenager wondering how much a guy likes me. Get over it, Jasmine. This is not the time to be starting a new relationship.*

While she drove to Luigi's, she turned on an oldies station and her thoughts spiraled back in time to her high school years. Back then, the pizza parlor was the place to hang out after school. Of course, the same cliques that existed in school continued on at the restaurant with each group marking their turf. Since their trio really didn't belong to an "in crowd" getting a booth or a stool at the counter wasn't always easy.

They had to get there as soon as possible after classes ended or wait until seven when the crowds and families cleared out. Much of the time, they ended up getting a slice and a soda which they ate and drank in one of their cars. They'd turn on the radio and pretend they were inside with the others having a fabulous time with the best of the best. The other kids weren't mean to them, but they didn't even notice their presence.

Jasmine wanted to be noticed, which is why after college she happily took a job on the other side of the country to recreate her identity and be someone of significance. If she was good at her job and got results, that mattered more than any high school popularity contest.

And she worked best when paired with Stefan. Their collaboration was remarkable on the job and with anything work related. Outside of business, they really didn't click, which she ignored thinking they'd blend together better with more time. But he liked hanging out with the guys at a sports bar in the evening – or that's what he told her he was doing. In time she learned the truth. Would a relationship with Trevor end the same way it did with Savannah and Derek?

She hadn't been to Luigi's for almost three years and did a double take when she drove into the parking lot. The restaurant had expanded into the store that was once adjacent to theirs. Their old flashing neon sign had been changed to a classy looking dark green sign with a gold border lit by hanging lanterns. Jasmine frowned wondering if the only thing that was the same with the restaurant was the name on the sign.

Then she opened the door, and a smile spread across her face. The wonderful fragrance of spicy tomato sauce and baked dough hung heavy in the air. She was glad that hadn't changed, though most of the interior of the restaurant had been updated. Gone were the glossy travel posters of Italy that had yellowed with age and the red and white checkered vinyl tablecloths over chunky wood tables. Now there was a large mural on the entry wall depicting a Tuscan vineyard and patio. The remaining walls were painted to give the impression of granite walls you'd expect to see in an Italian villa. Black linen tablecloths under thick glass tops now covered the sleek new tables.

It was still as popular as ever. Animated conversations with breaks of occasional laughter filled the room. Jasmine wondered if it would be as hard getting a table now as it was back in high school. Then she heard her name called and she turned to see Lexie waving. She weaved her way to the table resisting the urge to pull off a piece of pizza from a moving waitress. The scent was intoxicating, and her stomach had already started to grumble.

At the table she gave quick hugs to both Lexie and Savannah, before taking her seat. Her timing was perfect as the waitress had just left a small plate of garlic knot rolls on the table. "Wow, I'm so glad they still make these." She picked one up and inhaled the aroma. "Seems the same recipe with that wonderful butter glaze and sprinkle of parmesan. Thanks for ordering them in advance."

"Same recipes, only it's a bigger venue and Luigi, or I should say Lou, which is really his name, turned over control of the restaurant to his son and a nephew last year. From what I understand, he lent them the money to expand saying it was a good investment on his part for the interest and the free meals he'd get," Savannah said as she picked up a roll.

Lexie held up a roll. "They've added new items as well. They've got a dessert pizza, that is to die for, and a great antipasto platter. I like those items, but you still can't beat their classics like these rolls."

"Well, before we get involved in eating, let's say a quick prayer of thanks," Lexie said. She reached out her hands to the two women beside her and bowed her head. "Heavenly Father, thank you for the many years of friendship we've had. Thank you for the memories we've shared together. Guide us in the years ahead. And we especially thank you for the talents of the wonderful chefs who will be preparing our meal. Amen."

Jasmine broke off a piece of a roll and then stopped before she brought it to your mouth. "Lou or Luigi's last name is D'Amico, right? Weren't you dating or hanging out with a Mike D'Amico in our senior year for a while?"

"Well, there was nothing really romantic about us. We were just two friends who shared a love for eating pizza and all things junk food, but that's ancient history now." Lexie replied. "Oh, but he is one of the partners in this restaurant now."

"Yeah, I remember you and Mike. He always had a great sense of humor," Savannah added.

Lexie snorted. "Isn't that what you say about someone who isn't a hottie? They have a great sense of humor or a great personality. I remember my mom saying that about me back in high school when she was trying to fix me up with sons of her friends."

Jasmine patted Lexie on the shoulder. "And look how we both turned out with a little extra motivation. Guys would definitely call you a hottie now."

"Yeah, I do look good now, don't I?" Lexie fluffed out her hair and showed a dazzling smile. "Oh, yeah, we all look good."

Savannah tapped the table. "Your dating history in high school wasn't much to talk about either, Jasmine. The guys you hung out with were the jocks you were tutoring or nerds you worked with on science projects together."

"Yes, I was an overachiever in getting guys to be with me as long as I could help them get better grades. But you…" Jasmine paused. She was about to say Savannah was the lucky one for having found the love of her life. Only it didn't turn out that way.

The awkward silence was broken by the waitress coming to the table to take their order. After the decisions for meals were made and the waitress left, Savannah opened the conversation again. "I know you both wished you had a boyfriend like I had with Derek in high school but look how that turned out. Don't get me wrong, we were happy for a while. The romantic glow went away when the daily everyday life hit Derek. I think he longed for the glory days of high school when he was number one. To feel that way again, he went searching for other women to idolize him. And now he's found someone younger who dotes on him like I did in high school."

"You are not to blame for his straying ways. You were a good wife to him." Jasmine squeezed Savannah's hand.

"And Derek's new chickee-poo has nothing on you but a few less years." Lexie winked and made a circle with one hand. "I'll bet there are several men here who wouldn't mind taking you out and showing Derek the right way to treat a lady."

Savannah hung her head and blew out a breath. "I thought he was my forever love. I didn't date anyone before Derek. Now I don't know how to act on a date. Then there's Carolinda. What would she think about me dating someone that's not her daddy?"

Jasmine shook her head. "That didn't stop Derek from dating other women. What does she think of her daddy dating these other women?"

"Well, it was a little awkward at first, but he made sure they did fun things together. She enjoyed the attention she gave him. He made sure the few women she did meet were only with them for a few minutes and were played up as chance meetings. Carolinda didn't pick up that they were someone Daddy was dating, but the way she told me about their meetings I saw right through them. This is the only woman Carolinda has said has shared her dates with her daddy. She said she was Derek's special friend. And apparently now a very special friend."

Jasmine saw the pain in Savannah's eyes with those last words. It reminded her of the pain she felt in seeing Stefan with Kayla, the woman she thought was her friend. At least this woman wasn't someone Savannah knew. "Savannah, we're your best friends and know how wonderful you are. If Derek doesn't see that it's his loss. He's had more than enough time to reconsider his error in moving out and then signing the divorce papers. If you're not ready to start seeing any guys even as friends, then find something else to fuel your passions."

"And that doesn't mean you need to become a helicopter mom. You do a wonderful job in raising your sweet pea, but it's time you find something else just for you."

Savannah reached out and squeezed her friends' hands. "You are the best friends. Thanks for cheering me up. Now it looks like it's time to eat up. That's our food coming over."

The server laid the plates on the table in front of each of the women and they looked appreciatively at their meals as they inhaled the tantalizing aromas. Their talking had ended for a while except for the occasional laudatory comments on the taste of the food.

As their empty plates were removed, Mike D'Amico dropped by their table. "It's good to see the fabulous trio again. You ladies are looking lovely tonight. Seeing you together again brings back good memories from high school and when you let me hang out with you and eat pizza."

"Well, the food is just as good as ever," Lexie said. "And what you've done with the place gives it a nice touch of class that lots more people can appreciate."

Mike smiled and gave a quick pat to Lexie's shoulder. "Thanks, Lexie. You were actually part of the inspiration for the changes. You remember how we talked about what you'd do if you owned a restaurant?"

Lexie's eyes grew wide. "I'm surprised you remember. That was silly teenager talk wishing we were in charge."

"Well, you encouraged me to think forward and now I am in charge with my cousin. And we're doing pretty well with dine in and takeout. Come by mid-afternoon on a Saturday or Sunday and I'll show you what we've done with the kitchen."

"Sure," Lexie nodded. "I'd like that."

"Good," Mike smiled. "Thanks for stopping by ladies. Hope to see you again soon."

Once Mike was a good distance away and out of earshot, Jasmine whispered. "I cannot believe that is the same Mike we knew in high school. Even in his T-shirt and apron you can't help but notice his trimmed down body and muscles."

"And that goatee is really sexy looking," Lexie added.

Savannah pointed at Lexie. "Yeah, and I saw him checking you out as well."

"So, are you going to take him up on his offer?" Jasmine asked.

Lexie smiled and nodded. "We were friends in high school, so why shouldn't I do it. The man is easy on the eyes and he knows how to cook. Maybe I'll even get a free meal like back in the day."

Savannah gave Lexie a knowing wink. "And maybe your old friendship can be the starting point for something new."

Lexie laughed. "Hey, I'm the one that's the super romantic. Don't cut into my turf. Let's see what happens with my kitchen tour."

"Just remember to keep us in the loop so we can enjoy any budding romance vicariously."

"As long as you do the same, Jasmine, with what's happening with Trevor."

Jasmine fist bumped with Lexie. "Deal." She hoped there would be more to a romance with Trevor when they got together again, even if it were only temporary until she was offered a new job which was not yet in the near future.

CHAPTER 16
Disaster in Falcon Creek

On Thursday morning, Jasmine woke early and couldn't wait for the day to begin. Her shower was rushed, but she took extra time in deciding what to wear. Today she'd be seeing Trevor. Butterflies fluttered in her stomach in anticipation of their meeting. Donetta would fill in at the shop in the afternoon. Over the past few days, she and Trevor shared numerous phone calls and texts. The more they chatted, the more she liked him, which scared her. She still had the emotional scars from Stefan and feared getting hurt again. She was falling hard for Trevor and that wasn't in her plans. Whatever they had would need to be only temporary. She still had her career to consider as she'd first planned when she returned to Falcon Creek.

At the bakery, Jasmine re-directed her thoughts away from her date with Trevor. She concentrated on rolling, cutting, and filling the almond croissants on the counter. With a few quick turns of her fingers, they became half-moon shapes. As she finished the tray, she covered it for the final rise. The process continued with the next dough batch. As she worked, she hummed one of her favorite songs.

"Someone's in a good mood," Jasmine's mom turned and smiled. "What makes you so happy today?"

Jasmine looked up from her work. "What do you mean? My mood's the same as yesterday. And I'm happy about how some of those leads from the fundraiser have resulted in contracts, nothing more than that."

Mom walked over and tapped Jasmine on her nose leaving a touch of flour. "You can't kid me. I'm your mother. Could it be your afternoon off to see Trevor?"

Jasmine wiped the flour off her nose with the back of her hand. Then she picked up a pinch of flour and tossed it at her mom playfully. Her gaze returned to the work in front of her for a moment and then she looked up. "Well, there is that. Only I don't want to make too much of it."

"And why is that?"

Jasmine shrugged and picked up a tray of mini pies and brought them over to the oven. She removed the finished brownies and took a deep whiff of the fragrant chocolate and caramel filling. Once she placed them on a cart, she added the pies to the oven. "My last boyfriend turned out to be a disaster. I don't want to have my heart broken again."

"Everything you've told me about Trevor makes him sound like one of the good guys."

Mom gave Jasmine's shoulder a quick squeeze as she walked over to the refrigerator to get some butter

"Stefan was like that in the beginning, too. Everything about him seemed perfect." Jasmine joined her mom at the refrigerator and pulled out the dough to make Danish.

"Oh, honey, you're way too young to be that cynical. If I had closed my heart to love after my first big break-up, I would never have met your dad."

Jasmine sighed as she rolled out the pastry on the counter. "Mom, times were different back then. When you started dating, you didn't even have email."

Mom flicked a towel at Jasmine. "Don't go try making me sound ancient. I'm not that old."

"I know." Jasmine chuckled. "I was only teasing." She stopped her work and stared directly at her mom. "Seriously, though, how did you let yourself fall in love again after a break-up?"

"It was your dad's persistence," She chuckled. "He wouldn't take no for an answer. I don't mean in a stalker kind of way. When I told him I wasn't ready for a relationship, he simply agreed with me." Mom tilted her head and her eyes glistened. "That's when he really started romancing me, which began with sweet gestures -- like bringing meals from my favorite restaurant when I had to work through lunch, sending funny cards to make me laugh when I felt discouraged or bringing cold medicine when I was sick. He did everything he could to let me see he was the one for me."

"He was always so thoughtful and kind to others in all his volunteer activities." Jasmine's eyes started to well up. "Dad was a great role model. I sure miss him."

"Me, too." Mom walked over and hugged Jasmine. "He was one in a million. All the years we had together were a great blessing. One day you'll have a love like that, too. It may be Trevor or someone else. God has someone in mind for you. So don't let your cynicism close the door to love."

"Okay, I'll try my best to not shut off my feelings." She wanted to trust Trevor, but how could she be sure he didn't have a girlfriend or two in San Antonio?

"Good. Now let's get back to work before people arrive." Mom patted Jasmine on the back and smiled. "Don't want customers coming in while we're still prepping for the day."

Jasmine returned to her duties, but her thoughts were about Trevor. *God, you know my heart. If Trevor is the one for me, take away my fear of loving again*. She walked to the oven and checked on the mini pies. Scents of apple, caramelized sugar and cinnamon wafted from the open oven door. The golden-brown color of the crust was picture perfect. The old adage of *the way to a man's heart was through his stomach* popped into her mind. Trevor had a passion for food and understood the importance of tantalizing the taste buds. A love of cooking and enjoying new flavors was something they had in common. Perhaps when he dropped by this afternoon, they could make a dinner together.

"Mom, would you mind if Trevor and I made a meal..." She stopped mid-sentence at the sound of a low rumble followed by the floor shaking with the sensation traveling up her legs. "What in the world is that? If I were in California, I'd have called it an earthquake, but this isn't earthquake country."

"Oh, my Lord, what in the world is happening?"

They both ran outside the front door to the street. Dawn was just breaking so no one was on the street except the two of them. Fire truck sirens wailed in the distance. Toward the northwest side of town, huge plumes of fire and thick, black smoke billowed and spread across the sky. In the distance, repeating booms sounded, followed by burning debris arcing up in the air.

"Oh, no. Those flames look like they could be near the elementary school. Thank God, it's too early for anyone to be there. But there's train tracks nearby" Her hands tightly grasped her apron. "Could there have been some sort of train derailment?" Jasmine eyes widened and her hands twisted the edges of her apron.

"I'll call my friend who's a sergeant at the police station." Mom pulled a cell phone from her pants pocket. "Jeremy, it's Belinda. We're at the bakery and heard an explosion. You've had other calls...I see... That's terrible... Yes... Yes...Of course... I'll say a prayer for the fire fighters... I'll talk to you later."

"Boom... boom...Both women jumped when they heard the latest blasts. The skies lit up with tall orange flames and ominous looking grey smoke.

Jasmine grabbed her mom's sleeve. "So, what did he say? What's going on?"

"A train derailed when it hit a tractor trailer stuck on the tracks. The truck carried something combustible that caused a chain reaction with something else on the train."

Jasmine's jaw dropped. "That's horrible."

"There's concern over the fire mixed with the winds, so they're setting up an evacuation center at Hartwell High School." Mom shook her head and sighed. "Lots of help will be needed at the school. We need to take what we've made so far and take it there.

Jasmine nervously bit at her fingernails. "Sure. Hope the winds stay away from the homes over there. That could be devastating."

"Let's pack up and head over to the school to lend a hand." Mom put her hand on Jasmine's shoulder as they walked back on the sidewalk. Before they reached the front door, they heard a car's horn beep and they both turned.

The car slowed to a stop and the driver rolled down his window and called out. "Are the two of you headed to Hartwell?"

Belinda stepped over to the car. "Yes. Have you heard any news of injuries, Stewart?"

Stewart, one of their neighbors, looked like he'd just jumped out of bed with hair askew and unshaven face. He leaned out the window. "Talked to my cousin, Mac, who lives by Crockett Elementary. Says there's no damage to the school. They're watering it down to stay that way. The nearby Briarbridge Apartments weren't so lucky. Winds blew sparks that ignited several roofs in the complex. They're going up like tinder boxes."

Jasmine's hands came together as she closed her eyes and said a silent prayer. *Lord, Jesus, please wrap your loving arms around the people who live there and give the firefighters the power to put out the flames.*

"The fireman are evacuating everyone nearby until they know what else might be on that train. Emergency crews have been called from neighboring communities."

"That's good," Belinda nodded. "Sounds like it will be a busy day for all those crews.

"You bet." Stewart said. "I've got some med tech training and will pitch in where I can."

As Jasmine listened to the conversation, she ran her hands up and down her arms in a vain attempt to squash the goose bumps growing there. Her gaze kept returning to the flickering flames in the distance.

"The hospital's emergency room won't have room to treat all the minor injuries, so they'll probably set up a treatment center at the high school." Belinda added.

"Yep, my thoughts, as well. See you up there." Stewart waved goodbye and drove off.

Jasmine shivered thinking of the people running from the buildings. "With the evacuations, there's sure to be lots of people with frazzled nerves. They'll be hungry, too." She pulled her buzzing phone from her pocket and looked at it. "That was a timer. My pastries are ready. We can pack them up plus the other items that are cooling."

"I'll pull out our big coffee urns and get some other supplies together. Could you pack up the van?" Belinda asked as they hurried into the bakery. "While you're doing that, I'll get a prayer chain going and make some calls to organize other supplies for those using the school as shelter.

While her mom made calls, Jasmine assembled the needed supplies and packed them in the van out back. Then she boxed up the pastries as they finished baking.

Mom strode into the kitchen as Jasmine finished putting the final items in the company van.

With a deep sigh, her mom began counting out the details with her fingers. "The prayer chain is going strong and our church is setting up the fellowship hall for any overflow space that's needed. The Lunch Box and Jim's Barbecue will be putting together sandwiches. Family Market will be supplying bottled water. Creekside Inn and the Old Grist Mill will be putting together dinner meals." She clutched Jasmine's hand. "Lord, let your light shine through us, so we can comfort others."

"Amen to that. Let's roll." Jasmine closed the van's side door then took her seat on the front passenger side.

CHAPTER 17
Breaking News

Trevor woke at six a.m. and went for his morning run in Brackenridge Park which was just minutes from his condo. During the early hours of the day, the park's meandering tree lined path was mostly vacant except for other runners. However, on the weekends it would be a bevy of activities. But for now it was quiet and serene with only the occasional tweets from the birds who made their home there. As he went through his paces, he mentally laid out his day's activities. High in priority on his list was seeing Jasmine. That wouldn't happen until later in the afternoon and he still had work to complete.

When he finished his workout, he felt exhilarated, but he wasn't sure if it was from the run or the idea of seeing Jasmine again. Returning home, he tossed his sweaty clothes on the side rim of his laundry basket, then took a hot shower. and dressed for work. He turned on the big sports-sized flat screen TV in the living room to see the traffic updates while he pulled together a few things for breakfast. Though he ate in a grand style at restaurants he was reviewing, at home his meals were simple. Today it would be smashed avocado with a little salsa on multi-grain toast and Greek yogurt with peaches. This was his regular morning routine and it was a time to relax before the day got busy. But life doesn't always go as planned. He caught his breath as he stared at the TV screen in disbelief.

"Breaking news… There's been a massive explosion in the Hill Country community of Falcon Creek early this morning. The blast was so intense it could be heard miles away and sent a wave of destruction across this small community…"

The TV screen showed the scenes of devastation around the blast. He rushed to his nightstand, picked up the phone, and called Jasmine. Instead of hearing her voice, he heard, "All circuits are busy. Please try again, later." Again and again, he got the same results. "Aargh. I hate technology. It never works when I really need it." In frustration, he threw his phone on his bed and paced the room as he processed what he'd just heard. He reached for his phone again and called Nick. "I'm heading up to Falcon Creek to see what's going on."

"That's not your beat, Trevor."

"I'm not going there for the story; I'm going to help out." Trevor paced as he spoke.

"They may limit traffic into the city. You could be turned back."

"Then let me go with a news crew. I'll stay out of their way." He closed his eyes and clenched his free hand. "I need to be there."

"Okay. A van's leaving in a few minutes. I can add you to it and have them wait. How soon can you get here?"

Trevor shot a glance at the time stamp on the TV screen. "It's still early enough for light traffic. I'll be there in ten minutes."

"Okay, they'll be waiting by the delivery doors in the back. Be careful up there."

"Will do." Trevor ended the call and pulled the shirt over his head without unbuttoning it and tossed it on his bed. He switched into jeans, a T-shirt and boots. With keys in hand, he locked up and headed out to his car. He called Jasmine's number again but still received the frustrating "all circuits are busy." The radio news did nothing to ease his mind. Eyewitness accounts sounded frantic and distressing.

At the Times building parking lot, he saw the news van and a group of familiar people standing nearby. He jumped out of his SUV, locked it, and ran to the vehicle. "Okay, guys, are you ready to go?"

One of the paper's best photographers, Jon Strickland, slipped into the driver's seat. "Let's do this. It's anybody's guess what traffic conditions will be like up there."

Francine Mott, the lone female reporter in the group, climbed into the front passenger seat and snapped into her seat belt.

Immediately, she scrolled through updates on her tablet.

Trevor sat in the back with Patrick Withers, a new reporter he hadn't met until that moment. Patrick mumbled an uninterested "hello" without breaking his concentration on the computer screen on his lap. On his other side was a photographer he knew well and often requested for his special interest stories, Benito Rodriguez.

"This looks like one horrendous story," Benito turned to Trevor. "One hundred or more people have been injured. It's going to be rough. Are you sure you're up for this? This ain't a messy kitchen throw-down."

Trevor glared at him. "Don't patronize me. I'm not cutting into your news story. I'm heading up there to help. If it's as bad as it sounds, they'll need volunteers."

"It's bad, man. There's no mistake about it." Jon said as he glanced at Trevor in the rear-view mirror.

Trevor gritted his teeth and stared ahead. He hated not knowing where Jasmine was and whether or not she was okay. Based on the time the disaster occurred, he assumed she would be in the bakery prepping for the daily opening. Only he didn't know if she did any morning deliveries. If she did, she might have been in close range of the explosion site. He called Jasmine's number again and now had the immediate busy signal. *Dear God, please keep Jasmine and Belinda safe.*

During the trip, heads mostly stayed down checking computer screens. Occasionally someone would chime in with new information.

Through it all, Trevor kept silent. He wished he were in a helicopter instead of a van, so they'd be there already. From time to time, he'd check his phone and review the streaming videos of the disaster in hopes of seeing Jasmine safe. Her image never showed up.

Ten miles from Falcon Creek, the traffic slowed. A number of drivers didn't wait for exits and began cutting across the grass to reach frontage roads, which locals called "doing a Texas exit." Trevor fidgeted in his seat. He wished they could speed through the traffic, but side roads were already full. He grabbed the back of the front seat. "Isn't there another way to get there quicker?"

Jon shook his head.

Trevor threw his head back against the seat with a deep sigh. Police lights flashed alongside the road. Their vehicle received clearance to move ahead, but to an alternate route. Trevor's gaze darted from one window to another. Streams of emergency and fire vehicles rushed past them on the shoulder of the road.

When they reached the outskirts of the town, a police officer motioned for the van to stop. Jon rolled down his window. "Where's the closest we can get to photograph the accident location?"

"We're not letting any vehicles, including yours, anywhere close to the scene. The fires are not contained. You'll be directed to the high school, which is an evac center. We've set a command post there. Just follow the directions from the other officers along the road."

Jon rolled up his window and drove in the direction where the officer had pointed.

"As long as we have sight of the disaster area, I can get telephoto shots," Benito said, tapping his camera as they drove on.

"Okay, you take that angle and I'll do the human-interest side and look for the face of tragedy," Jon replied glancing in his rear-view mirror at Benito.

"Let's just get to the high school," Trevor said through gritted teeth. "We have no idea who's hurt. Or what the damage really is. We've got to find out."

"Sure," Benito said. "We'll get the details of the fatalities. What they were like. Tug at the heartstrings stuff."

"Pulitzer Prize-winning stuff," Francine added and then high-fived Benito.

"Really?" Trevor said as he frowned at her. "These are real people. They're devastated by what happened this morning. How would you feel if someone you cared about got hurt in the explosion? Show some compassion."

"Wow," Jon replied. "What's with you?"

Trevor raked his hand through his hair. "I've been trying to reach someone who lives here. I keep getting the 'all circuits are busy' response when I call." His voice softened to almost a whisper. "I don't know if she was caught in the explosion or if she's safe."

Francine leaned toward the back seat and faced Trevor. "When disasters like this hit, they usually have a place where you can check in for those who are missing, injured, or are fatalities. They'll be someone handling that at the high school. I can help you check names. Let me know who you're looking for."

"I need to find a mother and daughter who run a bakery here. The mom is Belinda Cattrell and Jasmine is her daughter. More likely than not they were at the bakery. Have you heard any details of businesses that were affected?"

"What I've seen is pretty sketchy so far. Only read about the train, the trailer truck, Falcon Creek Elementary school, which thankfully was empty at the time, and Briarbridge Apartment complex," Francine replied as she scrolled through her news feed. "The apartments were the closest to the accident. One building is totally toast. Hope she didn't live there."

CHAPTER 18
Arrival in Falcon Creek

Once they found a place to park, Trevor bounded out of the van. Sounds of sirens erupted every few seconds and the smoke in the air blotted out the early morning sun. With quick strides, he headed for the high school entrance, which had streams of people moving in and out the doors. He stopped the first EMT he saw. "Excuse me; I'm trying to find the status of someone I know. Can you help?"

The EMT turned and pointed down the hall. "Go inside the cafeteria. They've started working up lists to keep track of people. Look for someone with a clipboard."

"Thanks, man." Trevor turned on his heel down the corridor. He passed doors leading to classrooms with the absence of any students. Further down he heard the chatter of multiple voices and saw people moving in and out of swinging doors. He hastened into the room and his focus zig zagged throughout the groups of people around the long metal benches searching for someone carrying a clipboard. His gaze locked on a female with her back turned to him. She was handing out steaming cups of coffee to people. *Could it be?* He hurried towards her. "Jasmine?" At the sound of his voice, Jasmine spun around. He gripped her by the shoulders and blew out a deep breath. "I'm so glad you're alright. I was so worried."

She stared wide-eyed and sputtered. "Trevor, how…how did you get here? Why…why did you come?"

"I heard about the explosion. I came with our news van like all the other news sources who are converging on the scene."

Her shoulders slumped and she looked down with a sigh. "Yes, I guess this makes for a pretty big news story."

He caressed her cheek and lifted her chin in his hand. For a moment, he gazed intently at her glad to see she'd been unharmed by the blast. In a soft, solemn voice he said, "I didn't come for the story, I came for you. I care about you. I needed to know you were safe. I couldn't get through the phone lines.

Jasmine nodded as her heart skipped a beat while he wrapped her in his arms. "It's been so frenetic here. I haven't even paid attention to my phone."

Trevor smiled. "Well, I'm here to help. What can I do?"

"I'm glad you are." She gazed into his warm, caring eyes. *This is someone I can count on. He's not anything like Stefan.* She let herself relax in his comforting embrace and closed her eyes. A moment later, her reverie abruptly ended when someone bumped into them.

"Excuse me." said one of the evacuees, before she shuffled away.

Jasmine turned and gazed at a slim middle-aged woman with disheveled hair who stood a few feet away. She wore a "Go Spurs" T-shirt, faded jeans, and sandals, which Jasmine assumed, were the closest items at hand to dress in before she had to evacuate.

All at once, the woman began to shiver.

Jasmine scooted over and gripped her shoulder. "Ma'am are you okay? Let me get you a blanket."

Nodding, the woman stared at her but didn't seem to focus.

Trevor stood on the other side of the woman and gently put his arm across her back as they walked together to one of the lunch tables and sat her on a bench.

Jasmine stepped away and returned with a blanket for the woman. She leaned down and wrapped it securely around her shoulders and gave them a slight squeeze. "Is that better?"

The woman nodded again, but her blank expression didn't change.

"What's your name? Is there something else I can help you with?" Jasmine gently held the woman's clammy and shaky hands in hers. The woman tilted her head and looked at Jasmine as if she were asking a complex question.

"Maria... My name is Maria Rodriguez. I can't... find my husband, Eddie. I... got off my shift at the... They won't let me... go back to my apartment." Maria's gaze flitted between the two of them like a frightened, wounded bird.

Jasmine bit her lip. If this woman couldn't go back to her apartment, she probably lived in Briarbridge. Her husband could be hurt or worse. She sat next to Maria and put her arm around the woman's shoulder. "We'll find out about your husband." She turned to Trevor. "Can you find one of the EMTs and see who has an update on the victims and injured?"

Trevor squeezed Jasmine's hand. "Sure. I'll be back soon." He turned and walked away.

"So you work the night shift. Have you been doing that for long?" Jasmine spoke softly to Maria. She had no idea how to deal with someone in shock but hoped a simple conversation would at least calm her.

"About two months now. It was rough at first, changing my sleep. The pay is good, so I stayed. Tried to get Eddie a job with me..." Maria's head twitched with quick glances from one part of the room to the other... "So we could have more time together. Only nothing's come up yet."

Jasmine nodded. "That would be nice. You could drive in together." She anxiously looked around for Trevor.

"Don't like driving at night by myself. The morning's good though"

Trevor headed toward them with two people trailing behind him. He stopped at the bench and placed a hand on Maria's shoulder. "These folks are going to help you. This is Jacob Svenson. He's an EMT and wants to check to make sure you're okay."

Maria gave him a slight nod.

"This is Cassie who's in charge of helping get families back together." Trevor motioned for Jasmine to give her seat to Cassie, who slipped right in place beside Maria.

Trevor put his hands on Jasmine's shoulder and whispered in her ear. "Let's give them space to do their job."

She slipped her hand into Trevor's as they walked away. Her voice caught. "She's one of the many who've come in this morning in shock and bewilderment. It's so heart breaking. In between helping folks I've been in constant silent prayer." Jasmine wiped a tear away from her pooling eyes. "Last I heard there were thirty people unaccounted for. Maria brings that number back to twenty-nine."

A loud moan caused them turn toward where they had just been. Trevor shook his head. "Doesn't look like Maria received good news about her husband."

Jasmine let the tears fall down her cheek as she clutched Trevor's hand tighter. "I feel so sorry for that woman. This is all so horrible."

Trevor wrapped his arm around her shoulder and pulled her close. "Hopefully, others will receive better news. By the way, where's your mom?"

"She's in the kitchen getting refills for the coffee." Jasmine pointed to the back of the room and blew out a deep breath. "Can't seem to keep up."

Trevor raised up her chin with his fingertips. "What can I do to help?"

She blinked and gazed into his eyes. "Seriously, you're not here for the newspaper?"

He stared straight back. "No, the others I came with have that job. I came for you and to help. Now show me what I can do."

Jasmine was in awe for the moment seeing the compassion in his eyes. Then she cleared her throat. "Hmmm. You've told me you're good in the kitchen, so why don't we put you to the test."

"I'm game. What do you have in mind?"

"Mom's arranged for all sorts of food to come in. Fruits and veggies need cutting. Would you be willing to do that?"

"Gladly. Let's go to the kitchen" He swept his arm forward for her to go first.

She led the way with a smile on her face, which she covered with her hand. *He cares.*

He came to make sure I was okay. And he's here to help. How wonderful.

The school's industrial style kitchen was full of people scurrying about intent on their duties of laying out supplies, preparing food, boxing it to go and general clean up, but Jasmine quickly spotted her mom and headed that way. "I've got a new volunteer for you."

"Reporting for duty, ma'am." Trevor tapped his first two fingers to his temple. "I'm good at chopping, slicing, peeling. Whatever you need."

Belinda put her hands on her hips and smiled. "Trevor, what a surprise and a blessing. We certainly need extra hands today." She led him over to one of the stainless-steel tables. "We're going to make a soup. Aprons are over by the wall, get one and put it on. Pull one of those huge stockpots off the shelf and fill it halfway with water. Then start dicing the potatoes as a base for the vegetable soup."

"Will do." Trevor filled the pot halfway, placed it on a burner and turned up the heat. He picked up a ten-pound sack of potatoes, ripped it open and pulled out several. Next, he gave them a quick scrub, found a peeler and knife, and began the peeling process.

Jasmine found a chopping board and a good knife and began dicing the peeled potatoes. "Lots of stressed and scared people out in the cafeteria. We were pretty far from the train crash and the explosions, but it rattled me, too."

"You sure you're okay?" He reached over and gripped her hand.

She felt a tingling sensation from where their hands touched. For a few short moments all that mattered was the two of them being there together. Then the clanging of a tray hitting the floor from a nearby workstation brought her back to her senses, as she felt heat rising on her face. She slipped her hand from his and scooped up a handful of chopped potatoes and added them to the pot. "Yes, um, I'm fine. We're blessed. We've lost nothing. Unfortunately, others can't say the same. I've been praying they'll be able to find hope in this situation."

"This story will bring in tons of volunteers and people who want to donate to help the locals get back on their feet." Trevor paused and leaned a hand on the table. "I could help whoever's in charge of fundraising get the word out with the newspaper."

Before she could add a response, she heard her name yelled from across the room.

"Jazzy, Jasmine, where are you?"

She turned and waved to get Savannah's attention. "Excuse the interruption. That's one of my best friends from high school."

"She called you Jazzy," he said with a raised eyebrow. "I thought you preferred Jasmine."

"I do." She rolled her eyes. "It's a throwback to our high school days. Although sometimes I think she calls me that to annoy me."

Savannah strode to Jasmine's side, gave her a quick hug and asked, "And who is this good-looking guy with you?"

Jasmine cleared her throat and put her arm around Trevor's back. "My great helper here is Trevor."

"Is this THE Trevor?" Savannah asked wide-eyed.

Trevor wiped his hand on his apron and extended it to Savannah. "It's a pleasure to meet you."

Savannah gripped Trevor's hand and gave him an appraising look. "I've heard about you."

As he pulled away his hand, Trevor chuckled. "I guess you have."

"Oh, nothing bad, I assure you, but she does have a nickname for you. It's --"

"So, Savannah, are you here to drop off supplies or to assist?" Jasmine glared at her friend.

"I dropped off supplies, but I could stay and help. Especially, if I could work with the two of you. I'd like to get to know Trevor better and see where this relationship between the two of you is going."

"What?" Jasmine's jaw dropped. She reached over, grabbed her friend's arm, and whirled her around. "I'll be back in a minute. I

know just where Savannah can do the most good."

Once they were out of Trevor's hearing range, Jasmine blurted, "Are you crazy? What in the world are you trying to do? We're getting to know each other. There's no real relationship. We're only friends."

"Your mouth may say friends, but his eyes say girlfriend. I noticed how he smiled at you when I asked about your relationship."

Jasmine grabbed a strand of hair and twirled it in her finger. Butterflies fluttered in her stomach. "Well, I like the sound of it, sort of."

Savannah pointed a finger at Jasmine. "Sort of? Now who's talking crazy? Trevor looks like a great catch."

"Yes, he's wonderful, but I don't know if I'm ready for a relationship. I'm still crushed from what happened with Stefan." Jasmine locked her arms across her chest.

Savannah shook her head. "You may have a college degree and good business skills, but you've got no sense about men. The best way to get over one guy is to start dating another. You know, it's like that old adage about the horse. If you get thrown off, get back on again."

"Well, I'm steering clear of horses and men for the time being." Jasmine replied.

"Hmmm." Savannah tapped a finger over her lips. "So, then you wouldn't mind if I cozied up to him since he is one-hundred percent available?"

Jasmine eyes widened and her nostrils flared. "Why, um, why would you do that?"

"See you do care about him." Savannah said. "What are you going to do about it?"

"I don't know. I may not even stay around here." Jasmine rubbed her hands on her apron and shook her head. "You know I'm still trying to get back into advertising. A new job could take me anywhere."

"Well, you better start doing some self-promotion if you have an interest in this guy. Otherwise, someone else will make the moves on him. There are several single ladies here who are just itching to do that."

"That's not going to happen here. It's an emergency situation." Jasmine said as she swept her arm about the room.

"To some women, not having a man in their life is an emergency. Oh, look, who's that who took your place next to Trevor?" She nodded her head to the pass-through window of the kitchen that was visible from the cafeteria.

Jasmine turned to see the florist shop owner down the street from the bakery laughing with Trevor. "How dare she? ... I mean, I better go save him, so he doesn't accidentally disclose his secret identity as a food critic." She winked at Savannah and headed towards Trevor.

"Yeah, save him. For yourself." Savannah mumbled as she followed Jasmine into the kitchen.

Before they made their way to where Trevor stood, Belinda was motioning everyone out into the cafeteria. "Let's join the others. There's going to be some kind of announcement."

They all shuffled out to the main room quickly. Trevor rested his hands on Jasmine's shoulder and Savannah stood next to her.

One of the people in charge blew a whistle to break through the chatter in the room. When it quieted, she said, "Excuse me, everyone. I need your attention. I know many of us have been busy here for the last few hours and haven't had any updates on what's happened. The mayor and the fire captain will be here in five minutes. Everyone take a break so you can hear what they have to say."

Jasmine shivered. "This is going to be hard. We're a small community and we know one another at least by sight and most times by name."

Trevor rubbed her shoulders. "I'm here. I'll help you through this."

She looked into his eyes and smiled before she leaned against his chest and let him wrap his arms around her.

Jasmine and Trevor worked late into the evening until other volunteers could take over and continue the steady routine they'd started. By now, the deceased had been moved to morgues and their identities verified. The local hospitals housed those needing additional treatment. The people remaining at the high school were those who either were now homeless or couldn't return to their homes, as they were deemed unsafe. As they walked through the auditorium on the way out, Jasmine stopped multiple times to give someone a hug or a word of encouragement, as did Trevor. With each step, her heart ached for their loss. In her mind she kept repeating, *Lord show them your peace.*

Once outside Jasmine sighed deeply. "Are you as exhausted as I am?"

Trevor ran his fingers through his hair and yawned. "Didn't know I could get this tired without falling asleep."

"Me, too. I can't wait to plop down in my bed."

Trevor pointed to the bright stadium-style light stands that focused on the shadowy debris of what was once a series of apartment buildings.

"Looks like a war zone." Jasmine's nose scrunched up from the acrid smell of smoke in the air as she gazed over the area.

"It will take a long time to heal from the devastation." He wrapped his arms around her. "Are you going to be okay?"

Jasmine nodded. "Yes, Mom and I are resilient. Hope others in the community are as well." The warmth and comfort of his embrace gave her a sense of peace after a long day of stress. After a couple of minutes, she gently pulled away but still entwined her fingers with his. "There's my mom." She pointed and waved to her. "We're going home and do some serious sleeping. Do you have a place to stay?"

"Yes, the senior editor confirmed rooms for us before we left expecting we'd be here overnight. I'll text Jon, our crew driver for a pick-up. Do you think you'll open the bakery tomorrow?"

"I'll check with Mom." She shrugged. "Don't know if we'd serve people better by opening the bakery and feeding people from there or here at the school. I can barely think right now. I'll let you know in the morning."

He cupped his hands under her chin and pulled her close in a kiss until they heard an "ahem" behind them.

"Sorry to interrupt." Belinda patted Trevor's arm. "Thanks for coming up to help. Are you ready to go Jasmine? I don't want to fall asleep on the parking lot."

"I'm ready, Mom." She gave Trevor a hug. "Thanks for your help. I'm really glad you came up here."

"Happy to do my part. See you tomorrow." Trevor gave her a wave and turned away.

As she walked to the car with her mom, Jasmine let a smile fill her face thinking about how Trevor spent the whole day helping the victims and first responders. Stefan would never do that, unless he got some positive publicity from it. His way of helping people was writing a check. She liked Trevor's way better.

CHAPTER 19
Rebuilding Falcon Creek

Like all disasters, the survivors pressed on and kept doing what needed to be done. For the next few weeks, Jasmine and her mom continued to do their part in preparing snacks to sustain the first responders and those in temporary shelters. Church groups came in to lend a hand in rehabbing houses that were damaged but not destroyed. Samaritan's Purse and the Red Cross provided emotional, spiritual, and medical support. Donations from around the state and the country poured in to fill the gaps where needed.

The emotional scars and personal loss of thirty-four of the townspeople touched everyone. As she drove through the town, Jasmine's eyes would tear up as she saw the demolition of the charred remains of apartments and other structures that once were filled with joy and laughter. The tragedy brought a greater reality of cherishing her time with friends, her mom, and Trevor. Unfortunately, most of her contacts with him were by phone and text since work assignments kept him in San Antonio.

A month after the disaster, when the bakery was empty of patrons, Jasmine and her mom took a break and sat at a nearby table. Mom sipped her tea and then heaved a heavy sigh. "We've been able to handle the revenue losses to help the community from my "Rainy Day Blessing Fund," but that fund is now empty."

"I'm surprised it lasted as long as it did, Mom, with all we were doing." Jasmine reached over and squeezed her mom's hand.

"Thanks, honey. The influx of volunteers and the curious have made up for some of our daily local foot traffic; however, we've also had event cancellations. We need to find a way to make up for the loss."

Jasmine rubbed the back of her neck. "With all that's happened lately, we haven't done much with those leads from the "Taste of South Texas" event."

"That's right! Some of those leads might be cold, but we can still follow up. If I watch the front of the bakery, will you go to the back and start making those calls?"

"Sure, they're probably still in the card file we put together that night." Jasmine picked up her cup and stood. "I did go through a few already, but hopefully something good will be found with the remaining ones." She walked to the office, pulled out the box, laid out the interest cards on the desk, and made her first call.

Several calls were a bust as the potential clients had already contracted with other caterers. For others, she was able to set up appointments for events later in the year. Still nothing led to a booking now. She tapped her pen on the desk and picked up the business card from Cooper Benedict. "Well," she mused. "Let's see what Benedict Enterprises might offer as a potential client. If you're trying to sell me something, you're about as much out of luck as I am today."

She dialed the number and waited for the call to pick up. A receptionist asked her name and her business. Once she explained the call was a follow-up on a request from Cooper, her call was put on hold. Instead of listening to music, she heard an infomercial about a number of TV shows, which seemed odd as she half-listened while working on the computer.

A couple of minutes passed until she heard a live voice on the phone. "This is Cooper. Would you refresh my memory again of how we met?"

"You came by my booth at the "Taste of South Texas" and asked me lots of details about our bakery in Falcon Creek."

"Oh, yes, now I remember. I was in San Antonio finishing a show. You say you're from Falcon Creek. Isn't that where that horrendous train and truck explosion happened recently?"

"Yes, it is." Jasmine wrapped her arm around her stomach and clutched at her apron. The memory of all the pain she saw that night made her catch her breath. In a somber tone she added, "The damage to lives and property was staggering. Several funds have been set up for those who want to help, but I didn't call to ask for donations."

"No, no. I understand. But you are from Falcon Creek. You could do a lot to keep your community's needs in the spotlight and I'm in a position to help."

"In what way?"

"I produce a TV series called *Topped* where I put bakers from around the country to a test with other bakers to create something fabulous out of unique ingredients. How would you like to be a contestant? You'd need to do a short video, about two-minutes. This would highlight your business and the needs of your community. We would air that video during the show when you're introduced. If you aren't eliminated and continue on a contestant, each subsequent show would feature that segment to keep people reminded of who you are and the fundraising aspects to rebuild your city.

Jasmine was speechless. This was the last thing she expected from the phone call. She'd watched the show a number of times but had never paid attention to who the producer was. "I don't know. The show sounds intriguing, but I don't know if I can afford to take off the time from the bakery at this point."

"Not an issue. We do pay for your time; give you a daily stipend and a place to stay."

As she listened to the details, she'd jotted down notes and asked additional questions. In calculating the money, she estimated there was enough to allow her mom to bring in Donetta and Robbie, who could use the extra hours, and still have something left for the business. "Yes, I'll do it."

"Great. Give all your contact info to my assistant, Chelsea. We'll send out a contract for your signature and a detail sheet of what you need to know before you arrive. So, start thinking about what you want to feature on your video and plan it out. We don't expect a movie quality video, but we do want it to be fun and interesting. Let our viewers see why they should be rooting for you and your town. My assistant will give you all the specs we need for the video and where to send it. Depending on how well you do in the contest, you may be here as little as a couple of days or a couple of weeks, so plan for the long end just in case."

After Jasmine gave the information to his assistant, she hung up the phone and danced about the room. In a whisper not to be heard outside, she exclaimed, "I'm going to be on TV. I'm going to be on TV."

When the initial thrill subsided, she composed herself and returned to the front counter. Several customers were in the bakery, but she wanted to wait until they were alone so Mom would be the first to know. However, she couldn't keep a big grin from being plastered across her face. When questioned about her smile, her vague responses seemed to satisfy the regulars, but Mom gave her a puzzled look.

Finally, when the bakery was temporarily void of customers Mom blurted out, "Okay, what is it?"

Jasmine threw her hands up in air in a celebratory cheer. "I'm going to be a contestant on a TV competition show called *Topped*."

Mom screamed in delight and jumped around with Jasmine. "Praise the Lord. That's so exciting."

Now they both were grinning as they worked. When Savannah came into the bakery with her little girl, Jasmine spurted out her good news immediately.

"Oh, Jasmine, I'm so happy for you," Savannah said.

Carolinda clapped her hands and cheered as well.

Jasmine leaned down and gave the little girl a high-five. "It's pretty exciting isn't it? I'm going to be on TV."

"You are definitely going to win that competition," Savannah added.

"The competition?" Jasmine leaned against the counter and shook her head. "I didn't even think that far. I've been so excited about being on the show and telling people about the bakery, I didn't think ahead." She slapped her hand against her head. "I didn't even begin to consider the competition and the challenges. No one wins these contests on talent alone; I need to be able to think outside the box when they bring up those odd ingredients;"

"Have you told Lexie, yet?"

"No, other than Mom, you're the first to know." She took her phone out of her pocket and called. After she told Lexie the news, she held the phone away from her ear, hearing the screams of her friend.

Savannah spoke into the phone that was now between her and Jasmine. "We've got to get together to give our girl some practice tests."

"I'll review past episodes to get an idea of what the producers throw at the contestants to assess their skills. How about we get together Tuesday night?" Lexie asked.

"Sure," Jasmine said.

"Sounds good," Savannah said. "Can we get together at my place again, say 7:45? That will give me time to put Carolinda to bed, so we won't be interrupted by her lovable antics."

Lexie laughed. "She is a cutie. But this is business and we've got to do our best to help Jasmine be the winner."

"Yes, I need all the help I can get. I'll see you then." Jasmine ended the call, reached down and gave Carolinda a big hug. "And what would my little sweet pea like today as a treat to celebrate?"

"Chocolate-chip walnut cookie." Carolinda's eyes gleamed with delight.

"If that's okay with mommy, I'll get you one." Jasmine looked up at Savannah and gave her a big grin.

Savannah nodded her approval, took her daughter's hand, and walked to the counter. Once her daughter received the cookie, she tussled her hair. "You can't eat it all now." She split it in half and gave her daughter one side. "We'll share it and then save some for later."

Carolinda nodded and walked over to the closest table to eat her treat. Belinda, Jasmine, and Savannah joined her as well. While she nibbled on her cookie, they chatted.

"Have you watched these kinds of shows a lot?" Savannah asked.

"To be honest, I haven't as much I should have now," Jasmine replied. She tapped her fingers on the table. "The pressure of the show and mixing unique ingredients together can easily turn into a disaster. I've certainly had that happen when I've mixed things up a bit in my baking." Jasmine grimaced. "Have I gotten myself in over my head? Before coming home, I only baked for fun and friends."

Savannah reached over and squeezed Jasmine's hand. "Sounds like you're getting a case of the jitters. That's natural. I'm sure you'll do fine. You have a knack for putting things together in a unique way. You just need to practice. We'll brainstorm to get your mind thinking creatively."

"I've taught you everything I know about baking." Belinda put her hand on Jasmine's shoulder. "But you've learned to innovate on your own. Remember, ask God's guidance and you'll do fine,"

"Thanks, you two. I'll do my best to prepare for the show and see where God leads me."

"Sounds like a good plan," Savannah said as she broke off a piece of the cookie.

"Sounds like a good plan," Carolinda repeated.

"Yes, sweet pea, it is." Jasmine rubbed the little girl's head and smiled. "Now, I need to get back to work." She got up and headed to the display counter to assist her mom with customers who walked into the bakery. As she filled orders, she imagined some of the ways she could change the pastries by adding something out of the norm – like fried oysters, vinegar, or broccoli. She shook her head at their absurdity. Then she realized *Topped* would be about bringing something unique to the table that stood out, like bacon and chocolate or a mix of sweet and salty in a muffin. Trevor understood how flavors worked together. Once the shop closed for the night, she'd call him, tell him the good news, and ask his advice.

That evening, Jasmine propped her back against her pillow, leaned against the bed's headboard and made a call. A grin filled her face as she waited for Trevor to answer the phone. After a quick hello, she got right into her big news.

"I can't believe it. I've been selected as a cooking contestant on a TV show. I've often wondered what being on TV would be like. Now I'll get to feel it first-hand." She kicked her legs gleefully on the bed.

"That's fantastic. When is the show going to be taped?"

"They're sending out the contract and consent form. I'll have it in a day or two. I need to do a video about me and the bakery." She winced. "Are you any good with videos? I've only done them with my phone, and I want something a little more professional."

"I don't have a video camera, but the newspaper photographers do. I'll see if I can borrow one. Or maybe you could bribe one of them with pastries to do it for you?"

"I'd be happy to bribe anyone who's got a sweet tooth and is willing to help me." Jasmine's finger aimlessly drew loops on the bedspread. "Do I need to bribe you, too?"

Trevor laughed. "No, I don't need to be bribed. I'd be happy to help you make a great impression. I like spending time with you."

Her heart skipped a beat when she heard those words. "I like spending time with you, too. When do you think you could come up to Falcon Creek?"

"I'm working on a new feature. Friday is my deadline. Would next week be okay? Or too late?"

"No, that should work." Jasmine wished it could be sooner, but she understood his schedule. "Hope I don't look so bad in front of a camera that we can't get any usable footage."

"I doubt that'll happen. I'm sure you're look great on camera."

She closed her eyes at that comment. In high school, she shunned cameras as much as possible because of her weight and bouts with acne. With God's help, she'd moved past those times but still had anxious moments concerning her looks. "Thanks, I need that encouragement."

They chatted for a few more minutes about his story before she hung up. Next, she reached for the TV remote on her nightstand and scrolled through the channels looking for a cooking challenge show. When she found one, she stopped to watch it, but first picked up a pen and a notepad from her desk.

On this show, the challenge for the participants was to make a dish without using a key ingredient to see how they could come up with unique substitutions. As the show progressed, she sighed and shook her head when one the contender's shoulders slumped in disappointment over the comments on his results.

Her old insecurities came roaring back. Would she go down in flames with the first episode? Should she cancel before she made a total fool of herself in front of thousands of people? *Lord, you've given me this opportunity. Help me focus to be the best I can be.*

CHAPTER 20
Preparing for The Show

On Tuesday evening, Jasmine joined her friends for a brainstorming session. To get them in the right frame of mind, Savannah had crafted numerous props to give an illusion of being on the show. At the front door, Jasmine was greeted with a crayoned sign of many colors that read "Savannah and Carolinda TV Production Company."

At the kitchen table, there were judges' signs and clipboards for Savannah and Lexie. A banner proclaiming "Test Kitchen" hung over the kitchen island with mixing bowls and an assortment of pantry items on the counter.

"You really want to have fun with this, don't you?" Jasmine asked. "And it looks like your little one helped with the signs, too."

"Of course, she did." Savannah hugged Jasmine. "She thinks it's wonderful you're going to be on TV and can't wait to watch it."

"Me, too. I just wish they had a TV audience so we could be there with you to cheer you on to victory," Lexie added.

"Thanks for your help. I'm going to need it. So, where do we begin?" Jasmine asked.

Savannah pointed to the counter. "Stand in the kitchen behind the counter like you're ready to participate in the show. I'll be the announcer and judge with Lexie. We'll sit at the table."

Once they were all in their places, Savannah began her role playing. "On tonight's episode of Topped we're featuring Jasmine Cattrell from Falcon Creek, Texas. Tell us about yourself and your baking experience."

"What do you want me to say?" Jasmine asked.

"Wow us like we're big celebrity bakers with multiple bakeries and awards," Lexie said. "Get into the role playing so it'll seem natural when you're in L.A."

Jasmine closed her eyes for a minute and gathered her thoughts. When she opened them, she leaned forward, smiled and pretended she was doing a presentation for one of her past big-wig clients from the ad agency. "Hi, y'all, I'm Jasmine Cattrell and I hail from the charming town of Falcon Creek, Texas between Dallas and San Antonio.

We're a small town with a big heart who recently had its heart broken by a terrible train disaster where 34 people died and multiple homes and businesses were destroyed. But we're resilient and will grow stronger, but we still need help."

Lexie clapped her hands. "That was great. I loved how animated you were. And it sounded so natural."

Jasmine bowed. "Well, I've been thinking about what to say on the promo video. So, I guess you can say I've been practicing those lines."

"That's good," Savannah said. "More practice will help make it flow easier. So, keep working on it. Now let's move into the competition. You're not actually going to make the items but pretend what you would make and talk about what you'd add to make your creation." She pointed to the paper in front of Lexie. "You read the notes for the first competition."

Lexie cleared her throat and squared her shoulders. "Okay, contestants, your first mission is to make a savory breakfast muffin. But you can't use eggs in your mix. What will you use as a substitute for eggs in your muffin?"

"That's a challenge to make a muffin without eggs as they add moisture and leavening to help them rise. I could try the standard replacement of oil but that would make it greasy. Applesauce is a popular egg replacement, but I don't want to make a sweet muffin. The best thing to use would be a mixture of ground flaxseed and water, which will add the moisture and binding needed. Then I'll also add baking powder or vinegar to help with leavening."

"Is that for real?" Lexie asked.

"Actually, it is, though it sounds odd. I saw it on a show about emergency substitutions in baking. I've also made pancakes without milk by substituting cream soda instead of milk to give them a nice vanilla flavor to make them light and fluffy."

"That's something I'll bet Carolinda would love to try on a Saturday morning as a special treat. You'll have to give me your recipe."

"You don't need a special recipe. Just use an ordinary box of pancake or waffle mix. Use the same amount of soda as you would milk. She'll love it."

"Too bad you're busy with the bakery on weekends," Lexie said. "It would be fun to have Saturday morning sleepover breakfasts like we did in high school when your mom would leave us yummy cinnamon rolls ready to heat in the oven."

Jasmine's memory drifted back to those days especially when the Friday nights were special dance nights at the high school, and they lacked dates – except for Savannah who usually went with Derek. Rather than going together and looking pitiful, they watched rom-com movies while nibbling on popcorn and candy. Then they'd whisper long into the night about which movie actors they wished were their boyfriends. Funny how life changes. In high school Savannah had a devoted boyfriend and they had the fairytale wedding, only it didn't end in the happily ever after. Her mom had that. She thought she had it with Stefan. Would Trevor be her happily ever after or her unhappily ever after?

"Earth to Jasmine. Did you hear what I just asked as your next question?" Savannah asked.

"Oh, uh, sorry. I got caught up in remembering those sleep overs. They were a lot of fun. What was the question?"

"What would your savory ingredients be?" Lexie replied.

Jasmine tapped her finger to her lips. "Let me see. Rather than use meat, I could use soy bacon flavored bits, then add chopped chives, and shredded smoky gouda. If I needed to add a side, I could do a fruit salad with a hint of basil. How's that sound?"

"Like I want to try it now," Lexie said.

"Do they have those type of ingredients in the show's pantries?"

"I won't know that until I get there. However, they said I could bring in five of my special go-to ingredients. And we do get to do some shopping before the taping starts for fresh items that we think we might want for our bake-offs."

"Wow, they give you advance info on the challenges." Lexie gave a thumbs up. "I would definitely need that."

Jasmine shook her head. "Not exactly. We'll just be given the categories – such as something savory like Savannah suggested, or a gluten free item, or making a fabulous fake like an entrée that looks like a dessert. I hope they don't try that. It's an art I've yet learned to master."

"Then that's something you need to review just in case it does happen."

Lexie's phone's ringtone started playing, "Bruno Mars, "Just the way you are," "Oooh, sorry ladies, I want to take that call." Lexie picked up her phone and walked out of the room.

"Someone must be working out well for Lexie. She only assigns that ringtone to a boyfriend."

"That could be Mike D'Amico," Savannah said. "She's commented on things he's said in the last couple of weeks, but she hasn't come out and mentioned that they're dating."

"That's a possibility. They did get along well in high school and I think he did have a crush on her though he never actually said it. How about you? Any romance in the making?"

Savannah shrugged. "I've accepted the idea of Derek's marriage, especially since his wife is showing a baby bump now. He's moved on and I need to as well. At work, I usually go out with a group for lunch, but I've had a couple of single lunches with one of the guys there. It's nice, but it's hard for me to consider it as a date."

"Has he has asked you to go out with him after work or on the weekends?"

"Not exactly, but he has asked what types of activities I like to do on weekends."

"Could be he's trying to find a way to ask you out. Are you ready for that?"

"When Derek started dating openly after our divorce and had Carolinda meet a couple of women, I asked her how she felt. She was confused about it at first but came to accept it. She likes Derek's new wife. About a month ago, I asked her how she felt about me dating other men. She frowned and asked if I'd leave her like Daddy did and live with the new guy."

"Oh, my, what a frightening idea that must be to her?"

"Yes, that surprised me, but I reassured her that she would always live with me. If I moved, she would be with me. That seemed to make her feel better. Plus, I told her she would have to approve of anyone I would consider marrying and said that would be a long way off."

Jasmine clasped Savannah's hands. "It's good to hear that you're willing to look for love again. I'm sure God's got someone special who'll bring joy into your life and your daughter's."

"That would be nice. And this time with a happily ever after."

"You and me both. Judging by Lexie's smile, someone brought joy into her life by that phone call."

Lexie clasped her phone to her heart as she sat next to Savannah at the makeshift judges' table. Her grin resembled that of an expectant child waiting to open birthday presents. "You're probably wondering who called since I walked off from our roll playing so easily. That was Mike D'Amico. We've had a couple of mini dates like meeting at the farmers market or for coffee get-togethers in the late afternoons. I feel so comfortable with him. He's like a warm sweater you want to have wrapped around your arms. It just feels right."

"Does Mike feel the same way?" Savannah asked.

Lexie nodded. "He says he's never known a woman who he could talk to so easily. He wants to spend more time with me. Monday is his day off. We're going out to dinner and then go to a jazz club to listen to some music."

"Ooh, now that sounds like a romantic evening." Jasmine said.

"It does. And I am so looking forward to going out together. I'm sure I'll be changing my mind multiple times as to what to wear between now and then."

"Well, I'd be willing to let you borrow something of mine if needed. I remember when you helped me pick out clothes for my first semi-date with Trevor and how you kept finding clothes you wanted to wear."

"Oh yeah, I remember that." Lexie clapped her hands together and laughed. "You didn't want to let me interrogate him and interfere with his first impression of you as a date by pretty much pushing me out the door. But I do remember going through your closet and wouldn't mind going through it again for my choices. But enough about me. Let's get back to your show. We want to make sure you make the best first impression with the judges on your TV debut."

Savannah and Lexie began their next series of questions with Jasmine considering ways to make a sweet creation with veggies, combining salty and sweet combinations, and adding sushi ingredients to a dessert. When Jasmine hit a mental roadblock, they brainstormed ideas until a solution to their questions occurred.

At the end of the evening, Jasmine was mentally exhausted, but liked how her brain was rethinking new food combinations. They planned to do at least two more sessions before she left for L.A. With Trevor giving her tips as well, she was beginning to feel confident that she could be the winning contestant. But before she became too full of herself, she thanked God for giving her this opportunity and asked for his wisdom and guidance.

CHAPTER 21
Returning to L.A.

Jasmine looked out the plane's window as it made the final approach to Los Angeles International Airport. Looking down, she noted the heavily trafficked roads that stretched between the neighboring cities coming into L.A. which made it look like one endless city. She recognized the major thoroughfares and mentally followed them to the area where she once lived. In the past, she remembered how happy she was when returning to California after business meetings and conferences.

This time her stomach churned as she recalled unhappy memories. Most prominent was discovering Stefan had been two-timing her after proclaiming he loved only her. And having that woman being someone she considered a friend at work made it worse. She willed those memories away and replaced them with good times when they strolled on the beach under the moonlight and talked about their future. They had a good life together even though it was short-term. But that was in the past and there was nothing she could change about it. Now it was time to look forward.

Since she moved back to Texas, her life had improved dramatically. She rediscovered her love for baking and this opportunity to highlight those abilities on TV gave credit to her skills. Developing a relationship with Trevor was icing on the cake for her even if she didn't know what would happen if she was offered a new job out of state.

Once the plane landed and everyone stood impatiently waiting to rush out the door, her anxieties hit full force. She closed her eyes, trying to squelch the fear of crashing and burning in L.A. again. *How I wish Trevor were here. He would know what to say to calm my fears.*

At least she had her phone to keep him close. Following the lead of the other people, she headed for baggage claim and retrieved her items, then scanned the signs held by drivers waiting for their passengers. Since this was Los Angeles, the home of celebrities and wanna-be celebrities, it took a while to review all the signs before she saw her own name.

The driver, who had been provided by the studio, welcomed her to the city, picked up her bags, and directed her to a sleek white limo with a buttercream soft leather interior. This definitely made her feel like a celebrity and calmed her anxieties. As he drove along, he began to give a travelogue of the city.

"Thanks for the details, but no need." Jasmine smiled and nodded. "I used to live here. I've only been gone a few months."

"Feels good to be back, I bet." The driver smiled at her in the rear-view mirror.

"Yes, but not for the reasons you'd think. I'm here as a contestant on a TV show."

"Ah, good for you. Hope you're a big winner."

The stop and go traffic to the hotel was as hectic as she remembered. She was so glad she didn't have this daily commute anymore. You'd only see occasional gridlock on Saturdays in Falcon Creek when tourists flocked to town. When they finally arrived at the hotel, the driver retrieved her bags and dropped them at the front steps for an awaiting hotel staff member.

The hotel was a Hollywood landmark that was built in the 1920s. Even a century later it still oozed glamour from its gleaming marble floors to the intricately carved ceilings and stunning chandeliers. Jasmine could imagine seeing the luminaries of Hollywood's golden age striding through the lobby to the elegant restaurants as cameras flashed. Though she was far from being a celebrity, she still received a gracious welcome and given the impression that she was a valued guest.

Once she breezed through check-in, she immediately headed to her room with her bags to settle in. She'd been to the hotel in the past for fundraisers, but this was her first overnight stay. The room was a mix of the old and new. The classic parts included the box-beamed ceilings, dark oak floors, and an oversized fabric headboard matching the king bed's luxurious satin quilt. Modern amenities included flat screen TVs in the bedroom and the bathroom and a jetted tub. The view from her window was a panorama of Hollywood stores and restaurants. The studio had even provided a small welcome basket with two small bottles of sparkling water, energy bars, a gourmet bag of popcorn, and a box of chocolate truffles. All great snacks for binge watching TV, but that wasn't on her schedule for tonight.

The studio where she'd be working was about two miles away, but it wasn't visible from the window. Considering rush hour traffic in the morning, she wondered if it would be easier to walk. However, once inside the gates she had no idea how far it would be to the specific production studio. Since transportation was included as part of the program, she called the limo company and arranged a morning pick-up time.

Jasmine considered calling her old friends from the agency for a get-together but decided against it. This was not the time to party late into the night with friends. Her schedule for the week showed an early morning meet and greet with the other contestants and judges. She had no detailed bios of the other contestants. Were they seasoned caterers, restaurant chefs, food truck owners? Or somewhere in between like she was? No matter what, she had to be on her 'A' game tomorrow because every moment with the judges counted.

After unpacking, she returned to the concierge for dining recommendations nearby. When he reminded her about the iconic Mel's Diner a few blocks away, she chose it.

The Hollywood location still had a classic feel, with its location in the fabled Max Factor building. As she sat at a counter chair, she wondered how many of the people dining or working there had hopes of being on TV and wished they had the opportunity she'd been given. She shook her head and sighed. *It's funny. I never had the chance to be on a TV show when I lived here. If I had, maybe I wouldn't have moved back to Texas.*

The counter waiter dressed in a white shirt and paper hat smiled at her. "Hey, pretty lady what can I get you?"

She glanced at the menu. "I'll have the grilled chicken sandwich with the soup of the day and a vanilla yogurt shake."

"Great choice. I'll have your shake ready in a minute." The waiter wrote down the order and walked away.

"Jasmine?" A voice called behind her. "Is that you?"

When she turned around, she saw Felicity, one of her past co-workers from the agency. She still dressed in Melrose Ave chic and her hairstyle had the signature cut of one of the local celebrity stylists. "Wow. This is the last place I'd expect to find you." Jasmine stood and hugged her old friend.

"Great to see you." Felicity pulled away and chuckled. "I know, being here is a bit of the touristy thing and not my normal style, but I'm here for these two." She held out her arm and brought in the two teens near her. "These are my nieces, Gracie and Victoria. They're visiting and this was *their* choice."

The two girls smiled in an awkward teen way and briefly waved at Jasmine before their gaze began to scour the room.

"Are you back in town with a new job?" Felicity asked.

"In a way, yes. I'm one of the latest contestants on the cooking show called, *Topped*, but I don't know how long I'll last on it."

"You're going to be on TV? That's awesome!" Victoria said.

"Can you get us in to see the show?" Gracie asked.

Jasmine laughed at their excitement. "The show's only in the preliminary stages right now. Tomorrow, I go to the studio for the first time. Once I know what's going on, I'll see what I can do to arrange a tour for you. But don't get your hopes up; I don't know if they'll even allow guests."

Felicity patted Jasmine on her shoulder. "Don't go out of your way for a pass to a taping. There's lots of other stuff I can show them. Why didn't you call and tell me you were coming? I would have met you at the airport."

"The show provided a driver to pick me up. The reason I didn't call is I'm a bit nervous about the show. I don't know if I want to brag about it, if I end up getting ousted in the first episode."

"You'll do fine. You're creative, cute and talented." Felicity pointed behind Jasmine. "Looks like you got your shake, and your food is on the way. But let me fill you in on a little gossip before I leave." She leaned closer to Jasmine's ear. "Stefan split with the woman who caused your break-up. Seems she didn't live up to his standards. When I ran into him last week, I got the impression he misses you. Has he called you?"

"He's texted me a few times with suggestions for jobs but nothing much more than that. He's not about to ask me out when we live hundreds of miles away." She reached over to the counter, picked up the shake, and took a quick sip.

"Well, you were great together. If you do well on the show, it might open up some opportunities here. You could possibly get back together."

"No way." Jasmine adamantly shook her head. "That story is over. I am not going back there again."

Felicity held her palms up and shrugged. "Just telling you what I know. It's your decision."

Gracie tugged at Felicity's sleeve, "C'mon. We've got a table."

"I better get these girls fed. Call me." She hugged Jasmine and walked away.

Stefan is alone, Jasmine mused. *Too bad for him. Not my problem.* She sat at the counter as her sandwich and soup arrived. Her thoughts stayed on her ex-boyfriend. She recalled when they first met at the agency. They worked so well together on their initial campaign; they stayed a team thereafter. The staff dubbed them the "dream team" and their plans for a future together soon followed.

Trevor has a drive to succeed like Stefan. Would Trevor's career become the "other woman" and destroy their new relationship? Lost in thought, she jumped when her phone buzzed in her pocket. The caller ID showed it was Trevor.

"Did you have a good trip, and do you miss me yet?" He asked.

"Yes, to both questions. I'm here at Mel's Diner in Hollywood."

"Sounds pretty noisy there. Mel's must be a pretty popular place. Is the food any good?"

She sipped the shake. "The food's a mix of the standards of burgers, fries, and shakes, but it also includes specialty appetizers and trendy sandwiches. But the location is the reason people show up. They're on the lookout for celebrities, but that's a rarity. Wish you were here to share the meal."

"Me, too. I'd love to see what the Hollywood scene is all about. If your stay gets extended, I might have to come visit so you don't fall for some Hollywood heartthrob and forget about me."

"You beat any heartthrob competition I've seen so far." She visualized his face and how well his nickname of 'Dreamy Eyes' fit. "Besides, I don't have time to look for hunky guys; I need to focus on this show."

"A bit nervous?"

Jasmine let out a deep sigh. "Yes, I want to do well and win."

"Be yourself. Let your sparkling personality shine through. The judges want people who are authentic so the TV audience can relate to them. You fit the criteria. I'm going to keep calling you to remind you of that fact. And continue to send up prayers for you."

Jasmine felt a warmth fill her heart. Stefan never mentioned saying prayers when one of them faced a challenge. His standard response was, "Let's cross our fingers for luck." It was a simple difference between the two men, but it made a world of difference to her. *Thanks, God for bringing Trevor into my life.*

CHAPTER 22
A Surprise Ride to the Studio

The next morning Jasmine dressed in her favorite scoop neck blue and green print shirt and pale blue pants. She finished off the look with a low wedge shoe that would be comfortable enough to wear all day on what she expected would be a concrete floor at the studio. With one last look in the mirror and a nod of satisfaction, she picked up her purse and left her room. As she took the elevator downstairs, her phone buzzed and she saw a text from Trevor.

Don't know if you'll be able to take calls today at the studio. Stay focused. Be yourself. You're the best. You're in my prayers for great results!

While she was reading his note, another text buzzed in from her mom. Additional texts came from Savannah, Lexie, and Donetta that she read as she walked through the lobby. The sound of a familiar masculine voice behind her stopped her in her tracks.

"Let me get the door for you."

Stunned, she turned and saw Stefan. His blue eyes twinkled in delight and she couldn't help smiling in return. As he reached for her arm, she admired the custom-fit suit that accented his lightly tanned skin and sun-bleached hair. He looked every inch of what a Hollywood Prince Charming should be. "What…what are you doing here? I have to be somewhere."

He gently put his arm around her shoulder and whispered in her ear as he led her outside. "Yes, I know. I want to make sure you get to Benedict Enterprises safely and in comfort." He pointed to the waiting limousine at the curb.

"How…how did you know where I was going?" Her eyelids fluttered nervously as she inched forward.

"Your questions can be answered in the car. You know how hectic traffic can be this time of day. We'll talk on the way."

She slid across the backseat with Stefan slipping in next to her. This was so surreal. *Did Felicity call Stefan and tell her she was in town? Maybe. However, the details of where and when she'd be doing the show were unknown to Felicity.*

"Texas seems to suit you. I like the way your hair falls on your shoulders, but you really should drop the frown. That definitely doesn't fit you." He laughed and leaned forward to hand her a tall Styrofoam cup. "Here's one of your favorites, Vanilla Rooibos Tea Latte."

She raised her eyebrow and gave him a quizzical look while she took the offered drink. "What is this all about?"

"Jasmine, honey, I've missed you. I know I was a fool to mess up our relationship."

He reached over to clasp her hand, but she pulled it away and wrapped it around her other hand holding the cup.

"I'm trying to make it up to you." Stefan wrapped the edge of one of her curls in his fingers. "That's why I arranged your meeting with Cooper Benedict."

Her eyes narrowed. "What do you mean *you* arranged it? I met him in Texas. I called him and he asked me to be on the show."

Stefan gave her a sly smile. "I was the one who suggested he look you up when he was in Texas. We play golf together from time to time and I know he's always looking for new talent. I told him you'd be a great fit for one of his shows. I thought he'd drive to Falcon Creek, but then he ran into you at that "Taste of South Texas" thing. You had my strong recommendation, but your baking talent clinched the deal."

She stared at him unblinking. Could that really be the truth? From her history with him, it probably was. Only she didn't understand why. Taking a sip of her latte, she considered what he said. "Well... I guess I should say thank you."

"Good, that's a start." He gently pried away one of her hands from the cup and caressed it. "I really am sorry about the way it ended with us."

His voice was so soft and sincere. Jasmine felt herself falling under his charm. Then the memory of his words, "I'm not a one-woman man" brought her to her senses. She pulled her hand back and leaned away from him. In a clipped tone, she replied, "In what way? That I discovered you were seeing someone else? Would it have been better if I stayed blissfully ignorant?"

He shrugged. "Maybe. It didn't take me long to lose interest in Kayla. And we'd still be together."

Her eyes widened. "Do you even hear what you're saying? You're not apologizing for cheating on me. You're saying it's just one of those things that happen. I thought our relationship was an exclusive one. We talked about marriage."

Stefan lowered his gaze. "It was exclusive… mostly. And yes, someday, I'd like to get married and do the family thing."

She turned and gazed out the window. "It doesn't sound like marriage is anywhere in your game plan now."

"Maybe you could convince me."

Stefan entwined his fingers in hers, but she gently pulled her hand away again. She dropped her gaze to her cup, ran a finger around the rim and took in a deep breath. Being away from him brought a clearer perspective. Jasmine raised her head and sighed. "Stefan, I shouldn't need to convince you. When you're ready to make a commitment you should want it – not be dragged into it. You only want someone to keep you company and boost your ego. Maybe all I wanted us to do was play the rising executive couple. But when we broke up, I knew something wasn't right with our relationship, outside of your other girlfriend."

"How can you say something wasn't right?" Stefan raised his hand in a questioning manner. "We were great together."

"It's the big C word – commitment." She drew a big C in the air. "We didn't come first to each other, our jobs did." Her eyes narrowed. "And there was something else I shouldn't have ignored."

"What else? I said it was over between me and Kayla."

"My faith. You made it seem unimportant."

Stefan shrugged. "Hey, you practice your religion your way and I'll do it mine."

"You don't practice any religion. When we were together, you'd go to church with me at Easter or Christmas, but otherwise you stayed home. I tried to pretend that your disinterest in Biblical precepts wasn't important to me, but it is. Reading the Bible, doing daily devotions, going to church on Sunday is *who* I am. That's what I want in a partner. We don't fit that way."

"Hmmm. I don't understand the need for all that religious stuff."

"That's the problem. It's not stuff to me. For me, it's real and has meaning."

Stefan put his hands up in surrender. "Okay, okay. I understand where you're coming from. But that's not me." He turned and looked out the window.

They rode in silence for the next couple of minutes and Jasmine could feel her eyes welling up, which she quickly dabbed at to keep her make-up fresh. *Why did it take me so long to realize there wasn't a future for Stefan and me? Now I know better.*

When they finally drove through the studio entrance, Stefan spoke. "We may not be getting back together, but I still want you to do well on this show. You have a great passion for cooking of all sorts. I hope you'll easily sail through to the next round of the show."

"Thanks. I appreciate your encouragement." Jasmine smiled.

He motioned for the driver to make a turn and then pointed where to stop. "Here you are. Have fun in there today. Knock 'em dead."

The driver opened the car door for Jasmine while Stefan got out on his own and came around to meet her. He pointed to the entrance she needed to take. "This is your big shot. Do well." He placed his hands on the sides of her cheeks, kissed her on the forehead and then let her go. "I won't be here when you're through later today. So go ahead and take the studio's ride."

"I understand. Thanks, again." She walked towards the door and then turned back to wave to him, but he was already in the car and moving away.

CHAPTER 23
Meeting the Other Contestants

The day in the studio was non-stop activity, which began with signing all sorts of legal paperwork covering non-disclosure of the show's outcomes before airing, pay schedule, expectations of the producer, contestants and limits of liability. The room where she sat had about two dozen other people filling out paperwork as well. The show started with only twelve people, so some must have been there for other shows. After she turned in her papers and clipboard, she scanned the faces around her wondering who was her competition.

When she noticed a familiar face, her jaw dropped. It couldn't be. She closed her eyes and opened them again. The woman to her far right caught her attention. Yes, this was definitely someone she knew. Kayla -- the woman Stefan had been dating while he was supposed to be in love with her. *What were the odds they'd both be auditioning for a show at the same time? Is this some kind of weird game Stefan is playing?*

She tried to remain calm by mentally singing one of her favorite Christian praise songs, but her thoughts returned to the woman who sat the other end of the room. Kayla was once her friend, but it didn't stop her from making a play for Stefan.

The room became quiet and everyone turned when the door to an adjoining room opened. A woman carrying a clipboard in her hand entered the reception room, stopped a foot into the room and smiled. "Hello, everyone. We're excited about meeting you as new contestants. We'll be taking you by group into our initial interview room where we can get to know you. Our first group is the contestants for *Topped*. Please stand and follow me."

Jasmine glanced about as the others rose and moved forward. They were a diverse group of people from their mid-twenties to fifties with spiked hair, tattoos, some short, some tall -- all looking determined. Thinking this was the full group, she let out a sigh.

Then Kayla rose, straightened her short skirt, and joined the rest of the group. Jasmine kept her distance from Kayla to make sure she could choose a chair away from her.

Inside the room, the contestants sat around a large conference table. At the far side of the table, a geeky looking guy stood and let his gaze go from one person to another. "Welcome to *Topped*. My name is Stuart and I'll be working with you on and off today. This is where you can get to know your fellow contestants as we ask questions of the group. We'll start with introductions from my right and going clockwise. Please tell the group your name, where you're from and one of your favorite food items you like to order at a restaurant."

One by one, each of them told of their favorite comfort foods, from French fries to specialty coffee drinks. Their comments elicited nods and the occasional laughter.

When it was her turn, Jasmine said "salad," which elicited quizzical looks from several of the contestants. "I love food like the rest of you, but I feel salads are underrated. They are the start of a meal and should be a wonderful mix of colors, textures and blending of opposite flavors. The dressing should enhance and not overpower the greens. If a restaurant can make a salad that tickles my palate, I know I'm in for something great for the rest of the meal."

"That sounds so sweet," Kayla said jumping ahead of the two people between them. "But I want food to stand up and get my attention like a nice juicy burger with grilled onions and gooey, melted cheese. Of course, I want to keep my figure, so I only have them rarely which makes them all the more enticing." She smiled and flitted her eyelashes at Stuart, "Forgive me for jumping ahead of my turn. I'm a bit nervous."

Stuart smiled back at Kayla and continued with the remaining contestants.

Once they all responded, he added, "Since I've probably made you hungry with all this talk about food, it's time for a ten-minute break. Snacks and beverages are set up on tables down the hall. Enjoy."

As they walked, some of the contestants chatted with each other. Jasmine turned and smiled at the short woman with grey hair who walked beside her. "You're Becca, right? What do you think of this set-up so far?"

"I like how they're easing us into the show." Becca replied. "Once the actual challenges and the competition begins, it will be much more stressful with everyone trying to rise to the top."

Kayla eased herself between the two women. With a sweet smile beneath challenging eyes, she wrapped her arm around Jasmine's elbow. "What a surprise to see you here. I know you've dabbled in baking in the past, but I thought it was a passing fad with you. Now here you are. Didn't you move to some tiny burg in Texas?"

"Excuse me," Jasmine said. She raised both of her arms up over her face with the pretense of sneezing to get Kayla to remove her arm. She then moved over a couple steps to put some distance between them.

Becca turned to Jasmine. "Where do you live in Texas? I have a cousin who lives outside of Houston."

"I live in a wonderful town that's northwest of San Antonio. The town may be small, but there is a real sense of community there. It's called Falcon Creek."

"Still it must be a drastic change for you." Kayla said.

"Oh, my, isn't that the town where that horrible train crash and explosion happened?" Becca asked.

"It was," Jasmine replied. "But as I said about it being a community, we all helped one another. Outside help is still coming in to rebuild some parts of the town, and we'll still need the extra aid for a while. My mom and I were blessed not to have sustained damage either at home or at work so we're doing our part to help others."

"Good for you," Becca replied. "Giving back is good for the soul."

"Jasmine is such a caring person," Kayla replied. She rolled her eyes at Jasmine, which was unseen by Becca.

The food tables held an assortment of sodas, bottled waters and juices in a huge ice filled tub next to an assortment of sliced fruit, trail mix and granola bars. Another table had Danish, mini bagels, and donuts plus a large urn of coffee. Most contestants headed for the coffee. Jasmine tried to keep her distance from Kayla by going to the opposite end to pick up a chilled vitamin water bottle and a small bag of trail mix.

Chairs were absent so they stood and clustered in small groups. Jasmine returned to stand beside Becca, with Kayla joining her,

Jasmine turned to Becca. "Do you watch a lot of these food challenge shows?"

"Of course, don't you?" Becca replied.

"Not really," Jasmine sipped her water. "I've been working on new promotions and marketing plans for the bakery. That takes a lot of my extra time after regular shop hours. When do you find the time?"

Kayla shook her head. "Jasmine, you really have to learn to multi-task better. Maybe that is why you couldn't hold on to your boyfriend. You just couldn't find the time for him."

Jasmine glared at Kayla who stared right back at her in defiance. She could tell Kayla was trying to get her riled up and lose her temper. Then she'd act the innocent, no doubt. Well, she wasn't going to play into that game. *God grant me the serenity to accept the things I can't change like Kayla, and the wisdom to keep my mouth shut from lashing out at her.* She smiled and turned to Becca.

"You know, sometimes it's hard to know what your priorities should be. Things didn't work out well with my last boyfriend, but I think that was a blessing. Now I'm working full-time in baking, which is something I love. Plus, I'm using the skills I learned from working in an ad agency to promote the business. The move turned out to be a win-win situation for me. And I have a new boyfriend." With her final statement, she smiled and turned briefly to Kayla.

"Well, I - -" Kayla stopped in mid-sentence seeming uncertain as to how to respond.

Becca patted Jasmine on her shoulder. "What's that adage? When one door closes, another is opened. That apparently worked for you."

"Yes, it did. Hope it holds true here, too."

"Don't expect me to wish you too much luck there." Becca laughed. "After all, we are competitors and I've done my research. I've watched all the episodes of *Cupcake Wars, Ace of Cakes,* and *Chopped.* My dream has always been to be on one of these shows, so I know what it takes to be the winner."

"Well, I've been to the final tapings of some of these shows, so I've seen the really interesting backstage stuff." Kayla stuck her chin out in an air of superiority.

"That's nothing compared to Chad over there. He trumps both of us. He's been a contestant on two other shows," Becca replied.

Jasmine's eyes grew big. "Really? Did he win either of them?"

"No, if he had he wouldn't be eligible to compete again, unless it was a battle of the winners show." Becca's voice became softer. "He washed out pretty early in the competition. However, the producers seem to like him because he's quirky and funny and does a good job of breaking the stress."

"Well, aren't you the one with all the hot gossip." Kayla smirked as she tossed back her hair. "That might make him one of the harder people to beat in this competition."

Jasmine tilted her head towards Becca and crossed her arms. "Watch out when Kayla gets one of her devious looks like you're seeing now. Who knows what schemes she has planned?"

Kayla twirled a lock of her hair around a finger and fluttered her eyelashes in wide-eyed innocence. "Honestly, Jasmine, I have no idea what you could mean. I'll just do my part to make sure the best woman wins."

"I'm for that, especially if it's me. I've got the best shot of anyone here," Becca said with her head held high. "Baking is my life. I'm in charge of the desserts and breads as a restaurant pastry chef."

"I can see I've been warned. I'll make sure I bring my A-game to the table." Jasmine playfully put up her fists in a battle-ready position towards Becca.

Stuart strode down the hall to the group. "Sorry my hopeful super stars, but your break is over. Now it's time for make-up, then we move on to your personal promos."

After the make-up was completed, she smiled at the results. She took a quick selfie and sent it to Trevor, Lexie, Savannah, and her mom with the caption...*I'm ready for my close-up and the show. Keep me in your prayers for success.*

When the time came to shoot the video, Jasmine felt she was in her element. She pretended the camera was a client during a pitch session and concentrated on good posture, clear diction and an unhurried pace. After several takes to fix a couple of minor verbal flubs, both she and the director seemed happy with the results.

Once the videos were complete, the contestants reassembled in the main room where Stuart met them. "Only one more exercise remains. We're giving you an hour in the show kitchen. Use the time to familiarize yourself with the supplies and the equipment. Each contestant will be given the opportunity to request five items that they don't see stocked to add to their kitchen area.

You'll be working as three-person teams on your first day of competition. The judges will be watching to see how you can work as a unified team and do the job without egos getting in the way. The three teams with the best scores will advance to the next day, while the lowest scorers will go home."

Jasmine held her breath and prayed silently as Stuart went through the list of names. A smile crossed her lips when Kayla landed with another group. She happily moved over to her own team as they made their introductions.

Chad spoke first. "Well, as you may or may not know, I'm an old pro at these shows having been on them. My name is Chad and I specialize in catering weddings. So I'll lead us off to make sure we make it through the first round."

"Hi, I'm Aisha. I do the menus for a hotel's weekly gala buffets." Her face scrunched up. "How can we make a list when we don't even know what the food challenge will be? I like using flavoring extracts, but which one should I include?"

"That's where we need to think outside the box like mixing bold flavors with a sweet undercurrent, Aisha," Jasmine added. "I work in a bakery and am always looking for ways to make savory

Chad patted Jasmine's shoulder. "That's the idea. Think creatively. Now let's discuss our strengths and possible weaknesses so we can be one of the winning teams."

Together they walked through the kitchen assessing what was available and what could be added to successfully complete the first round. At the end of the hour, Jasmine felt confident that they would work well as a team.

CHAPTER 24
The Baking Competition Begins

The first day of the cooking challenge proved successful for Jasmine's team even though it felt awkward. Their dishes weren't perfect, but their presentation had flair and squeaked ahead of the lowest scoring team. The teamwork was stressful, but the adrenaline rush of continuing on the show diminished any anxieties.

Next day they'd work independently and wouldn't be able to count on a team member to pick up any slack. Knowing their every move on the set would be filmed was a bit daunting, but she knew that meant she'd need to keep laser focused.

With the help of the hotel concierge, she ordered food delivery for dinner. She wanted the quiet of her room to revive and prepare for tomorrow. Once her meal was finished, her first call was to Trevor, but it went directly to voice mail. *Maybe he's working on a review and doesn't want any distractions.* When the beep at the end of the message came, she said, "Wanted to give you the good news that I've progressed to the next round. Hope your day went well, too."

Eager to share her good news, she called Savannah next. "I did it, I did it. I made it through the first round," Jasmine squealed as soon as Savannah picked up the phone.

"That's fantastic. How many more do you have to conquer to make it to the winner's circle?"

"Four more. Tomorrow is a food art challenge only using fresh, raw ingredients, nothing baked. They want to see how we can create around a theme. I'll work on my own this time. They haven't given us any other clues, so I'll have to imagine a variety of ideas and hope one of them fits."

"Wow that sounds a bit nerve-racking. You've catered themed events before, haven't you?"

Jasmine bit her lip and started doodling some sketches. "Sure for birthdays or weddings where we do cakes. However, I won't have a cake for a base. I'll be using fruits or vegetables."

"Then start with the biggest thing you can for a base, like a watermelon split in half."

"Sure. Or any other melon variety. Pineapples clumped together could create a rugged look."

"Jasmine, that's good. You're a natural at this."

"Mom's done a lot more events than I've done. I'll get her feedback, too."

"Good idea. Maybe Trevor could help you as well."

Jasmine tapped her pen on the desk and frowned. "I tried calling him earlier, but it went to voicemail. "I just realized I haven't heard from him since yesterday morning."

"Maybe he's on deadline for some big story?"

"Sure. That's probably it. Oh, I have some really weird news about the competition here."

"You're not going to have to eat or cook bugs, are you?"

"I hope not." Jasmine stuck out her tongue. "But it's something even stranger. I ran into my ex-boyfriend. Stefan told me *he* set up the meeting with the show's producer."

"Is he trying to win you back?"

Jasmine shrugged. "I think he hoped that once I returned, I'd want to stay." She brought her hand to her chest in mock devotion. "And I'd fall in love with him again."

"What about Trevor and the bakery?"

"Don't worry. I am so *over* Stefan. We are *never* getting back together. I don't want to live here. The only reason I'd stay is if I win and they offer me a show. Even then I'd head back home to Texas until they're ready to shoot the episodes."

"Oh Jasmine, that's great. I'm glad you want to stay in Falcon Creek. It's fun having our trio back together again. And your mom probably loves having you around, too."

"Stefan wasn't my only surprise. My old friend, stab-me-in-the-back Kayla, is a contestant as well."

"Wait. Isn't she the one who caused the break-up between you and Stefan?"

"The one and only. She's been throwing daggers at me, well not literally, since the competition started. Thank God, we didn't have to work on the same team. I don't know if she's aware of how Stefan helped me, but she acts as if she wants me gone. If anyone had a reason for wanting payback, it would be me."

"Maybe she thinks if you're back in town, you'll try to win him over."

"Stefan told me they had already broken up."

"Who knows, she may think you caused their break-up because he couldn't get over you."

"Don't think she's considering him too much. She's been playing up to the TV director between takes, probably hoping he'll find some other shows for her if this one doesn't work out."

Jasmine heard a child's scream of "No. No." in the background. "Is that Carolinda?"

"Who else? Miss Prima Donna doesn't like it when I've been on the phone too long. Plus I just told her it's time to take a bath."

"Well, it sounds like you have a challenge on your hands. We'll talk again tomorrow."

Her next call went to her mom who answered after the second ring. "Hi, Mom, hope I didn't wake you."

Mom smirked. "Hardly, it's barely nine. From the tone of your voice, I'm guessing you had a good day and aren't being sent home tomorrow."

Jasmine smiled, listening to her mom's sweet and comforting voice. "Yes, Mom, I'm still in the game. And I called to get your advice on how to make sure I stay in."

"Really? You're asking my advice. Thank you."

Jasmine could almost see the broad grin that was probably on her mom's face. "I need your suggestions for making an edible centerpiece. I don't know the theme, but I know you have tons of experience and can give me some great ideas."

"Well, honey, with a bunch of toothpicks and an assortment of fruits and vegies you can make anything."

As they chatted, Jasmine's thoughts flashed to the many times Mom encouraged and made her feel like she could achieve her dreams. Of course, Mom always added that it should be within God's will and by his grace.

When she started her career in L.A. years ago, she'd forgotten about the God part. She was in command of her future. That's also when she began thinking Falcon Creek was too small a town and L.A. was the place to be. Though L.A. had lots of opportunities; after returning to Texas she'd come to the realization of how special her hometown was.

CHAPTER 25
The Competition Heats Up

The next day when Jasmine awoke, she had a text message from Trevor… *Sorry I've missed your calls. Left my cell phone at home. Had a family emergency. Grandma Merle went to the hospital after passing out. Turned out to be an issue with her meds. She's going home today. Keep her in your prayers. You're definitely in mine for the final win on the show–and then home again with your cheering fans—especially me.*

She immediately texted him back… *Sorry about your Grandma's health scare. Glad she's doing better. Saying prayers now. Call you after the show. No cell phones allowed on the set during taping.*

As she showered and prepared for the day, she recalled how her early interest in baking began. In high school, the bakery had been an escape for her introverted personality and a haven for comfort foods. She enjoyed making the recipes beside her mom and tasting the results, but she never considered it as a career.

When a job came to go to L.A. after college, she jumped at the chance to move there. She loved the beach lifestyle, the chance of running into celebrities, and all the bars and clubs L.A. had to offer.

The reality didn't fit her expectations. Her long hours at work left little time to spend at the beach. The celebrities she met were spokespersons for their campaigns and many turned out to be demanding divas.

Dining out and attending galas were mostly business related. The one activity she truly enjoyed was having dinner parties and creating unique menus.

The move back to Texas made her realize how much her life in California left her empty. The money was great, but there was little time to enjoy it. Working at the bakery gave her a daily opportunity to do something she loved -- creating new recipes and improving on old ones.

Whether or not she was the winner on the show, wouldn't change that. *Lord, inspire me today to do my best.*

At the studio, the tension in the air was evident. The room where they were assigned had no windows, but the walls were painted a calming seafoam green and multiple can lights in the ceiling gave a warm glow like natural light. Three long high gloss white tables were placed together in a U-shape. The chairs were all on one side so they would be facing each other. In front of each chair was a composition notebook with pens and pencils.

Occasional off-pitch nervous laughter erupted, and contestants displayed nervous twitches of nail biting, tapping their fingers on the table, or occasional pacing. With three contestants already booted off, they couldn't escape the fact that any of them could be next. Chad did his part to act like the old pro on the set to lighten the mood when staff was watching. He told anecdotes from his other shows and lightheartedly poked some fun at himself.

When Stuart walked into the room, he patted Chad on his shoulder and gave him a wink. "You've been standing around, but now it's time to sit at the tables we've provided. Feel free to chat amongst yourselves, but today you will work independently. You'll all work on the same theme, but no cheating." He clucked his tongue and wagged his finger mimicking an elementary school teacher. "We want original ideas. You'll have one hour in this classroom to sketch out ideas. Then it's off to the kitchen to create them. Is everyone ready?"

Jasmine nodded along with the other contestants and rolled her pencil between her hands in anticipation.

"Okay, today's challenge is a non-baked, or cooked in any way, food centerpiece depicting the perennial favorite of *The Sound of Music*. Your one hour begins now." With an overdone hand flourish, Stuart pointed to the clock.

Jasmine let out a sigh of relief when she heard the theme. She could definitely use Savannah's suggestion of using cut halves of pineapples as mountain shapes for the Swiss Alps and press slices of marshmallows on it to show bits of snow. She gleefully began sketching ideas to create the Abbey, Von Trapp home and people out of marzipan paste.

After she roughed out her sketches, she relaxed her neck and shoulders, then surveyed the others in the room. Becca had a furrowed brow and seemed to be deliberate in making her marks on the paper. Kayla was occasionally admiring her nails between short spurts of writing. Chad went from squeezing his eyes shut and pulling on his hair to furiously dashing off ideas on the paper. Her gaze returned to her sketches and she added additional touches and notes of what she'd need from the show's pantry.

The hands-on part of the competition began with a frenzy of activity with all contestants running through the different areas of the pantry and kitchen collecting their supplies. For inspiration, the movie soundtrack played throughout the set creating snippets of humming by the contestants as they worked. As they got closer to their deadlines, the sounds turned into groans and grunts when projects weren't working out as planned. Finally, the buzzer for the round sounded.

"Okay, everyone," Stuart said. "That's it. You can breathe now. Step away from your creations and take a break in the snack room. TVs are there to watch and hear the judging until they go into final deliberation."

Aisha came and stood by Jasmine. "Wow, that was more stressful than I expected. I do food centerpieces all the time for the hotel buffets, but this was much more focused and quicker."

"I know what you mean. I do creative cake tops for children's birthdays, but I have props that help and more time to try different options."

The others huddled nearby anxiously watching the TV screens as the judges moved from one display table to the other. Some grimaced at hearing the judges' remarks while others rocked on their heels in hopefulness. Soon, the judges stepped away from the display tables and left the room, with the TV screen focusing solely on the displayed centerpieces.

The deliberation of the judges took thirty minutes. All contestants returned to the show kitchen and told to stand by their creations. One by one, they heard the pluses and minuses of their movie centerpieces. Next came the call for the nine who would be staying.

Jasmine blew the judges a big kiss and bowed when she became number six. Two others were added, leaving only one spot left.

Kayla turned out to be last number. She smiled and waved to the judges and then slid in line next to Jasmine. "They saved the best for last," she whispered. "But will this be the last time you'll be on the winning side?"

CHAPTER 26
The Competition Pressure Continues

Two more days of competitions wore on until it was down to the final three remaining contestants -- Jasmine, Kayla, and Chad. All three would receive cash prizes with the winner also receiving a six-episode run for a new show promoting their branding and style.

The taping for the final episode would be the longest day in the studio. After they donned their aprons, the three contestants walked on to the set. The show's host smiled at them and with cameras rolling explained the final challenge. "Today we'll see who will come out on top. Your first challenge is to create a memorable appetizer..."

Jasmine listened carefully to all the directions and what needed to be included and repeated them to herself so she wouldn't forget. When she heard, "Your challenge starts now" she bowed her head and silently prayed. *Lord, inspire me. Keep me focused.*

At the end of the segment, they presented their plates to the judges and waited for their feedback. In turn, the judges told each contestant what worked and what did not work on their plate. Jasmine was the highest scorer for that round; however, there were two more cooking events that day. The one with the highest score for all three would be the winner. Having the initial lead was a relief, but her hands were still clammy, and she could feel droplets of sweat slipping down her neck. Her anxiety pumped up another level when Kayla turned and mouthed "watch out" and Chad glared at her beneath narrowed eyes and a cold smile. The pressure was on and each of them were on edge.

Before the second challenge began, the show's producer made an appearance and spoke to them without the cameras running. "I want to thank you for all the hard work you've done. I've watched the daily tapings and like what I see. As the final three, you have true star potential." He turned to the crew. "Let's give our stars a round of applause."

Once the applause died, the director gave them their cues as to where they should stand and where they should move. While he explained the details for the next round, Jasmine heard a muffled conversation that was distracting. She turned her gaze to the source and was surprised to see Stefan over to the side talking to the producer. They seemed to be on good terms if Stefan was given access to a normally closed set. This was not the time to lose focus and her attention, she quickly returned to the director.

Lights went on and the show's host gave his opening remarks and challenge for the contestants. The countdown clock started with the final three scurrying about to get their supplies for the entrée and the ingredients that were required to be part of their dishes.

Jasmine had memorized where all the supplies were in the show kitchen and the pantry so she wouldn't waste time. She methodically moved from one section to the other picking up what she needed from her mental shopping list. Her sweaty palms nearly caused her to drop a jar of sun-dried tomatoes that she quickly scooped into her apron as she headed to her workstation.

Out of the corner of her eyes, Jasmine saw Kayla make several trips to the pantry area for additional supplies she missed on her first go through. In one instance, she nearly collided with Chad because her head was down trying to see how to best balance what she was carrying.

"Watch where you're going." He hissed at her.

Ten minutes later, Kayla did an abrupt turn to head to the oven and almost collided with Jasmine who was returning from the cooking area.

"Be careful, Kayla," Jasmine chided quietly. "We still have plenty of time." She shook her head and then pushed away some loose hairs with the back of her hand and returned to her prep area. After that near collision, she did her best to keep some distance from Kayla who seemed oblivious to anyone else. There was no time for any slip-ups or mistakes with the clock ticking down. Adrenaline rushed through her veins and she took a few slow, calming breaths to bring her racing pulse in line. She snuck a quick glance at her competitors to see how they were faring.

Kayla was wiping away sweat from her furrowed brow. In her haste to reach over for a package of fresh basil, she knocked over an open jar of marinated Cipollini onions that scattered on the floor. She gasped as she stared at the chain reaction to her clumsiness.

Chad was walking back from the oven with a pan of roasted root vegetables. His foot slipped on the onions and liquid, causing him to lose his balance and toss the vegetables in the air and on to the floor.

Chad sat on the floor looking dazed for a moment. Then he quickly jumped up, grabbed a knife from the counter and headed towards Kayla. "You stupid cow!" he screamed. "Look what you made me do. You're trying to ruin my chances." Within seconds, he was in front of her and slashing at her with the knife.

Kayla moved to the left, but the knife tip nicked her blouse and cut into her shoulder and she let out a piercing scream.

Chad lunged for her again and the blade barely missed the side of her face. "This should have been my competition win. I was ready for it. You're going to pay."

Jasmine's eyes widened in disbelief at what was unfolding. There had to be something she could do to help Kayla. But what? She picked up a large platter and held it in front of herself for a bit of protection. As calmly as she could make her voice sound, she spoke to Chad. "Take it easy, Chad. We all know Kayla's a klutz. You're doing so much better than Kayla or me in this competition. You do deserve to win. The judges like you and I'm sure they'll give you extra time because of her. So let's calmly get back to the competition."

Chad stopped his aggression against Kayla for a moment as if considering what Jasmine had said. Then he made an abrupt move, got behind Kayla and wrapped his left arm around her neck. His right hand held the knife in the air near her neck as if he were considering slashing her throat. A crazed look came over him like a dog ready for an attack. "Don't anyone come closer." He slowly turned keeping Kayla as a shield in front of him. "You're all against me."

"That's not true. The other contestants love you. And the judges must as well since they keep bringing you back." Jasmine whispered the words softly to him and took a step closer.

"Stay back," Chad screamed. "I don't want to hurt you."

Jasmine turned her head slightly to see how the crew was reacting. Most looked like they'd stepped back into the shadows except for the unarmed security guard who was making slow advances toward Chad. Would he be able to apprehend Chad before he caused any more harm to Kayla? Her gaze returned to Chad and saw his hand holding the knife was shaking.

"Everyone stay away," he screamed again. "I need to figure this out."

Dear Lord, please bring some calm into this situation to keep Kayla safe. Jasmine prayed. In the far corner of the room, she saw an exit door open, and Stefan enter soundlessly. He stopped in his tracks and stared at the scene in front of him. His eyes narrowed and they seemed to scan the area. She looked at him quizzically as he picked up a small, round metal plate and seemed to balance it in his hand.

Chad's back was to Stefan with his attention on the security guard who was coming closer. He stepped back a couple of steps shrinking the gap between him and Stefan, whom he had not noticed.

Jasmine held her breath as she watched Stefan jiggle the plate in his hand. Then she watched in utter awe as he changed his stance. He was getting ready to toss the platter. Her mind rushed back to the many times she watched him use a Frisbee with expert skill. She'd throw an object up in the air to see if he could hit it. He often made wagers with his buddies that he could knock off all sorts of things on the first try and always won. He had perfected Frisbee throwing to a skilled art.

In what seemed like slow motion she watched as the plate left his hand and swiftly crossed the room. His aim was for Chad's hand holding the knife. Just like the days in the park, Stefan's aim was precise. Chad wailed in pain as he dropped the knife. The few seconds of distraction gave the security guard time to rush forward, kicked away the knife, and push Kayla away from Chad. Once that was done, the guard slapped on a pair of handcuffs and began to lead him away.

"I'm sorry. I'm sorry." Chad cried. "I don't know what got into me. It's all Kayla's fault. I don't deserve this treatment."

Deep sighs of relief echoed throughout the room. Stefan rushed over to Kayla who was holding a hand to her shoulder. He wrapped his arm around her. "Hey, Babe. Are you okay?"

Kayla closed her eyes and leaned her head against his chest. "I'm a little better with you holding me."

Jasmine walked over and gave him a playful jab to his shoulder. "That was some pretty fancy plate throwing. All those days of playing Frisbee certainly paid off. Guess you never thought you'd save a life with that ability."

He smiled. "No, that never would have crossed my mind. You did your part as well in trying to calm him down. I watched it from a preview camera in the other room." He stepped forward with Kayla still leaning on his shoulder and wrapped his other arm around Jasmine.

The camera operator never stopped filming the show and he got a great shot of Stefan kissing Jasmine on the forehead with Kayla on his other arm.

CHAPTER 27
A Life Threatening Event

When the paramedics came to treat Kayla, several members of the press followed behind. TV producers always welcomed publicity, especially when they could shape the message. For the next hour Kayla, Jasmine and Stefan answered questions, amidst numerous cameras, as to their take on Chad's mental breakdown.

Afterwards, they were given their release for the day. No decision had yet been made as to how they would proceed with the show. The producers would meet with their legal department to determine the best course of action. They'd be notified in the morning as to the production company's decision.

Stefan stayed in the reception room until they were both ready to go. When they came out of their meeting, he got up. "The press has gone so we can walk freely to my car and driver. I'm sure you're both exhausted and probably hungry. Where would you like to go? It's my treat."

Jasmine trudged towards the car. "I want to head back to my room and curl up in front of the TV and forget about all this. If we could get some Chinese to go, that would be great." She stepped into the back seat with Kayla following her.

"Not me," Kayla chimed in. "I want to celebrate being alive. That nut job almost slashed my throat. I want to be wined and dined like a queen." She settled in the middle seat.

Stefan moved in next to her and gave the driver an address for one of his favorite Chinese take-out places. He dialed his phone and turned to Jasmine. "What do you want?"

"How about an order of Lemon Chicken and a side of sautéed mushrooms and snow peas."

He repeated the order into the phone and gave them his name. "That's done. Now for Kayla." He sat back, put his arm around her and kissed her cheek. "What can I do to please you and make you feel special? What about sushi? I can usually wiggle a reservation at Matsuhisa Restaurant."

Kayla smiled at him and leaned on his shoulder. "I'd like that." She turned her head towards Jasmine. "I guess I should thank you for trying to calm down crazy Chad. I don't know if I would have had the nerve to do that if our places had been swapped."

Jasmine sighed." I feel sorry for him."

"Why?" Kayla glared at her.

"He wanted to win so badly. When that tray of food scattered in the air, it seemed he lost all hope. And he couldn't cope with that."

"Well, hopefully he'll win a prison sentence," Kayla said with disgust.

Jasmine shook her head. "No, he needs medical treatment.."

"Don't worry about Chad," Stefan added. "A good lawyer, will have Chad's sentence served in a medical facility."

"I hope so. That's what he needs." Jasmine replied.

"Well, not me. I want him to pay for the stress and fear he put me through."

"Can't you forgive him? Didn't you hear him crying out?"

Kayla snorted. "That was because he was caught. Saying he was sorry was his way of trying to get out of his insane act. And I don't forgive him for that."

Jasmine shut her eyes for a moment and sighed. Then she leaned forward and faced Kayla. In a soft, deliberate tone she added, "You don't understand forgiveness. It's not about whether the person deserves it. Forgiveness lets *you* get past the anger and hurt." She hesitated a moment and held her hands open to Kayla. "I forgave you a long time ago for how you came between me and Stefan. At the time, I was shocked you thought so little of our friendship that you would betray me like you did. I wanted to hate you, but the anger was eating me up inside.

I asked God to open my heart to forgive you. By trusting in Him I found peace. What I thought was a bad situation, turned out to be good. Because of my move, I've reignited my passion for baking and learned how much I love the ambiance of Falcon Creek. So, any hurt I may have felt from the betrayal and break-up, has turned into a true blessing."

"Well Stefan played his part in the break-up, too." Kayla pouted.

"Yes, he did. I forgave him, too." Jasmine leaned over and patted his hand. "And he's made his amends. I think we're on good terms with each other."

Stefan nodded.

Kayla sneered. "So do you expect me to make some sort of amends, too?"

Jasmine shook her head. "You don't get it. Making amends has to be your choice, not a reaction to a challenge."

'Well. I... I'm sorry." Kayla said barely above a whisper.

Jasmine leaned back against the car seat again and closed her eyes. She never expected she'd be sitting in a backseat together with Kayla and Stefan. Judging by their closeness, maybe the two of them would give their relationship a second chance. Being with them gave her a sense of closure. The life she had in California was over and her new one was in Texas. She reached in her pocket to send a text to Trevor, but her phone wasn't there. It wasn't in her purse either.

"What are you looking for?" Stefan asked.

"My phone. I must have left it in my locker at the studio."

"They closed that area up for the night, so you'll have to wait until the morning." Stefan replied. "Check back after 8:00 AM when someone will be there to handle calls and set up a time to pick it up. You'll probably be back sometime during the day for a final wrap up anyway."

The driver pulled into the restaurant parking lot and stopped the car. Stefan handed a twenty dollar bill to the driver. He quickly exited the car to get the order.

Stefan stroked Kayla's cheek. "You sure you don't want Chinese take-out?"

Kayla scrunched up her nose and shook her head. "You promised me Matsuhisa and I'm not settling for less."

The driver returned a few minutes later d handed the order to Jasmine. The 'cate scent of lemon and the aromatic ʳance of garlic oil from the vegetables the car as she placed the order on the ℩ front of her. "That works for me. I can't kick back, relax and dig in."

ʋ don't have to wait on our account," aid. "If you want to eat as we drive go

at's okay. I can wait." Jasmine k in her seat and closed her eyes vished she could call Trevor. y, she didn't even know his ause she had programmed it into

258

her phone. Calling him would have been nice, but she wished he could be with her. She imagined sitting in her kitchen with him and sharing the food whose aroma was making her mouth water. A smile crossed her face as she recalled when they first met. Back then, she'd told him how much she missed the L.A. scene. Now she was homesick for her wonderful small town of Falcon Creek. The gentle whoosh of the car running down the freeway and her thoughts of home eased her into a relaxing sleep.

The next thing Jasmine knew, Kayla was nudging her shoulder. "Hey, sleepy head we're back at the hotel. Time to go to your room and enjoy your meal."

Bleary-eyed, Jasmine stared at Kayla and began to focus. "Can't believe I fell asleep." A slight grumbling sound from her stomach made her chuckle. "It looks like my stomach didn't fall asleep. Good night. See you sometime tomorrow." She stepped out of the car with her food and purse and headed into the hotel. As she walked into the lobby, she steadied herself by leaning on a chair for a moment as the stress of the day hit her, leaving her limp. After a couple of deep breaths, she headed to her room and went inside.

Chapter 28
Missed Calls and Misconceptions

Trevor tried calling Jasmine again after his evening run, but her phone kept going to voice mail. That seemed odd to him but perhaps the show had numerous re-tapings. Yesterday, she was anxious about the finale and he texted her words of encouragement, but wished they'd been able to talk as well.

He tried again after his shower, but the call still went to voice mail. It frustrated him not knowing if she was happy or sad about the show's final outcome.

Hopefully, she was out celebrating with old friends rather than holed up in her room and feeling depressed. As he dressed, he turned on the TV evening news to take his mind off worrying about her.

The newscaster opened with a breaking story… "A TV cooking competition show nearly turned deadly today in Los Angeles. One finalist apparently took the competition too seriously and tried to eliminate one of his competitors. Here's the details from our local affiliate KTLA and Thomas Drummond."

"Good evening. The filming of the widely popular series, *Topped*, went horribly wrong today when a finalist tried to end the show for another contestant..."

Trevor plopped down at the edge of his bed and stared at the TV as the story continued with video coverage of the security guard handcuffing the contestant, Chad Strothers, who had lost control. Additional footage showed Stefan Galanos with his arm around Jasmine and his kiss to her forehead. Trevor didn't hear anything else the announcer had to say as he froze the image on his TV.

He recalled Jasmine mentioning her ex-boyfriend's name was Stefan. Since it was such a unique name, this had to be the same guy. Only the picture on the screen didn't make him look like an ex-boyfriend at all. His lips pursed as he recalled her saying she'd probably feel like an outsider going back to L.A.

Apparently that wasn't the case. It looked like their romance had continued where it left off. Galanos had probably spent all week with her and convinced her to stay in L.A. permanently with him.

There was no other possible scenario looking at the image of the two of them together.

He clicked off the remote and threw it on the bed. In their first meeting, she'd talked about how hard it was to get accustomed to small town life after living in L.A. Now she could go back to the life she once loved.

Images of his previous girlfriend drifted through his mind. He could never do enough for her. She wanted someone who would buy her anything she wanted. When he didn't meet those expectations, she quickly found someone else who would.

He stared at the TV screen. Stefan looked like a celebrity with his tailored suit, perfectly tanned skin and professionally styled hair. Too slick for his tastes, but that's apparently what Jasmine still longed for. Any hope of a future relationship with her was gone. He felt betrayed and wanted nothing more to do with her.

At least when he dated Giselle he knew where he stood. She'd told him she was on a quest to find her personal millionaire and would be his dining fill-in until Mr. Richly Right showed up. He got a kick out of the envious smiles from other men when he walked through a restaurant with Giselle on his arm because no one knew it was only for show. That suited him. Real relationships didn't work.

He didn't need a female in his life. He was fine on his own. Unfortunately, he wasn't the only one kicked to the curb. He felt sad for Jasmine's mom who would need to find a new replacement at the bakery as well.

CHAPTER 29
The Show Makes the News

The next morning Jasmine woke to a ringing hotel phone. She flapped her hand around trying to find it as she blearily opened her eyes. The excited voice of Lexie on the other end of phone brought her fully awake.

"Oh, my gosh, Jasmine, are you okay? I saw the news about the show. That must have been awfully scary at the studio yesterday. Did you have nightmares? You didn't get hurt, did you? I don't know how you didn't just faint."

"Whoa, whoa, slow down on the questions. You just woke me. Give me a chance to focus."

"Oh, sure, it's just I've never seen anyone I knew on national news before."

"What do you mean about national news?"

"You, Miss Celebrity. They showed news clips with the guy from your TV show who went bonkers."

Jasmine bolted up in bed and turned on the TV to mute as she flipped through the channels. "What exactly did the news report say?"

"It said he held a knife to a contestant's throat, and you tried to calm him down. That's not all. The newscast also showed you with this super-hot hunk named Stefan. Is he the one who cheated on you? Or is it merely a coincidence?"

"You saw me with Stefan?" Jasmine ran her fingers through her bed-head hair and yawned.

"Yes, the guy who looks like a magazine cover."

"How is that possible? We were taping on a closed set."

"I don't know, but it's all over the news. Are you two together again?"

"Not at all." Jasmine slammed her hand on the mattress and shook her head. "We're through, but he might be back in the picture with the person who broke us up before I came back to Falcon Creek."

"Oh, that's too bad. You two looked so great on TV. And I liked the idea of having a friend who had connections in Hollywood."

Jasmine sat cross-legged on the bed and held a pillow to her chest. "First off, I don't have any Hollywood connections. I've merely been a contestant on a show, which is now probably cancelled due to the disastrous life threatening show. We didn't even get to the end. My show business career has come to a screeching halt."

"You are going to get paid, aren't you?"

"Yes, we had a set amount to be paid at the end of the show for our time here, but that's all. No prize money because we didn't finish the competition."

"So what are you going to do now?"

"I expect there will be a meeting today and I'll hear their decision."

"Well, keep me informed."

"Sure. Talk to you later." Jasmine ended the call and turned up the volume on the TV. She finally found a local channel airing the story from yesterday... *Terror in Tinsel town. The final taping of the latest Topped Cooking Challenge almost became deadly as one contestant brandished a knife and held another hostage...*

Jasmine watched the film footage of the security guard hauling Chad away in handcuffs and Kayla fainting. Even though she'd been in the middle of it, the scene looked scarier now. Chills ran up and down her body. If her mother saw the news report, she would no doubt be worried sick. Immediately, she turned off the TV and dialed the bakery from the hotel's phone to put her mom at ease.

As soon as she heard her mom's voice, she blurted out, "I'm okay, Mom, no need to worry. Actually, everyone on the set is okay. I wanted you to hear it directly from me before you saw the news clip on TV."

"Was there some sort of accident on the show? I didn't turn on the TV last night or this morning since I was feeling a bit under the weather. And of course there's no TV here at the bakery."

"Well it started as a mishap. Then Chad, one of the contestants, snapped. He attacked another contestant. With quick thinking by someone there, he was able to disarm Chad. The poor guy was arrested and is probably under medical care to find out why he flipped out."

"Good Lord that must have been terrifying."

"Yes, it was. By the grace of God, no one was hurt. I'll probably be coming home tomorrow. I'll let you know when it's definite."

"And you didn't get hurt at all?"

Jasmine sensed the concern in her mom's voice. "No, Mom. Really, I'm okay. He didn't come near me."

"Well, I'm glad you'll be coming home soon. I'm going to call Donetta to see if she can fill in for me for a few hours. Feel like I have a touch of the flu and my back is hurting a bit. I'm sure I'll be fine by the time you return."

Her mom was never sick and one to take off work. Jasmine bit her lip. "Maybe you should go see a doctor?"

"I'm sure it's nothing to be concerned about. I'll just come home and rest."

"Well take care of yourself. I'll text you with my return details, once I get my phone back from the studio. Just make sure you check your phone for text messages after you take a nap." Jasmine could hear the tiredness in her mom's voice and hoped she wasn't underestimating her symptoms.

"That would be nice. I've really missed you at the bakery. See you soon. Love you."

"Love you, too." Jasmine hung up the phone but had a sense of uneasiness. She closed her eyes and said a short prayer. *Lord, watch over my mom. Don't let her overextend herself.*

Turning to the nightstand, she saw the hotel phone light flashing. The voice mail from the studio informed her of the decision to end production of their show. Her final check and plane ticket home would be ready for pick-up at ten at the studio. Jasmine sighed, "So much for my TV career."

Her thoughts turned to Trevor. How she wished she'd memorized his number. She'd call him as soon as she retrieved her cell phone at the studio. Since her flight ended in San Antonio, she hoped they could meet before she headed home.

After her shower, she dressed and called the studio to request a pick-up. While she packed, a wave of sadness washed over her. At the beginning of the week, she had great hopes for making it to the final episode. The cash bonus would refill the empty reserves of the bakery and it could pay for some new equipment. Now she'd only receive the minimum guaranteed rate. She was neither a winner nor a loser. There had to be some sort of lesson to be learned here, but as yet she didn't see it. She grabbed her bags and headed out of her room.

The driver, who had picked her up on other days, waved to her as she exited the lobby. "Ready for a final ride to the studio?"

"Guess so, Drake." She moved forward with her luggage.

"Let me take your bags as a final gesture of hospitality. I like to do that for all the winners."

She snorted. "Only I'm not a winner."

"Oh, but you are." He held the car door open for her. "Anyone who makes it to the show is a winner because they dared to reach for their dreams."

She gave him a quizzical look before stepping into the car. "But trying isn't winning.

"True, but when you *are* willing to take a risk, you're a winner in my book. Most people don't want to step out of their comfort zone. These TV shows are way past that. Contestants push themselves beyond their normal limits."

He placed her things in the trunk and slipped into the front seat. "What makes winners is how they rise to the challenges before them and what they do next." He gave her a wink and started the car.

Drake had a point. This cooking show tested her abilities and made her to focus on each step. She'd learned to stretch her creativity and thinking outside the box. Being there brought real closure over her break-up with Stefan and her anger with Kayla for her part in it. Those were all winning points. She leaned forward and gave him a big smile. "You know, you're right, I am a winner. And you're a winner, too, for being such an encourager."

Drake smiled in the rearview mirror and gave her a salute before he drove out into the street.

While Drake handled the stop and go traffic, Jasmine brainstormed marketing concepts to bring more revenue to the bakery and jotted them in a notebook. By the time they made it to the studio, she had a full list of possible options. Some were a bit bizarre but keeping them on the list might spur more realistic options. With a renewed sense of hope, she hopped out of the car and headed into the production company office.

When she entered the reception area, she was surprised to see Kayla and Stefan seated there. "I thought I was only coming in to sign off on some paperwork and leave. Is there some kind of meeting?" Her eyes narrowed as she noted how content they appeared and had a sinking feeling. She gulped and asked the question she didn't want to hear the answer to. "Are you here to talk about some new show they want you to be in?"

Kayla and Stefan glanced at each other and then shook their heads.

"No, probably like you I'm here to pick up my final check. The assistant went into the main office to get the papers." Kayla replied.

Stefan leaned forward. "You know, I could pitch some ideas for shows they could do. All I would ask in return is that we could pick up the marketing campaign for them."

"Maybe this could be a new marketing niche for you." Jasmine sat in a chair at a diagonal from them. "Who knows? You might get your own agency sooner than you think."

Kayla squeezed his knee. "You'd be good as a boss. I think you should go for it."

He hugged Kayla and kissed her cheek. "All in good time. That's my goal. I know I'll succeed."

Jasmine tilted her head and put a finger to her chin. "Looks like there's something else you could be successful at – being a couple again. After all, you did save Kayla's life, which means you're now responsible for her."

Kayla leaned on his shoulder. "You're not responsible for me. I can handle my own life." Then she turned and looked into his eyes. "However, I do like the idea of us being together. Of course, showering me with gifts from time to time would be a great way to show your sense of responsibility for my life."

Stefan chuckled. "What have I gotten myself into?"

"Something good," Kayla replied giving him a quick kiss.

"What about you, Jasmine? Is there someone new in your life? Or are you all work and no time for relationships?" Stefan asked.

Jasmine looked off to the side for a moment as she thought about Trevor. They'd really been getting closer lately and she hoped it would continue. "Yes, there is someone new. We're still in the early stages, but I think there's something that goes deeper."

The assistant returned with two clipboards in her hands. "Oh, good, you're both here. This paperwork terminates your contracts with the show. Please review and sign the final disclosures, then I'll give you your checks. For you, Jasmine, there's also your flight ticket home." She handed the clipboards, papers and pens to both women. "One last question before we finish, did either of you leave anything in your personal lockers on the set?'

"Yes, I left my cell phone. Could I go get it?" Jasmine asked.

"I left a small cosmetics bag," Kayla added.

"I'll call down to the set and have someone bring your things to the reception area while you complete the paperwork." The assistant turned and headed back to her desk.

After they received their checks, and personal items, Kayla and Jasmine hugged one another briefly before heading out the door.

Jasmine stepped happily into the car with Drake for the drive to the airport. Immediately, she called Trevor and was disappointed the call went directly to voice mail. "I'm sorry I missed you again. If you've seen any video on TV about the show, don't worry. I'm fine. I'll be heading home today. My car is at the airport. Could you meet me there or anywhere else that would work for you? Leave me a message with your schedule. I've missed you."

Jasmine's trip had only one short layover before arriving in San Antonio, but the flight seemed to last forever. She was anxious to return home and try out her new ideas for the bakery. But mostly, she looked forward to seeing Trevor again. Once the plane landed, she dialed his number. The call went directly to voice mail, so she left a message again. Thinking he might have been in a meeting and not picking up calls, she sent him a text. *Just landed at airport. Hope we can get together for a light dinner before I head up to Falcon Creek.*

His text response came while she retrieved her checked bag from the airport luggage carousel. *Sorry, busy tonight. Surprised you're back. Thought you'd stay on in L.A. longer.* She frowned as she looked at the message. Why would he think she would want to stay in L.A.? She was about to text him back when her phone rang.

"Jasmine, this is Donetta. Where are you?"

"I'm at the airport. I just got all my stuff and I'm heading home. Why? What's going on?"

"It's your mom. They just took her to the hospital. You need to get home as soon as possible."

Jasmine's eyes bugged out as she gasped and dropped her suitcases back on the floor. "What happened? How is she? What hospital?"

Donetta's response came in spurts amidst sobs. "She wasn't feeling well... and was going home...then she said she was having trouble... breathing...I was so scared.

"What was it? What did the EMTs say?" Jasmine's one hand clenched the phone as if it were a lifeline, while her other hand grabbed at the corner of her jacket and held it in a fist.

"I heard them...say something about... a heart attack. They're taking her...to Riverview Medical."

"It will take some time for me to get there. I'll be praying as I drive." She stashed the phone into her jacket pocket, grabbed all her gear and ran out of the terminal. She frantically looked for the pick-up spot for the off-airport parking. Though she'd parked there numerous times and taken the shuttle, she couldn't seem to figure it out. After a couple of deep calming breaths, she re-focused and got directions for the pick-up area.

While the driver took her to her car, she called Donetta again. "Could you do me another favor? Please get a prayer chain started for Mom. The list is posted on the wall behind my desk by the phone."

"Right... I'm familiar...with the list...and will start the calls." Donetta sniffled.

"Call our pastor, too. See if he or the elders could go to the hospital. She should have someone from the church right there praying for her."

"I'm...I'm going to...close the bakery and head... for the hospital. I'll see you there."

"Thanks, Donetta, for being there for my mom. I'll see you at the hospital."

Jasmine hopped out of the van as soon as it stopped. She threw her bags in the trunk and jumped into the car. Her hand was a little shaky when she turned on the engine, so she leaned back into her seat and prayed.

Heavenly Father, I'm frightened. I don't know how to cope with my mom being in the hospital. Keep me safe as I travel. Please hold her in your care. Amen

CHAPTER 30
The Hospital Visit

Trevor arrived in Falcon Creek while Jasmine was speeding up the highway to see her mom. He had an appointment with Stacey Flanagan, the proprietor of *Chocolates and More*, who was doing the fundraiser with the local food bank. When he entered the shop, he stopped for a moment to inhale the scent of chocolate that permeated the room. He smiled and waved to Stacey who was busy with a customer.

"I'll be with you in a minute," Stacey called over to him.

He watched her describe the chocolates in loving tones as she pointed from one display case to another. From his previous samplings, he'd learned she was an outstanding chocolatier. Before he left, he'd be taking home a box for himself and one for his boss as directed.

"Sorry to keep you waiting," Stacey said as she reached out and shook his hand. "There's often a last-minute customer at the end of the day. Let me lock up and we'll go over the presentation. Geoff Whitestone is in the back setting it up."

She pointed to the back room. "I'm glad Geoff's teaming up with me. His shop, The Art of Cheese, is phenomenal and a perfect pairing for this campaign."

The room they entered was the storeroom for the candy boxes and supplies, which were all neatly arranged on floor to ceiling shelving units. There wasn't a lot of extra space, but Geoff had made the most of the work area he was given. As they walked toward him, Geoff was adding final touches to the display. He was a thirty-something with a neatly trimmed beard and dressed in professional chef's attire like Stacey. A tri-fold self-standing poster covered the back of the table. It explained how the program worked. In front of the table were sample boxes with images of what would fill them plus the details for pricing.

"I know my idea probably isn't unique. Businesses are always doing something or other for their communities," Stacey said as she pointed to the poster, "We've created what I call 'The Giving Gift.'" She picked up a box wrapped in luminescent paper and tied with ribbon. "This is a half-pound box of my signature chocolates. Who wouldn't feel special receiving a gift like this? For every 'Giving Gift' sold, we'll donate the equivalent of a meal to a local food bank. So it's a gift that gives twice." She handed it over to Trevor for his review.

"Superb packaging for gifting and you make a great chocolate."

"Yes, her chocolate is addictive," Geoff said. "Here's my design." He handed a small wooden crate to Trevor. This is my display. The actual cheese is an exclusive full-flavored triple-cream cheese that is aged for six weeks. It's washed with a salt-water brine that permeates the rind with a sunrise-orange glow. This cheese is blended just for the promotion."

"The packaging and pricing you show on the display should make it an easy seller." Trevor said.

"That's what we hope. Our community really came together aiding and assisting one another after the railroad derailment. A lot of families who were displaced by the fires still need help."

Trevor remembered the horrific disaster. He'd rushed up here to make sure Jasmine wasn't among the victims. Fortunately, she'd been safe. They'd formed a special bond helping those whose lives had been shattered. He felt a closeness to her that day.

She shared her hopes of expanding the business. He shared his dreams of running a small restaurant, something he had only previously mentioned to this family. Was their connection merely the emotional pull of the tragedy that had brought them together?

After he saw the story on the TV last night featuring Jasmine and Galanos, Trevor wondered if another near tragedy brought her and her ex back together again. He clenched his teeth and tried to maintain a smile. He was wrong to trust a woman again. "Yes, I remember that day. This will make a great feature story. Have any other local shops showed interest in joining in the campaign?"

"I talked to Belinda this week at *Sweet Delights.* She seemed interested, but she wanted to discuss it with her daughter who is a partner in the business. The daughter's been in L.A. for a cooking show competition. I think she might be finishing up in a few days and I'll check back with her then."

Geoff turned to Stacey. "Didn't you see the news last night or this morning? One of the contestants on that show had an emotional breakdown and threatened another contestant with a knife. Jasmine's okay. At least she looked that way on the TV."

Stacey shook her head. "Well, I guess with hot kitchens and high stakes it's almost inevitable that someone would reach for a knife. Glad no one got hurt, especially Jasmine. Belinda has really come to count on her since she came back home from L.A. It seemed like great timing for both of them."

Trevor's hands automatically balled up in fists at the side of his legs. Even when he wasn't thinking about Jasmine, someone else had to bring her up.

The geographic distance between them would now be even further, since Jasmine had made her decision about being with her boyfriend from California. She wasn't a small-town girl after all.

An hour later Trevor had the pictures and notes he needed to complete his feature story. As he drove through the town, he would pass by *Sweet Delights*, unless he wanted to take a wide detour. Since it was hours past their normal five o'clock closing, he didn't expect to see anyone there.

However, a handwritten sign on the front door got his attention. Curious, he pulled into a parking spot in front of the bakery and walked up to the door. The sign read, "Family Emergency. Bakery will be closed for the time being." He caught his breath and furrowed his brows as his gaze darted about to see if anyone could give him more details.

A click of a lock on a door sounded and his head abruptly turned to its location. Two stores down at the *Sass and Class* dress shop a woman had just locked up.

"Excuse me, ma'am," he called out. "The sign for the bakery says there was a family emergency and it's going to be closed for a while. Do you know anything about it?"

She squinted and looked him over. "There's another bakery two blocks away. It will be open in the morning, though it's not as good as *Sweet Delights*."

He gritted his teeth and took a deep breath. "No, I'm not interested in the bakery. I want to know about the people. Did Jasmine get in an accident?"

The woman shook her head. "Good Lord, I hope not. Belinda is the family emergency. Happened earlier, around mid-afternoon. An EMT took her out of the bakery.

I thought at first maybe she got burned, you know with the ovens and all, but I heard Donetta say something about a stroke or heart attack. She was a basket case seeing Belinda all hooked up with tubes and such. Seeing people like that gives me the chills. Reminds me how fragile life is."

Trevor rubbed his hand across the back of his neck and tugged at his hair. "Yes, life is. Do you know what hospital they took her to?"

"You're not from around here. There's only one hospital nearby. That would be Riverview Medical. You friends with Belinda and Jasmine or just a curious tourist?"

Trevor nodded and felt his throat go dry. His relationship with Jasmine might be over, but he remembered how impressed he was by the selfless attitude Belinda had during the train derailment emergency. She deserved at least a short visit from him. "No, I know them. "I'm sorry to hear about Belinda."

"Well, if you know Jasmine, why don't you give her a call? She'll be able to give you more details."

"Thanks, I appreciate your help." His voice drifted off as he headed back to his car. He sat in the driver's seat for a moment trying to decide what to do. The last thing he wanted was to run into Jasmine, but there was no way she could have made a flight from L.A. and driven from the airport in this short a time.

It didn't take him long to find the hospital using the GPS. When he arrived, he went to the information desk and asked for Belinda Cattrell's room number.

The woman smiled at him. "She's on the third floor, room 317. Only one or two people at a time in the room, but I know you folks want to be nearby and praying. Just do it softly."

He didn't know what the woman meant and shrugged it off. When the elevator opened on the third floor, he made a right and followed an arrow down the hallway. As soon as he did, he saw a large group of people in the hall, holding hands with their heads bowed as one person spoke softly in prayer.

He quietly passed by and noticed Donetta and Lexie were part of the group but didn't stop and interrupt their prayer time. He continued to the room, poked his head into the doorway, and then abruptly stopped.

Jasmine sat beside the bed and she was holding her mom's hand. How did she get here so quickly? He expected to be gone before she arrived. With a quick pivot, he turned around, but not before Jasmine noticed his presence.

"Trevor? Is that you?"

His shoulders sagged and he bowed his head. After taking a deep breath, he turned to face her. "I don't want to interrupt you. Just tell your mom I'll keep her in my prayers for a speedy recovery." He wanted to leave as quickly as possible.

"Wait, Trevor. Don't go. I want to talk to you." Jasmine rose and walked towards him.

"No need to. I saw the video of the show." He held up his palms and shrugged his shoulders. "There's nothing to explain. You've made your decision. I wish you all the best in L.A. where your heart is," he replied in a quick, dismissive tone and walked out and down the hall.

Her once ex-boyfriend was probably in the cafeteria getting coffee. The last thing he wanted was to run into him and deal with that awkward moment of seeing the two of them together. He didn't need that humiliation.

CHAPTER 31
Waiting for the Doctor's Update

Jasmine would have run after Trevor, but at the same time he left, she thought she heard her mom mumble something. Hoping Mom was waking; she returned to the bed and caressed her forehead. But there was no change. She was still asleep. Jasmine sat back in the chair, wrapped her arms across her chest and shook her head in disbelief.

What just happened with Trevor? It made no sense. Why was he upset? She glanced over at her mom, clasped her fingers together and prayed in a whisper. "Lord, I need my mom. Please heal her and help me understand what's going on with Trevor?" A few tears trickled down her face, which she gently wiped away.

Restless, she stood and turned toward the window. Clouds were rolling in and the wind was picking up. The sky seemed to mirror her thoughts which were being tossed from her concern for her mom's condition, to disbelief of what happened in that abrupt meeting with Trevor, and an uneasy feeling of what could happen next. To ease her mind, she sat by the bed, closed her eyes, and began to pray silently. *Lord, I know you hold the world in the palm of your hand, and you love me. Keep Trevor safe in this storm. Calm the fears and uncertainties of my heart as I wait for good news for my mom and a real conversation with Trevor.*

Knowing there was nothing more she could do at the moment, she stood and walked to the door. The prayer circle that had gathered nearby was breaking up. She waved to get Lexie's attention and motioned for her to come over.

Lexie gave her a quick hug and stepped back. "Didn't I just see Trevor go by? What made him leave so quickly?"

Jasmine nodded. "I don't know. Once he saw me, it seemed he couldn't wait to get away. Trevor said he didn't want to interrupt and would keep Mom in his prayers."

"Then why didn't he stay and pray with us?"

"I don't know. I was so happy to see him. I had forgotten to call him about Mom but he somehow found out on his own and came to be with me." She ran her hands down the sides of her thighs and shivered. A tear slipped down her face. "Only he didn't want to even hold me. I don't understand."

Lexie put her arm around Jasmine's shoulder. "Did he say anything else?" Jasmine closed her eyes and sighed. "Yes, something about me making a decision. I haven't made any decisions yet, I'm too worried about my mom."

"That is odd. Could he have been upset you decided to be on that show and could have been hurt?"

"No, that can't be the reason. He was incredibly supportive of my doing the show. His actions here don't make sense. I have no idea what set him off." Jasmine shook her head and leaned in to look at her mother.

"How is she doing?"

"Her heart monitor is steady and she's resting." Her finger touched the corner of her eye and blotted away more tears. "I hate seeing Mom hooked up to tubes and the monitor and hearing the blips."

Lexie gave Jasmine's shoulder a gentle squeeze. "Yeah, it's always hard seeing people at the hospital like that. Just remember, she's in God's care. Lots of people praying for her, not only here but throughout the town."

"I'd like to go back and sit with her. Would you mind getting me a cup of hot tea?"

"Sure," Lexie said. "Do you want herbal, black or green?"

"Full strength black, please."

"Will do. By the way, some of the nurses came over to the group and said they were praying for her as well."

"That's much appreciated. All prayers count." Jasmine turned, walked into the room, and sat beside the bed.

Her mom's eyes fluttered open and she looked around until her gaze rested on Jasmine's face. In a raspy whisper she asked, "What happened? Why am I in a hospital?"

Jasmine beamed in seeing her mom awake and reached over to hold her hand. "You've had a heart attack. They're monitoring your heart and pulse. That's why you're here."

Her mom looked up to the ceiling and stared for a moment. "I sorta remember saying I wasn't feeling well and then nothing. I guess I passed out." She turned to face Jasmine. "I'm glad it wasn't fatal. I'd hate to miss out on all the details of your trip."

"Mom, you're not going to die, at least not anytime soon." Jasmine bit her quivering lip. "You're going to be fine."

"Honey, no one knows how long they've got." She reached out for Jasmine's hand. "We're supposed to live like every minute counts because we don't know if it will be our last. I've certainly tried to do that, though not always successfully.

Jasmine felt a lump in her throat and could feel the tears welling in her eyes again. "Oh, Mom, don't sell yourself short. You've been wonderful to me and a blessing to the community."

"This scare or warning has me thinking about my life. After your dad died, I decided I didn't want to risk falling in love again. I didn't want to open my heart and lose someone again. Instead I threw myself into the business and helping others."

"Both of which you've done very well."

Belinda smiled. "I'm not looking for compliments. I'm saying not allowing myself to love again was a mistake. I don't want that to happen to you. I know you were badly hurt with your break-up with Stefan. Nurture what you've got going with Trevor. Don't snuff it out. Open your heart again."

"Mom, don't worry about me, let's focus on you." She couldn't bear to tell her mom they'd hit some sort of roadblock. Besides, with her mom's condition, maybe it was better to stay solo to focus on running the business.

"Remember, it's always much nicer to share your good fortune and fun with a partner beside you. Business can fail you, like it did with your last job. But I think your job loss was a blessing in disguise. It gave us the chance to work together again. I'm so blessed to see how capable you've become in running the business. Now if I ever decided to take a long vacation, I know the bakery will do well in my absence."

"Vacation?" Jasmine laughed. "When was the last time you took time off other than for a few hours?"

"I was afraid to leave work, even when I had a strong assistant backing me up. Guess I have a bit of a control issue."

Jasmine nodded. "Runs in the family, doesn't it? Like mother, like daughter."

Mom smiled, closed her eyes, and took a few deep breaths. Her eyes blinked open and she turned towards Jasmine. "Sorry, the show didn't work out for you. Are you okay with the outcome? I know you were excited about it and wanted to win, but I'm really glad you're back."

"The show was intense and tested my cooking skills. It was exhilarating until Chad lost it. So, I am definitely glad to be back."

"I'm feeling a bit tired, honey. Would you mind if I rested?"

"Sure, Mom. You go ahead. I'll be here when you wake."

While her mom slept, Jasmine thought about what had happened this week. The lure of becoming a TV celebrity had seemed so enticing. She didn't want a quest for fame to overwhelm her life and leave her emotionally devastated as had happened with Chad. *Thank you, God, for that lesson.*

Being back home in Texas was where she wanted to be. Having all those people in the hall praying for her mom felt wonderful. This was the life she desired – one with true friends who would always be there for her in times of crisis like they were for her mom.

Lexie came to the door with her tea and nodded for Jasmine to come outside of the room. Jasmine rose from her chair but blew a kiss to her sleeping mom as she left.

"I've only a few minutes to spare before I head downstairs to start my shift. Before I go,

I need to ask, how are you holding up?" Lexie handed Jasmine the tea.

"Better now since I was able to talk to my mom. She told me she was worried about me. Imagine that. She's the one in the hospital and is concerned about me."

"That's what moms do. They always worry about their kids even as adults. A nice blessing from God to remind us how much he cares for us."

"Amen to that." Jasmine tapped her Styrofoam cup to Lexie's.

"So how are you feeling now that the show is over?"

Jasmine blew out a deep breath and shrugged. "I've mixed feelings. I'm sad it's over because doing the show was exciting, but it also was gut-wrenching wondering if I'd make it to the next round."

She ran her finger around the edge of the cup. "The show reminded me of the stress I had with my previous job. Don't miss that stress. However, the show gave me the confidence that I can keep the bakery going while Mom's on the mend."

"Of course you can." Lexie playfully jabbed Jasmine on her shoulder. "Even as a teenager I was impressed with your baking skills."

"Are you sure it wasn't all the freebies you received?" Jasmine smirked.

"Well, there was that, too." Lexie giggled. "But you've got a gift with baking."

"I agree. I love creating foods that make people happy."

"Well, I may not know how to bake, but I could help with taking orders and running the register on Saturday when I'm not working."

"That would be great, but money's kinda tight now. Don't know how I could afford to pay you."

"Don't worry about it. Consider my work as a down payment towards the price of the wedding cake you'll make for me one day."

Jasmine looked at her sideways. "Are you holding out on me? Did something big happen while I was in L.A.?"

Lexie's face broke into a wide smile. She threw her hand over her heart in her usual melodramatic way. "Well, you know me. I am ever hopeful that Mr. Right is always just around the corner. Maybe he is this time."

"Ooh, sounds interesting." Jasmine gave Lexie's hand a quick squeeze. "Tell me more."

"Well, I met a guy this week at your bakery when I was waiting in line to pick up a snack. We started a conversation about anticipation. He made a cute comparison about kids waiting for Christmas and adults waiting for their coffee and Danish. After he received his order, he waited for me to get mine. Then we talked for a couple of minutes after we walked out.

"Did he ask for your phone number?" Jasmine's eyes widened with hopeful anticipation.

"He did and I gave it to him – the real one." Lexie replied as her face turned crimson. He called and asked me out to lunch the next day. And he paid for it without any credit card denials."

"Good, that's a positive start." Jasmine clapped her hands. "Anything else since the lunch?"

"He texted me today and said he'd like to get together again, but he'll be out of town this weekend and he'll call me when he returns."

"I'm happy for you." Jasmine smiled. "Hope this time he's more of a prince than a frog."

Lexie hugged Jasmine. "Me, too. Gotta start my shift now. I'll check back with you later"

"Thanks for the tea and your prayers." Jasmine's smile disappeared as her friend walked away. It sounded like Lexie was off to a good start with her new man and she hoped it would last. Too bad, it wasn't the same for her and Trevor. Earlier in the week he seemed like a Prince Charming, but the way he cut out of the hospital made her wonder if he had turned into a leaping frog. She'd call him later to get an explanation once she felt at ease with her mom's condition and had feedback from the doctors.

CHAPTER 32
Stopping at the Diner

Trevor stopped at Polly's Café, about ten miles from the hospital, before continuing to San Antonio. He'd done a review on the restaurant last year and recalled how it was a local favorite. Their colorful neon sign was aglow even though it was only late afternoon. The wind was picking up as well. He wouldn't linger here long as Texas storms were known to be unpredictable. They may start as slight winds and steady whisps of rain then break into to twirling winds and buckets of driving rain.

Though there were tables available, he sat at the counter for quicker service. After a short perusal of the menu, he ordered a coffee and the daily special. He didn't really care what he ate. It was only something to fill him until he got home. While he waited for his food, he looked around the room for a distraction. He caught a mirrored reflection of the booth where a couple in their late twenties sat. It was on the opposite wall from his stool. Though he only heard an occasional word here and there, he could tell they were having an argument by their frowns, glares, and pointed gestures. The woman said something about an "old girlfriend." He replied with "just talking." The man kept shaking his head while she glared at him. After that, she scooted out from the booth and spurted, "I know what I saw" before she ran off.

Then Trevor noticed the guy's reaction. He didn't show the guilty look of being busted. Instead, he looked baffled and confused like he was innocent. The man jumped up, dropped a few bills on the table and ran out the door. The large front window showed he'd caught up with the woman and brought her hands up to his chest in a gesture of pleading. Apparently, this woman meant a lot to him and he didn't want to lose her.

"Here's your special," the waitress said as she put the plate before him. "Can I get you anything else?"

Her question caught him off guard because he'd been so intent on watching the couple. He smiled and picked up his knife and fork. "No thanks." He took a bite and considered the man's reaction. Could it be the woman had misread what she saw? He picked up another forkful and held it in mid-air. Could he have misconstrued what he saw on TV with Jasmine? No, it couldn't be. He didn't imagine it.

Trevor continued eating his meal and occasionally watched the TV on the wall. *Hollywood Happenings* was on the air and the still picture on the upper corner of the screen featured a happy smiling couple. The sound was off, but the TV was set to closed captioning, so he'd be able to read the newscaster's remarks.

"Looks like a TV contestant cooked up some love this week. One of her competitors attacked Kayla Blegen, a popular local model and contender on Topped, the cooking challenge show; but it didn't end badly for her. Stefan Galanos, who saved her from the attacker, has popped the question. No date was given for the marriage, but we can be sure she'll be cooking up something special for the two of them."

Trevor's jaw dropped. There was Stefan again. And that wasn't Jasmine. Looks like he did get it wrong. He laid down his utensils and shook his head. What a fool he'd been. He paid for his meal and headed out to his car. The sky was now an ominous looking grey with occasional flashes of lightning. The wind whipped up and twirled bits of leaves and debris through the air. Trevor hunched his shoulders and pulled his sports jacket collar up. In the car, he scanned through the radio dials to find a local news channel covering the weather.

A series of long beeps interrupted the music on the radio and ended with an announcement. "A severe weather warning has been issued for Gillespie County. This covers the area in the northwest section of the county between Falcon Creek and

Merriville. You are advised to seek shelter and stay in a secure location." He looked through the upper part of his windshield. The rain was just starting. There was still a chance he'd beat the worst part of the storm. He had to get back to the hospital to see Jasmine. He tried calling her, but he only got the recording of "all circuits are busy."

As he drove along the highway, the rain fell in sweeping gusts and he could feel his car buffeted by the winds. Small tree branches and scattered leaves blew across the road. White knuckled, he clutched the steering wheel as he swerved occasionally to keep from hitting rolling trashcans in the street. At times, the rain was so severe it was hard to see past anything more than a few feet. He was driving by faith. "Please, God," he mumbled repeatedly, "get me safely back to Jasmine."

When he slowed at a yield sign just a few blocks from the hospital, a truck from the other side of the street lost control and spun out. Trevor caught his breath and gulped hard as he watched the vehicle head directly for his car. There was no time to move out of the way. He tried to brace himself for the oncoming assault.

The crashing of metal against metal and the sound of breaking glass were the last things he heard before his airbag was deployed and he lost consciousness.

CHAPTER 33
News of Trevor's Accident

Soon after Lexie began her shift in the emergency room, an ambulance brought in an accident victim. With the rains and high winds nearby, she expected her shift would be extremely busy. She took notes as the EMT gave his verbal report of the patient's vitals, but abruptly stopped when she heard them state the name on his driver's license – Trevor Lassitor. *How could it be? He was just at the hospital.* She turned and scrutinized his cut and bloodied face then gasped. *This is Jasmine's Trevor.*

Trevor's eyes were glazed over and he appeared disoriented but she heard him mumbling, "Jasmine. Need to see Jasmine. Important. Where is she?"

Lexie gripped her computer tablet tightly, took a deep breath and then turned to the doctor. "This is my best friend's boyfriend. He's asking for her. She's visiting her mom in the hospital. May I call her?"

The doctor listened to Trevor's voice and heard him repeating the sentences as Lexie mentioned. "Mr. Lassitor, do you want us to contact…" The doctor turned to Lexie. "What's your friend's name?"

"Jasmine Cattrell."

The doctor faced Trevor. "Is that who you want us to contact?"

Trevor closed his eyes and nodded. "Yes, Jasmine."

After Trevor's admittance was completed and there was a break in her workload, Lexie pulled out her phone and called Jasmine. "How's your mom doing?"

"Still resting peacefully. I'm getting used to the monitors and their blipping which sounds and looks regular without any spikes."

Lexie bit her lip. "That's good to hear." She hesitated for a moment and then added, "Umm, I don't have a lot of time, so I have to say this straight up. You need to come down to the emergency room. Trevor was in an accident. He's pretty banged up and has a broken humerus and fractured his lateral malleolus. He's been asking for you."

There was a moment of silence before Lexie heard Jasmine suck in a deep breath.

"Oh, no… I'll be right there."

"I'll be looking for you." Lexie hung up the phone and said a silent prayer for Trevor and Jasmine's mom before she returned to her duties.

Jasmine's heart pounded as she jumped out of the chair and headed down the hall to where her friends were gathered. Her eyes welled up as she choked out the words,

"Could someone sit with my mom? My boyfriend is in the ER. I need to go see him."

One of the women from her church reached out and squeezed her hand. "Go ahead, I'll sit with her."

Her lips quivered. "Please lift Trevor up in prayers, too." She dashed to the elevator and prayed silently. *Lord, please let him be okay. I don't want to lose him. He means too much to me.*

When Jasmine entered the emergency room lobby, her gaze darted about looking for Lexie. All around the crowded room there were anxious faces waiting for words on the condition of their loved ones, just as she was. Finally, she spotted Lexie, who was finishing up with a patient. Jasmine waved to get her attention and walked toward where she stood.

She gripped Lexie's hand and blinked back the tears in her eyes. "How is he? Can I see him?"

"He's in good hands." Lexie put her arm around Jasmine. "They're still running tests to make sure they don't miss anything. Right now he shows as having multiple facial lacerations and the broken humerus and lateral malleolus. Those bones will take time to heal but he's lucky that's all that happened."

Jasmine gasped. "That still sounds awful. He's going to be okay, right?"

"I'm sure he'll be fine once the bones heal. They'll do a CAT scan to make sure there's no internal bleeding or a concussion. You can spend time with him until he's moved to do the scan." Lexie pointed down the hall and started walking with Jasmine. "Just to let you know, he looks bad but he's not in critical condition. Don't faint on me, okay?"

"I'll do my best." Jasmine shook out her arms and took a deep breath when they came to the room. "I'm ready to see him. Will you stay with me?"

"I can for a minute, until you get over the shock of seeing him. Then I need to get back to work. Follow me."

They walked into a large room with curtained off beds. Lexie stopped at one on the left and opened the privacy curtain. She put her hand on Jasmine's shoulder and they stepped to the side of the bed.

Jasmine reached over and touched Trevor's cheek with a shaky hand. "Oh, Trevor. I'm so sorry you were in an accident." She turned to Lexie and blinked through eyes filling with tears. "He looks so pale."

"That's normal at this point. The doctors want to keep his vitals steady." Lexie looked at his medical chart. "He's been given painkillers for his injuries. The monitors are tracking his condition to make sure there are no changes."

"Do you think he can hear me if I talk to him?"

Lexie shrugged. "Hard to say. I don't think it could hurt, especially if you want to sit and pray. I'll let you have some privacy. I've got to get back to work."

"Thanks for letting me know he was here." Jasmine pulled a chair closer to the bed and sat. She wrapped her hands around one of his, closed her eyes and prayed silently. *Heavenly Father, I place Trevor in your loving hands. Bless and heal him and bring him back to me.* She continued to hold his hand but opened her eyes. No magical spark happened this time when their fingertips touched.

In a soft and gentle voice she said, "Trevor, I don't want to lose you. I wanted to tell you that when you came to visit my mom earlier tonight." She brushed her hand across his forehead. "The scare at the studio really got to me. Of course, I've tried to tell others I wasn't really scared, but I was. I didn't want to see blood spurting all about." She leaned closer and whispered in his ear. "You need to know that about me. I'm a bit squeamish about blood, so I'm glad you've been cleaned from the accident. I wouldn't want to faint and be a patient here as well."

Jasmine wiped away her tears and sat for a couple of minutes deep in thought. *Having to deal with my mom's condition is stressful enough, now here's Trevor. I don't understand why he barely spoke to me and left the hospital so quickly. We need to clear up whatever the problem is.* She stroked his cheek. "Please open your eyes and tell me you're okay. I can't stand seeing you so listless."

She squeezed his hand and attempted to laugh but it sounded hollow. "Not talking, huh? Well I need to find a way to change that, Mister Dreamy Eyes. Remember when Lexie told you I called you that name after we first met? Well, I'd like to see your beautiful, dreamy eyes again. And how about giving me one of your winning smiles?"

The scratching sound of the curtain pulled around its track caught her by surprise, and she jumped in her chair.

A man in a white lab coat and stethoscope walked up to the bed. "Sorry to disturb you." He glanced at his chart. "I'm Dr. Martinez and I'm here to get an update on Mr. Lassitor's vitals."

Jasmine gave Trevor's hand a final squeeze, rose from the chair and moved out of the doctor's way. She stood at the end of the bed, watched the doctor as he did various checks on Trevor, and made notes. She tugged at her shirt and nervously blinked waiting to hear the doctor's analysis.

When Dr. Martinez finished his work, he turned to her. "There are no changes to his condition since he was brought in. Pulse, heart rate and air are in acceptable ranges. The lack of consciousness may be due to pain and the medication. Until we get the results of a CAT scan, we can't be sure. We'll continue to monitor him. Are you a next of kin in case we need to do surgery?"

Jasmine's eyes widened and she gasped. "Surgery?"

"Ma'am it may not be necessary. We just need consent if something changes."

She shook her head and exhaled deeply. "No, I'm not his next of kin. I'm his girlfriend. His family lives north of Dallas – his parents and his brother. I don't have their numbers, but he probably has them in his cell phone. He should have had it with him."

"I'll see what they know at the nurse's station. We'll need their full names and info to reach them if consent is needed."

She clasped and unclasped her hands. With her voice cracking she asked, "Is there anything else I should know?"

"He needs to regain consciousness. Once he does that, we'll run another set of vitals and have a better idea. After that, he'll be assigned to a critical care area. When they're ready to move him, someone will let you know."

After the doctor left, Jasmine returned to Trevor's bedside. "Wake up." Tears fell as she kissed his cheek. "This is not the time for sleeping." She leaned over and gently touched his temple and brushed back his hair with her fingertips. "C'mon you need to talk to me. You need to explain why you left my mom's room so abruptly without even a hug.

Why were you upset at seeing me? No secrets. We need honesty." She laid her head gently on his chest and closed her eyes as she listened to his heartbeat, which was smooth and regular – unlike hers, which seemed to be pounding. Did she hear him mumble? She lifted her head and faced him. Was he trying to say something?

His lips moved but she only heard something like a moan.

Was it a moan of pain? "Is there something you need? Something I can do for you?" She put a hand on his cheek and closed her eyes to pray. *Lord, ease Trevor's pain. Fill him and my mom with your love and peace.*

The noise from the curtain moving in its loop caused her to open her eyes and sit up. A nurse had entered his area.

"Excuse me, we're taking him for a CAT scan. Then he'll be moved to a room. You can check at the front desk for his room assignment." The nurse held up her hand and pointed to the lobby.

Lexie wasn't in sight, so Jasmine walked over to the admitting area and waited in line for someone to assist her. When it was her turn, she learned Trevor wouldn't be in a room for at least thirty minutes, but she did get a room number. For the time being, she would return to be with her mom, but her thoughts would be continually on Trevor until she could talk to him.

CHAPTER 34
Waiting for Answers

After Jasmine left Trevor, she headed to the hospital's cafeteria. She hadn't eaten anything since her breakfast in California and the grumbling in her stomach plus a stressful headache told her it was time to remedy that situation. She sat at the counter and picked up one of the menus clipped on the metal stand. The options were limited but better than having something from a vending machine. In perusing the short menu, she decided on a combo of soup and half a roasted turkey sandwich with avocado.

While she waited for her order to be ready, she scanned the dining area to see if there was anyone she knew. On the far side of the room, she noticed Patricia Vasquez, one of the bakery's regular customers, sitting alone at a table. While she was trying to decide if she should go over and chat, Patricia glanced in her direction and waved her over.

"Good to see you, Jasmine. Have a seat. What brings you to the hospital?"

"I guess you haven't heard. Mom had a heart attack earlier today. She's resting now and seems to be okay, but they want to keep her here for at least a couple of days to make sure she's okay."

Patricia reached over and clutched Jasmine's hand. "Oh, I am so sorry to hear that. Your mom is such an active person, always helping others, and probably overworking herself."

Jasmine stiffened waiting for Patricia to add something about not working enough to help her mother. She recalled in the past how the woman discounted her assistance in the bakery as minimal, as she did as a teen, rather than putting in the full hours like her mom. However, her next words were unexpected.

"Jasmine, you know your mom is so proud of you. She's told me how hard you work at the bakery. And I can see you've added more life to the bakery with the new choices and ideas that make it fun to come into the shop. Your mom will probably need to cut back on her hours for the near future, but I know you'll be able to handle the situation to keep the business going strong. You truly have a talent for baking and marketing."

"Thank you, Patricia, for that lovely compliment. I will certainly do my best." In saying those words, Jasmine realized her job hunt would need to be put on hold while her mom recuperated. It struck her as funny that she really didn't mind staying on at the bakery for the indefinite future. She enjoyed the banter she had with many of the regulars and visitors at the bakery, plus trying out recipes of her own creation gave her a strong sense of accomplishment.

"What brought you to the hospital, Patricia?"

Patricia leaned back and waved a hand in the air indifferently. "Nothing quite as serious as what your mom is going through. I came to pick up a friend who had successful cataract surgery. The doctor is giving her the details of what to do and not do once she returns home. The first thing she can't do is drive. So, I'm her ride."

"That's sweet of you to help. I'm sure she appreciates that."

Patricia shrugged. "That's what we're supposed to do. Helping others brings me joy and shows my gratitude for the many ways I've been blessed – with one of those being the long-lasting friendship with your mom. When could I see her?"

"She's resting now and that's what she needs the most. I'll let her know you were concerned about her. Once we see what the doctors have to say after watching her overnight. I'll call and let you know her status. Right now visits are extremely limited. When she's more up to talking, I'll let you know. She'll definitely appreciate a short visit from you."

Patricia pointed behind Jasmine. "Looks like your order is ready. I'll wait for your call.

In the meantime, I'll keep Belinda in my prayers."

"Thanks, Patricia. You know how much my mom believes in prayers, so they are much appreciated." Jasmine paid the waitress, took her bagged meal, and walked to the lobby. Having Patricia praise her work lifted her spirits. And it seemed like another nudge that staying in Falcon Creek was the right decision.

CHAPTER 35
Praying for Good Results

The number of people in the hallway praying for her mom had dwindled to a few while she was in the cafeteria, but they were also ready to return home to be with their families. They said their goodbyes and promised to keep Belinda in their prayers. As they entered the elevator, Savannah was exiting it.

Savannah walked toward Jasmine and gave her a gentle hug. "Oh, Jasmine, so sorry to hear about your mom. And you've had a long day with your flight from L.A. How are you both doing?"

"I'm getting by. It's been a lot more stressful than I expected it to be today. Thanks for coming. I know it's hard sometimes getting sitters on short notice. Mom will definitely appreciate seeing you here."

As they walked down the hall, Savannah asked, "What have the doctors told you?"

"The doctor said she's doing fine, and all the tests are looking good with no major heart damage. She'll just need to take it a little easier."

Savannah gave Jasmine a quizzical look. "For someone who has good news, your face doesn't show it. Why the red eyes? Did they find other issues?"

"No, no. She really is doing well." Jasmine exhaled a deep breath and gripped Savannah's hand. "It's Trevor. He's been in an accident."

Savannah stopped and faced Jasmine. "Oh, no. Double the medical scare. How is he doing?"

"I saw him, and my heart ached." Jasmine wiped away a tear as her shoulders sagged. "He's got cuts all over his face and a broken arm and fractured the bone by his foot, plus he's not conscious. They're running more tests. Don't know if it's a concussion or something worse."

"Well let's keep him in our prayers." She gave Jasmine a hug and then put her arm on her shoulder as they continued down the hall. "Judging by the others I saw leaving; I'll guess lots of prayers have been offered up."

"Yes, our prayer chain is fully activated. Once Donetta gave me the news about what had happened with Mom, I asked her to start the prayer chain. She got everything in motion."

Savannah and Jasmine walked into the room together and greeted a church elder and his wife who had been sitting next to her mom and saying prayers. Jasmine thanked them for their support before they left to keep with the two-visitor rule for patients. She sat on the chair nearest Mom's face and Savannah sat on the other chair. The rustle of the bed sheets got Jasmine's attention and she moved closer to see if Mom was awake.

In a sound just barely above a whisper her mother said, "I know you're here and staring at me. Just like when you were little, and you came in and watched me, when I tried to take a nap. Do you want to talk about something?"

Jasmine wiped away a tear and smiled. "Moms don't just have eyes on the back of their head, but on both sides of their eyelids, too." She reached over and squeezed Mom's hand. "Savannah came to visit you as well."

"Hi, Mrs. C. Hope you'll be well, soon." Savannah leaned over and gave a quick squeeze to her shoulder.

"How could I not? I have a boatload of folks praying for me throughout the church. Plus, I had a little talk with God, and he's told me my time on this earth is not yet complete."

"That's right. You still have a lot to teach me, Mom."

"True, I need to bring you up to speed in running the business. I always hoped to hand it over to you. Your return to Falcon Creek was the answer to my prayers. You may have not made it to the winner's circle on that TV show, but you've always been number one to me." She opened her eyes and entwined her fingers with her daughter's hand. Then with a wink, she said, "There's more than the business to take care of. I want to see the next generation of bakers. You need to get started on giving me some grandbabies."

"Well, I should be married first, shouldn't I?" Jasmine snickered and clasped Mom's fingers. A lump formed in her throat and she forced a thin smile. "Nothing on the horizon for that at this time."

"What in the world is taking you and Trevor so long to realize you are meant to be together?" Mom rolled her eyes and shook her head.

Jasmine looked up at the ceiling and dabbed her finger at the edge of her eyelid to stop the tear that was forming there.

Savannah cleared her throat and then said in a soft tone, "Mrs. C, Trevor's been in an accident. They're running some tests on him. He's unconscious and she doesn't know the full details of his injuries."

Jasmine's mom gave the two women a steely stare. "As long as there's life, there is hope. Don't forget that. Let's join hands and pray."

Jasmine and Savannah gently reached for Belinda's hands making sure they didn't disturb any of the tubes and wires. They closed their eyes as she began her prayer.

"Heavenly Father, thank you for our many blessings of family, friends, and prayer warriors. Direct and guide the doctors as they treat Trevor and me. We trust in you for a good outcome and thank you in advance..."

As she continued to listen to her mom's prayer, Jasmine was once again amazed by the conviction and power in Mom's voice as she prayed. Her faith in action came from years of experience in talking to God daily and waiting for his leading. Her mom's favorite verse was from Hebrews 11:1 "Faith is confidence in what we hope for and assurance about what we do not see." She lived those words as a key part of her life.

When she was finished her prayers, Jasmine and Savannah added theirs as well. After an additional minute of silence, they all ended by adding, "Amen."

"Thanks, Mom. I really appreciate how you know the right words to say to keep me focused on what's important." She leaned over and kissed her on the cheek. *Thank you, God, for giving me such a wonderful role model and so many friends who are praying for Mom's recovery.*

CHAPTER 36
Hospital Updates

The next day, Jasmine was at the bakery early as usual. She needed to be working with her hands so her thoughts wouldn't be on the two people she held dear to her heart, who were in the hospital. Opening the door and heading into the kitchen without her mom eerily felt as if she had entered into an alternate time and space. The quiet and emptiness tugged at her heart. She'd come to enjoy the banter with her mom at this time of day. Once in the kitchen, she turned on the music to play contemporary Christian praise songs to fill the void and lift her spirits.

Since she was the only one doing the prep work for the day, she started with one of the basic dough recipes that could be used for an assortment of pastry choices. As she went through the motions of adding the ingredients together with robotic preciseness, she recalled years gone by when her mom was first teaching her to make the bakery's sweet delights. What joy she had when she brought out her first tray of pastries she had made on her own. The pride in her mom's eyes in seeing her accomplishment was something she had never forgotten. At that point, she had considered baking a fun hobby and not something she would do as a career. Then she went on to establish her skills in marketing and advertising and found joy in that.

She smiled and shook her head. Funny how life can throw you curve balls. Six months ago, she thought L.A. was the lifestyle for her, until that life was turned upside down. She closed her eyes for a moment and breathed in the heavenly scent of dough, sugar, butter, assorted spices and fillings that drifted through the room. This is what gave her joy and fulfillment now. This is the work she wanted to do. She'd let her mother know she'd be there permanently and together they would grow and expand the business.

The sound of the front door chimes startled her, and she wondered if she had accidentally left the door open. Then she heard Donetta's voice and relaxed. Looking up at the clock, she was surprised she'd already been there for over two hours.

"It smells wonderful in here. Have you been baking all night?" Donetta peaked her head into the kitchen and strode toward Jasmine. "How are you doing today? How's your mom?"

Jasmine noted the uncertainty in Donetta's voice and her lips pinched together. "When I left last night, Mom was doing well.

According to the doctors, she didn't sustain any major damage to her heart. But I'm sure they'll want her to rest. And it will be our job to make sure she does. I'll probably need to bring on another baker to assist me and I hope you're willing to learn to do some baking yourself."

A grin spread across Donetta's face and words spewed out. "I enjoy working out front and helping people, but I'm excited that you want to teach me the baking side. I've been wanting to learn but was afraid to ask. I didn't want to upset you and your mom's routine. I'll put in all the hours you need me for."

They worked together pulling out baked goods and filling the front cases until 8:00 when it was time to open. Donetta stayed by the counter to handle orders while Jasmine finished placing the last trays in the oven to bake.

Several of their regular customers asked about Belinda and Jasmine told them she was doing better. She appreciated their concern and prayers, but with each question she could feel a lump forming in her throat and a flutter in her heart as she wondered how her mother was doing at the moment and what Trevor's condition was.

When the morning rush ended around 9:30, Jasmine took off her apron. "I'm going to the hospital now to see Mom and Trevor. Georgia, one of Mom's part-time fill-ins, said she could help out between twelve and two. If you need anything, don't hesitate to call me. I know you've handled the store on your own before, so I know I can count on you again."

Donetta gave Jasmine a tentative hug. "Give your mom a hug for me and let her know I'm praying for her."

"I will." Jasmine picked up her purse and walked toward the front door."

Donetta raised her hand in a wave. "And I'll add prayers for Trevor as well."

Jasmine opened the door and gave a final wave. "Thanks. He needs them." As she drove to the hospital, she reflected on what she and Donetta had accomplished this morning. They worked well together and she could see that Donetta was ready to take on more responsibility. She hoped she was up to the task as well. "Lord, give me guidance in running the bakery for Mom and let me hear good news for both Mom and Travis at the hospital."

CHAPTER 37
Good News at the Hospital

When Jasmine arrived at the hospital, she immediately headed to the critical care unit to see her mom. One the way, she called Lexie to see if she could get an update on Trevor. She picked up the call on the second ring.

"Hi Jasmine, how's your mom doing?"

"I'm on my way to her room now, but I hope you can give me an update on Trevor." She held her breath as she waited for the response.

"I thought you'd be wanting to know that. So, I checked up on him. He was sedated most of the night and the doctor is with him now. I'll call you once he's done. Give your mom my best."

Jasmine let out her breath and clicked off the phone. She straightened her shoulders, smiled, and walked into her mom's room. "How's one of the best loved ladies in Falcon Creek doing today?"

Her mom was propped up in bed and smiled at her entry. Jasmine was happy to see her the color in her face had improved and her eyes were bright.

"Best loved? My that's a sweet compliment," Mom replied.

"That's not only my thoughts but those of our bakery regulars and friends who love you and are praying for a speedy recovery." Jasmine leaned over the bed and kissed her mom on the cheek.

"What a wonderful blessing. The doctor says I'm doing well. No new blips of a negative nature on my heart monitor. They still want me to stay another night to make sure. So, Lord willing, I'll be going home tomorrow or the day after at most."

Jasmine raised an eyebrow. "And you'll follow the instructions that the doctor gives you about taking it easy, right?"

Belinda raised two fingers over her heart. "Cross my heart. I'll do as instructed. How did it go at the bakery this morning?"

Jasmine pushed away some errant hairs on her mom's forehead. "You were missed, but Donetta and I got things done and Georgia will be mid-day to help out."

Belinda reached for Jasmine's hand and squeezed it. "I'm so proud of you. Now I know I won't have to worry about the bakery at all. But enough of me. I can see by your eyes something is bothering you. Did you hear something on Trevor's condition?"

Jasmine let out a deep sigh and sat. "According to Lexie, there weren't any new issues from last night. And the doctor is checking him out now. He looked so horrible last night. I hope he's doing okay.'

"He's in God's hands and I've been praying for positive results."

"You and me both."

"Knock, knock. Can I come in?" Lexie's head peered around the doorframe. "I hope you don't mind but I brought a friend with me. We won't stay long because I don't want to tire Mrs. C."

"Fine, Come in. You're always welcome," Belinda replied.

Lexie opened the door all the way. With a big grin on her face, she pushed the wheelchair forward that held Trevor.

Letting out a squeal, Jasmine jumped out of her chair and ran to him. She bent down to the wheelchair and gave him a big hug. Her brow creased in seeing he wore an ankle boot and arm sling, but his face had more color to it than she'd seen when he was unconscious and that was an answer to her prayers. "Oh, Trevor, I was so worried about you."

He winced in pain at her embrace. "Whoa, be a little careful of the arm. It's a bit tender."

She pulled away, but he grabbed for her hand to keep her close.

Trevor's deep blue eyes filled with concern as he held her focus "I'm so sorry I ran off the way I did yesterday. My ego got the best of me."

"What do you mean?"

"I saw the video of Galanos hugging you after the knife-wielding contestant was hauled away by the police." He hung his head and shrugged. "Since I knew the two of you had a previous history, I jumped to the conclusion that he had won you back."

Jasmine shook her head. "No, no, no. That is not the case at all. I told Stefan I had absolutely no interest in revisiting a relationship with him.

"Yeah, I finally figured it out when I saw a later video with him and that other contestant, Kayla. The news reporter said that love had bloomed between them."

"That's the impression I got, too. They fit together. Not him and me."

"And what about a relationship with me?" Trevor tilted his head and raised an eyebrow.

Jasmine squeezed his fingers tightly. "You really have to ask?"

He motioned for her to lean closer until they were face to face. "I guess not. I just want to make sure this is what you want."

"Take it out in the hall," her mom chuckled. "It sounds like the two of you need to discuss a few things."

Jasmine and Trevor smiled and let go of each other's hands. In a flash, she was behind the chair and pushing him out of the room and down the hall from the church members. Once they got out of hearing range, she stopped and turned the chair to face her. "Now, where were we?"

Trevor gave her a big grin and stared deep into her eyes. "I was going to tell you I don't want anything to keep us apart. For the short time we've known each other, we've already gone through multiple life-threatening events – the town disaster, your crazy show contestant, your mom's heart attack, my family's hospital issues and now my accident. All these events made me realize how precious every moment is. I don't want to lose you."

"I couldn't bear to lose you either." She hugged him more cautiously this time.

He whispered in her ear. "Then let's make it official. Say you'll marry me."

She pulled back and stared wide-eyed. Butterflies flitted in her stomach joyously. A smile started to form on her face until she broke out in a full grin. "I recall you once saying that a proposal should be a *private* experience between the two people at a place that's special. I don't think a hospital corridor fits the bill."

He stared dumbfounded for a moment, and then a spark of understanding began to gleam in his eyes. "Yes, a proposal should be a cherished and romantic experience just between the two people. Somewhere that has meaning for the two of them."

"Like a first date or when they first met," Jasmine said as she knelt beside the wheelchair to be eye to eye with him."

"And it would certainly not be at a bakery. There might be some difference of opinion."

Jasmine chuckled, "Yes, we wouldn't want a difference of opinion, but we can agree on the bakery to handle the wedding."

"Hmmm. Perhaps we could find a secluded garden-like setting for the official proposal. And having a restaurant nearby to celebrate afterward would be a plus."

Jasmine smiled and kissed him. "That sounds wonderful."

"You know it will take time for my bones to heal. I can't exactly do the one knee thing right now. Are you willing to wait?"

"A loving future is worth waiting for. We can take as much time as we need."

"I agree." He leaned close and kissed her again.

CHAPTER 38
Making New Plans

The next day Trevor met with his doctor for a follow up. It was awkward wearing the ankle boot and arm sling but felt blessed being told he could leave the hospital. Follow-up appointments with his regular physician would also be needed. Knowing his parents would have a fit if he didn't tell them about the accident, he made the call to his mom.

After the normal pleasantries, he broke the news about the accident. "Mom, I was up in Falcon Creek when a big storm hit. Visibility was bad, the roads were slick, and I had a bad accident."

There was an audible gasp from his mom and a tumble of words followed. "Oh, no. That's terrible. Are you okay? What are your injuries? Can I come see you?"

"The accident was scary, but I'll be okay. One arm is in a sling and my leg is in a boot, but I can get around. I'm being released today. Would you like to come see me?"

"I'll do more than come see you. I'm going to come down there and bring you home with us. Sounds like you're in no condition to drive and in no good condition to get around on your own."

He considered trying to talk her out of the suggestion but knew the rest and care she'd provide would be a blessing. Since his car was a wreck, he knew he'd need to make other arrangements for getting around, handling meals, and work. Being with his parents would make that much easier. Besides, she often complained he didn't visit them enough. "Okay, I'd appreciate that. If I get too burdensome, you can always send me home."

"Trevor, dear, I carried you for nine months. I think I can handle you for a few weeks, We can catch up, play cards, get some barbecue delivered or whatever else you might have a hankering to eat. Maybe I could even bring in a cute nurse to help you with any therapy you might need. A nurse for a wife would be a good idea."

Trevor rolled his eyes and shook his head. "I don't need any of your matchmaking. I'm perfectly capable of finding a wife and partner on my own. And there is someone, I'd like you to meet in that regards."

"Well, it's about time. Is she the reason you were in Falcon Creek?"

"Yes, we had a bit of a misunderstanding, and I stormed off. But we've cleared that up. We're doing fine and looking ahead to a future."

"My, my, that sounds serious. When did all this come about? When do I get to meet her?"

"Well, if you'd like, you can meet her at the hospital. She's not a nurse to fit your matchmaking idea, but she's a wonderful, creative baker. She's at the hospital with her mom who is recovering from a heart attack."

"Having to worry about the two of you in the hospital must be hard on her. If she's up to meeting me, I'd like that, but if she isn't, that's okay and we can do it another time."

"I'll ask her and if it's a go, I'll let you know once you get here." Trevor gave her the details on the hospital and his room number before they ended the call.

The next call was to Jasmine. He got an update on Belinda and what was happening with the bakery. Then he told her they were working on his paperwork to leave the hospital. "I'm going to recuperate at my parents. Mom's coming down to pick me up. Would you feel up to meeting my mom? If you feel too stressed out with your mom's condition, I'll understand."

"I'm happy you're being released. Mom had a good night. If this day goes well, she'll be able to leave tomorrow. That's good news, though I know she'll have to take it easy. I'd love to meet your mom, but I didn't exactly dress for making a stunning first impression."

Trevor smiled thinking of the first time he met her in the bakery. Her hair was a bit in disarray, but the way her face lit up when she discussed the bakery specials immediately drew him to her. "Just be you and you'll make a wonderful impression on her. The meeting you'll want to prepare for is the one with Grandma Merle."

"This is sounding serious having me meet the family."

"Didn't I make it sound serious last night?"

Jasmine laughed. "Yes, we both did. I'd like to meet your mom. Call me when she arrives. I'll be with Mom or in the hall with folks from the church."

When his mom walked into his hospital room, Trevor saw the look of concern on her face. He stood and opened his arms. "Come give me a hug but make it gentle. And don't worry, I'm really a lot better than I look. It's just bruises."

His mom gently wrapped him in her embrace. "I'm so glad you're going to be okay. I'll make sure you'll be able to get to whatever doctor appointments you need to make in San Antonio. Your dad and I will gladly make that happen."

Trevor slowly extricated himself from her arms and sat in the wheelchair behind him while his mom sat in the nearby chair. "So, where is Dad today?"

"He's got a big commercial deal closing today, so he's with the clients to make sure it goes smoothly without any last-minute surprises. You know he'd usually like to go out and celebrate, but this time he'll pick up the food from his favorite restaurant and make it a celebration at home. He's looking forward to seeing you and I'm sure he'll have a few questions about your new girlfriend."

Trevor reached for his mom's hand and squeezed it. "Mom, please go easy on Jasmine when you meet her. No third degree. I don't want you to scare her off."

"I'll be as sweet as pie," Mom replied in an overly sweet tone of voice. "Now when will that happen?"

"She's in the cardiac care center with her mom. She told me to call her once you arrive. Her mom's condition seems stabilized and if that continues, she'll be going home tomorrow."

"That must be rough on Jasmine, worrying about both of you."

"She's strong and has faith. Let me call and tell her you're here."

While they waited for Jasmine to arrive, Trevor gave his mom the details of how they met and the experiences she had with the TV show. He babbled on a bit because he was nervous about their meeting. What if his mom didn't like her?

Trevor's concerns dissolved when Jasmine popped her head in the doorway and smiled a hello. His mom immediately went over and gave her a hug. Soon they were chatting like old friends.

CHAPTER 39
A Future of Blessings

A few more weeks passed before Jasmine could get away from the bakery. Her mom was back at work, but only part-time. They hired another worker part-time who would fill in for the day, so Jasmine could do the two-hour drive to Georgetown to meet Trevor's grandma. Since Trevor had filled her in on Grandma Merle's attitude about the importance of knowing how to cook, she brought a small sampling of her favorite baked goods. A paper wrapper between each item cushioned them in the pastry box, which was tied with a mix of colorful ribbons.

When she turned into the street where Grandma Merle lived, Jasmine's mouth fell open. Trevor had said his grandfather had given her an open checkbook to do as she pleased to design the house, but she didn't imagine how deep that checkbook was. The house was definitely the showstopper in the neighborhood. Her family home in Falcon Creek, though well kept, looked shabby by comparison. The landscaping consisted of a mix of perfectly manicured shrubs of various sizes to add depth and fullness. Flowers accented the color of the house and each of the mature shade trees were circled with a river rock base around them. The home was stunning and exactly what you'd expect to see on the covers of prestigious home style magazines.

Jasmine's throat went dry. Maybe she should have done a bit of research on the home and Grandma Merle so she wouldn't feel like a short order cook who has been invited to prep the meals at a five-star restaurant kitchen. This home was easily worth three to four times the value of her mom's home. Would his grandmother think she was an economic inferior and not worthy of her grandson? Well, there was nothing she could do about that now. Once she parked the car, she did a quick check in the mirror to make sure she looked her best, picked up her pastry box, took a deep breath, and got out of the car.

Her first knock on the door was hesitant, but her additional raps had a more confident sound. If only her stomach wasn't doing somersaults.

When Trevor answered the door, she sputtered, "Your arm sling is gone. What a wonderful surprise."

He gave her a quick kiss and hugged her. "It's great to hold you close with both arms." As he escorted her inside, he whispered, "You brought treats. Grandma will be pleased."

A voice sounded from down the hall. "If that's some salesperson at the door send them away. If it's your Jasmine, don't keep me waiting. Bring the young lady to see me."

"Yes, Grandma. We're coming." Trevor continued in a whisper as he held her close. "She's in her queen bee mood, but don't let it rattle you. Smile and treat her with respect and she'll warm to you quickly, like I did. Mom's with her, so you'll have a second person cheering for you."

Jasmine swallowed hard and held her head high. They walked into what Trevor had said was his grandma's entertainment room. It was as stunning as the exterior of the home. The walls held paintings of beautiful western landscapes and the sofa table displayed a lovely bronze sculpture of a cowboy on a bucking broncho. Grandma Merle sat regally in the middle of a plush leather sofa. She held an elegant lacquer and mother of pearl cane. Her long white wavy hair outlined her face and set off her piercing steel gray eyes. Her blue pants and coordinating top looked like the clothes that were sold in the high-priced boutique shops in Falcon Creek. Jasmine almost felt the need to curtsy, until Grandma Merle beckoned her forward.

"No, need to keep your distance, dear. Come and sit with me. I don't bite." Grandma smiled, but gave her a quizzical look? "Did you buy what's in that box? Or did you make them?"

Jasmine sat beside her and handed over the box. "These are some of my favorites from the bakery. I hope you'll like them."

Grandma handed the box to Trevor. "Go put these on a platter and bring in a pitcher of sweet tea when you return.

Trevor took the box but didn't move.

Grandma wagged her finger at him. "Now go. This dear girl is probably thirsty and hungry from her drive. Show her some hospitality, like I taught you."

Trevor dipped his head and left the room.

"Now that he's gone, we can talk freely. What is it about my grandson you like?" Grandma leaned back against the cushion and was silent.

Jasmine smiled. "I didn't like him after our first meeting because he gave a bad review for something I baked. When I let go of my bruised ego, I realized what he wrote was the truth." Her voice changed to a serious tone. "Then I discovered we had a lot in common, especially our love of cooking. We balance each other with our culinary talents, and we strive to be our best and help others in the process."

Grandma reached for Jasmine's hand and squeezed it. "But will you love him for better or worse?"

"Oh yes," Jasmine replied. A broad grin spread across her face. "With all we've gone through already, there's no one else I would want to spend the rest of my life with."

"I can see you mean that." Grandma patted Jasmine's hand. "Yes. If you love each other like Mike and I did, you'll have a wonderful life together. When do you plan to marry?"

Trevor returned with the tea, glasses, pastries, small plates, and napkins. He set them on the coffee table in front of the sofa. "Grandma, you're jumping the gun. I haven't officially asked her yet."

"But I've unofficially accepted if he does a proper proposal," Jasmine said with a wink toward Trevor.

"And what exactly is a proper proposal?" Grandma asked, placing one of the pastries on her plate.

"One filled with romance to set up a lifetime of love." He handed his grandma a filled glass of tea. "I've got a reservation at the Old Grist Mill where we had our first date." He reached for Jasmine's hand and let their fingers entwine. "Will you join me on the garden bench by the mill tomorrow evening, Jasmine?"

Her body tingled with joy from her toes to her head. "Yes. I can't imagine wanting to be anywhere else tomorrow."

"That's wonderful," Grandma Merle said. "When you start a marriage off right it can be a sweet delight for the rest of your life."

Love is patient, love is kind. It does not envy, it does not boast, it is not proud. It does not dishonor others, it is not self-seeking, it is not easily angered, it keeps no record of wrongs. **1 Corinthians 13:4-5 NIV**

AUTHOR BIO AND BOOK LIST

Christine Henderson's short stories, poems, and inspirational pieces have been published in regional and national magazines and numerous anthologies about family life. Her recipes have also won awards. Other published works include sweet romance novels, children's picture books, devotionals, and a cookbook.

Her blog for writers and readers features weekly interviews with best-selling authors who discuss their upcoming books, tips on writing, and offer eBook giveaways. You can read it at https://thewritechris.blogspot.com/ Discover all her books and details on new releases at: **https://amzn.to/447yw09**

Thank you for taking the time to read this book. Would you do me a favor and leave a review on wherever you purchased the book? I would greatly appreciate that. And it would help other readers discover this book.

Inspirational Romance Novels
Finding Love at Christmas:12 Heartwarming Christian Romance Novellas for the Holidays: This box set of sweet romances stories can be pre-ordered at a discount. Release date is October 15. Her book takes place in Aspen. It's called

Falling in Love Despite Christmas Miscalculations

Christmas Moonlight Melodies. Nikki left her hometown and Michael for music fame. Devastated by her departure, Michael poured his heart into writing love songs and gained fame as well. Can their Christmas reunion reignite the sparks of love that still simmer?

Devotional and study guides
The First Noel–Digging Deeper into Christ's Birth – a 25-day devotional and study guide for individuals and families. Buy the book and support a cause. **All** royalties are being donated to a prison ministry that brings Bible teaching to prisoners..

Exploring the Bible: Prayers, Poems, Praises, Bible Verses and Fun Pages – 5-Star Reader's Favorite Rating. This book provides 15 lessons to engage the young reader. Each includes Bible verses to remember, poems, gratitude pages, and Bible related games, puzzles, & coloring pages.

A Closer Walk with Jesus: 52-Week Prayer Journal for Women - Transform your daily prayer life with this beautiful and inspiring women's prayer journal. Designed with the busy woman in mind, this 52-week journal provides a simple and organized way to deepen your relationship with God. Each week offers inspiring Bible verses, thoughtful prompts, space for reflection, and a guided section for writing out your thoughts.

Picture Books for Families to Read Together

A Special Digital Scrapbook Memory - Eek! Who wants to do homework? Certainly not Angie. She's too busy putting together an online scrapbook about all the fun her family had at the beach this summer. But class is back in session. Can't she just ignore her homework? That's last on her list - especially memorizing her Bible verses for class. But a conversation with her mom changes her perspective with happy results.

Jesus Loves Me This Much! And Guess What? He loves you, too! Through captivating illustrations and engaging storytelling, children will come to understand that Jesus's love is always with them, no matter what they do or where they go. Spark meaningful conversations about faith and love as you share this enchanting story with your little ones.

'Twas the Day Before Christmas: The story leads you past the hustle and bustle of the holidays with a group of carolers whose singing spreads cheer and touches the hearts of those who listen. The tale is told in the poetic style of Clement Moore's writing, but rather than focusing on Santa, this focus is on the first Christmas. You'll want to make reading this book a yearly tradition.

Please Let Santa Fly! Santa's on the naughty list? That has to be a mistake. Santa is the essence of good. Who is behind this push to make Santa the number one offender of being naughty? Could it be someone who doesn't like to be on the naughty list? You'll giggle and laugh at the funny antics around the North Pole. Then decide for yourself if you're on Team Santa Nice list or Team Santa Naughty list.

Cookbook
Let's Share a Meal: Comfort Food For Family & Friends
Come join me on my food journey as I share favorite recipes I've made over the years as well as those shared with me from family and friends. Though I consider myself a "foodie," these recipe ingredients can be found in most markets. The directions don't require fancy kitchen tools to make.